P9-CEI-728

Lauren watched as Gray smiled down at the child, the tenderness on his face almost more than she could bear.

"Mommy! Mommy, did you see me ride the horse?" Sarah glowed with excitement.

"I sure did, sweetie." Lauren met Gray's eyes only briefly. Even that contact sent an unwanted tingle up her spine.

Gray dismounted and lifted Sarah off the horse.

"I had this much fun!" Sarah exclaimed, holding her arms wide. "I want you to ride, too!" She looked expectantly from Lauren to Gray. "Please, Mommy?"

"I'd be happy to take you," Gray offered.

Lauren glowered at him, which only made him grin. "All right, all right."

Once Lauren settled on the saddle, Gray slid in behind her. His palm flattened on her abdomen and pressed her closer to his hard male body. She trembled at the feel of him. His fingers knotted in the cotton of her T-shirt, then relaxed.

He felt it too, she realized.

Gray Longwalker might like to pretend he was in control, but when it came to this attraction between them, he was as defenseless as she was.

Dear Reader,

It's February—the month of love. And what better way to celebrate Valentine's Day than with a Harlequin American Romance novel.

This month's selection begins with the latest installment in the RETURN TO TYLER series. *Prescription for Seduction* is what Darlene Scalera offers when sparks fly between a lovely virgin and a steadfast bachelor doctor. *The Bride Said, "Surprise!"* is another of Cathy Gillen Thacker's THE LOCKHARTS OF TEXAS, and is a tender tale about a secret child who brings together two long-ago lovers. (Watch for Cathy's single title, *Texas Vows: A McCabe Family Saga*, next month from Harlequin Books.)

In Millie Criswell's charming new romance, *The Pregnant Ms. Potter* is rescued from a blizzard by a protective rancher who takes her into his home—and into his heart. And in *Longwalker's Child* by Debra Webb, a proud Native American hero is determined to claim the child he never knew existed, but first he has to turn the little girl's beautiful guardian from his sworn enemy into his loving ally.

So this February, treat yourself to all four of our wonderful Harlequin American Romance titles. And in March, look for Judy Christenberry's *Rent a Millionaire Groom*, the first book in Harlequin American Romance's new promotion, 2001 WAYS TO WED.

Wishing you happy reading,

Melissa Jeglinski
Associate Senior Editor
Harlequin American Romance

LONGWALKER'S CHILD
Debra Webb

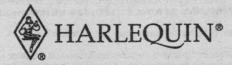

HARLEQUIN®

TORONTO • NEW YORK • LONDON
AMSTERDAM • PARIS • SYDNEY • HAMBURG
STOCKHOLM • ATHENS • TOKYO • MILAN • MADRID
PRAGUE • WARSAW • BUDAPEST • AUCKLAND

If you purchased this book without a cover you should be aware
that this book is stolen property. It was reported as "unsold and
destroyed" to the publisher, and neither the author nor the
publisher has received any payment for this "stripped book."

Thanks to a friend and fellow author Tina Leonard
for keeping me straight on my Texas facts.

This book is dedicated to the light of my life,
my little girl, Melissa. God gave me a very special gift
when he sent you to me. Be sweet always,
and remember that I will always love you.

ISBN 0-373-16864-0

LONGWALKER'S CHILD

Copyright © 2001 by Debra Webb.

All rights reserved. Except for use in any review, the reproduction or
utilization of this work in whole or in part in any form by any electronic,
mechanical or other means, now known or hereafter invented, including
xerography, photocopying and recording, or in any information storage
or retrieval system, is forbidden without the written permission of the
publisher, Harlequin Enterprises Limited, 225 Duncan Mill Road,
Don Mills, Ontario, Canada M3B 3K9.

All characters in this book have no existence outside the imagination of
the author and have no relation whatsoever to anyone bearing the same
name or names. They are not even distantly inspired by any individual
known or unknown to the author, and all incidents are pure invention.

This edition published by arrangement with Harlequin Books S.A.

® and TM are trademarks of the publisher. Trademarks indicated with
® are registered in the United States Patent and Trademark Office, the
Canadian Trade Marks Office and in other countries.

Visit us at www.eHarlequin.com

Printed in U.S.A.

ABOUT THE AUTHOR

Debra Webb was born in Scottsboro, Alabama, to parents who taught her that anything is possible if you want it badly enough. She began writing at age nine. Eventually, she met and married the man of her dreams, and tried some other occupations, including selling vacuum cleaners, and working in a factory, a day-care center, a hospital and a department store. When her husband joined the military, they moved to Berlin, Germany, and Debra became a secretary in the commanding general's office. By 1985 they were back in the States, and finally moved to Tennessee, to a small town where everyone knows everyone else. With the support of her husband and two beautiful daughters, Debra took up writing again, looking to mystery and movies for inspiration. In 1998 her dream of writing for Harlequin came true.

Books by Debra Webb

HARLEQUIN AMERICAN ROMANCE
864—LONGWALKER'S CHILD

HARLEQUIN INTRIGUE
583—SAFE BY HIS SIDE*
597—THE BODYGUARD'S BABY*

*A Colby Agency Case

Don't miss any of our special offers. Write to us at the following address for information on our newest releases.

Harlequin Reader Service
U.S.: 3010 Walden Ave., P.O. Box 1325, Buffalo, NY 14269
Canadian: P.O. Box 609, Fort Erie, Ont. L2A 5X3

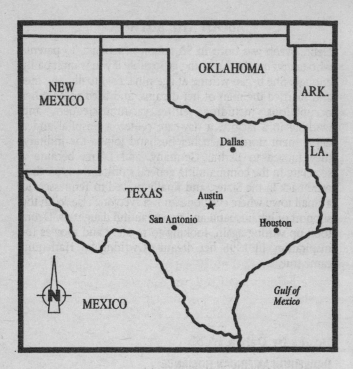

Chapter One

"I believe you have something that belongs to me."

Lauren Whitmore looked up at the tall raven-haired man filling her doorway. Wearing a black Stetson and duster, he all but blocked the bright morning sun, casting an ominous shadow across her threshold. His dark hair fell well past his broad shoulders, lending an even more roguish quality to his appearance. His face, all shadows and angles, was undeniably good-looking.

At first Lauren considered that maybe the handsome stranger who'd knocked on her door was lost, but one good look into his eyes changed her mind and stilled her heart.

Eyes that Lauren looked into every day of her life— the same intense gray eyes of her soon-to-be-adopted daughter. Fear slid through her veins.

"I'm sure you're mistaken, sir," she finally managed to say despite the rush of hysteria crowding her throat. Lauren grasped the tarnished brass knob more firmly and prepared to close the door. Please God, she prayed, just let me get this door closed and locked so I can get to the telephone and call Don. He will know how to handle this.

The man flattened one wide palm against the door,

halting its movement. "Wait. You *are* Lauren Whit-more."

Lauren knew he wasn't asking. This was the kind of man who calculated every move, every word. He knew exactly who she was before he stopped at her ranch and knocked on her door.

"Yes," she said, her voice strained with the effort of maintaining her composure. "I'm Lauren Whit-more." Panic snaked around her heart as she groped for some kind of plan—any kind of plan to get rid of him until she could make just one call. "But there's nothing here that belongs to anyone but me," she hedged. Technically it was the truth—she was alone in the house.

"This *is* your ad."

Another statement. He thrust the crumpled news-paper he held in his left hand in her direction. His expression determined, the angular features of his face slashed in granite.

Lauren moistened her dry lips and tried to swallow, but she couldn't. Her gaze dropped from his watchful gaze to the newspaper he offered. Concentrating hard to keep her hand steady, she took the paper and stared blankly at the ad circled in red. She didn't have to read the printed words…she knew what they said be-cause the ad did belong to her.

Ice-cold dread formed in her stomach. This was the nightmare Don, her good friend and trusted attorney, had assured Lauren would never happen.

Never, he'd emphasized.

Lauren drew in a shaky breath and met the man's piercing gray gaze once more. "Who wants to know?" she asked in the bravest tone she could muster. Her heart pounded wildly as she waited for the answer she didn't want to hear.

"Gray Longwalker," he said roughly, as if accustomed to a particular reaction to the announcement. A muscle flexed in his deeply bronzed jaw.

"I'll need to see some sort of identification," Lauren insisted. The delay tactic would prove futile, but she had to try. Though fear whittled away at her resolve not to run as fast as she could away from him, Lauren held her ground. She needed some inkling of his immediate intent.

One corner of his mouth lifted in a patient but weary gesture that wasn't quite a smile. She had the distinct impression that he had not smiled often during his thirty or so years. Somehow that thought disturbed her. Lauren tamped down the reaction. She would not feel anything even remotely related to sympathy for this man. This was the man who held the power to devastate the life she had built since coming to this town.

Lauren squared her shoulders and met his searching gaze. Taking his time so that he could analyze her more thoroughly, he reached into the back pocket of his faded jeans and removed his wallet. The March wind ruffled the duster around his legs, the flapping sound loud in the otherwise stark silence.

He flashed a Texas driver's license. "Gray Longwalker," he repeated, his tone wary now, as if he'd read her last thought. He shoved the worn leather wallet back into his pocket. "I've come for my daughter."

The words, though expected, echoed all the way through Lauren's soul. She blinked twice. Her skin felt clammy, and the hasty breakfast she'd wolfed down less than half an hour ago threatened to make a reappearance. She knew the symptoms and what would follow. She willed herself to calm, taking a slow, deep breath to fight the light-headedness already overtaking her. This was not the time to lose control. She focused on blocking the disabling sensations clawing at her.

"She's not here," Lauren informed him with surprising strength. She would not allow him to destroy their little family. Surely the man could be persuaded to see reason. But right now she had to get to Don's office.

"You're sure about that," he pressed, easing a step closer, putting himself in her doorway.

Lauren suppressed the desperate words she wanted to blurt out and struggled to think rationally. Gray Longwalker didn't know his child's name or what she even looked like, yet he had come to claim her. He had to be reacting on impulse. How could he expect to just take her away? His gaze shifted to the hall behind her, then settled intently back on her.

"I said she's not here." She resisted the urge to retreat a step from his stare.

"I'd like to know where she is, then," he said quietly, too quietly. *"Please,"* he added stiffly.

Lauren was certain that word hadn't come easily. Something resembling the same desperation she felt glimmered from the gray depths that marked this man as the father of the child Lauren had called her own for almost a year now. He was every bit as anxious as she was, but beneath the surface a storm was brewing. She could feel it emanating from him in waves. Gray Longwalker was holding back, restraining something that felt very much like rage. Lauren knew with complete certainty that she should be afraid. She should be very afraid.

"I told you she's not here." Lauren lifted her chin

in defiance of her own emotions. She had to be strong. She had to fight this man. He would not take her child away.

Something changed in his eyes then. The anger she'd felt simmering overrode his restraint. "Patience is not one of my strong suits, Ms. Whitmore," he warned, his voice low, lethal. "I'll ask you again, where is she?"

Her heart banged painfully against her chest, but Lauren ignored the ache. "I'll get my keys and you can follow me into town to my attorney's office."

He shook his head slowly from side to side. "I don't want to see your attorney. I want to see my daughter."

"Mr. Longwalker, if you have no consideration for my feelings, at least consider the child's." Lauren blinked back the sting of tears. "How do you suppose she would feel if you burst into her classroom and announced that you were her father?"

Realization dawned in his eyes.

Oh, God! Lauren realized at that same instant that she had just told Gray Longwalker where his daughter could be found. She could well imagine him roaming the halls of Thatcher Elementary, looking for a child he'd never seen and asking for a daughter whose name he didn't even know. Somehow he didn't appear the type to be thwarted by mere technicalities.

"Thank you for your kind assistance, Ms. Whitmore," he said tightly, then turned and strode away.

Not a single doubt existed in Lauren's mind that he fully intended to go straight to the school. He had already made it across the porch and down the steps before Lauren found her voice.

"Wait, please," she called after him. By the time he turned back to face her, Lauren stood on the bottom step, practically at eye level with him. She shivered when his gray gaze collided with hers. A strange spark of awareness arced briefly between them, and Lauren felt oddly violated, as if he had looked right through to her soul.

"What?" he demanded, seemingly oblivious to the zing of electricity that had passed between them.

Lauren dismissed the unfamiliar sensation as a part of the lingering shock of finding Gray Longwalker at her door, not to mention the monster headache threatening. "Think," she pleaded. "We both want what's best for Sarah—"

"Sarah...that's her name?" His features relaxed just a fraction, an almost-imperceptible vulnerability crept into his wary eyes.

"Yes."

He looked away. Lauren watched the smooth movement of muscle beneath dark skin as he swallowed hard. However cold and ruthless this man was rumored to be, hearing his child's name for the first time touched something deep inside him. That knowledge only served to increase Lauren's mounting anxiety. God, why had he come? He couldn't possibly love Sarah the way she did.

"Does she know *anything* about me?" His penetrating gaze locked back on Lauren's. All signs of vulnerability had vanished. Those gray depths were like hard, metallic points probing past her defenses.

"No," she said simply, and braced herself for his response.

Gray closed his eyes and then dropped his head. Lauren heard the heavy breath he released. She had expected him to explode into a rage, but he didn't. For one fleeting moment she wanted to reach out to him...to tell him she was sorry about the whole situation. That maybe they could work something out, then Lauren remembered the promise she had made Sarah's mother.

"Mr. Longwalker, I love Sarah. I must warn you that I'll do whatever is necessary to keep her happy and safe."

His head shot up, and his eyes blazed with a rage probably as old as he was. Startled, Lauren drew away from his fury as far as her precarious perch on the step above him would allow.

"Then we both want the same thing," he said harshly.

Lauren shook her head, unsure as to how he would react to the words about to tumble from her mouth, but they had to be said. He had to understand. "I made a promise to Sarah's mother on her deathbed that I would never let you take her child away and I intend to keep it."

Pain and betrayal flashed in his eyes. Gray adjusted his black Stetson and gave her one last heated glare from beneath the brim. "You'd better get to your attorney's office then, because you'll need one if you think you're going to keep my daughter from me." He turned away and continued toward his truck. His movements were graceful and sleek like a cat's, but at the same time more dangerous and determined than any animal's, domesticated or otherwise, she had ever seen.

Lauren wasn't a coward, but neither was she one to pick a fight—that fact didn't stop her from bounding down that last step and grabbing Longwalker's arm. She pulled him around to face her, which would have been impossible had she not taken him by complete surprise. He glared down at her, impatient and irritated by her lack of cooperation.

With a single lift of his shoulder, he shrugged off her hand. "You have something else to say before we go to your attorney's office?"

"How can I be sure that you'll follow me? What's to keep you from going to the school and trying to find Sarah instead?" Lauren set her hands on her hips and glared back at him, though she trembled inside. Every vicious story she had ever heard about the man flashed through her mind during the brief pause before he answered. Stories that would make the bravest woman fear for her safety in his presence. Especially alone.

"I'll be right behind you, Ms. Whitmore," he assured her. "You have my word."

Lauren almost laughed at the absurdity of his statement. "I'm afraid your word doesn't mean much around these parts, Mr. Longwalker."

He made a mirthless sound in his throat. "Tell me something I don't know." His somber gaze punctuated his words. "*You* have my word," he repeated then turned away once more.

Lauren watched as Gray Longwalker took the last few steps to his truck and seated himself behind the wheel. He made no move to start the engine; he just sat there and stared at her. Waiting, Lauren supposed, for her to get in her own car and lead the way.

Maybe she was a fool, but she believed him. Contrary to the rumors she'd heard, Longwalker didn't strike her as the sort of man who gave his word lightly. Deliberately Lauren turned her back on the man and went inside the house to get her keys. Despite the display of trust, she listened for the roar of his truck's engine as she searched for her forever-misplaced keys. The sound never came.

Lauren finally located her keys, grabbed her purse and headed for the door. In an hour she had a tele-conference with a client and his building contractor, but she would just have to miss it. Maybe she could call Rosemary from Don's office and have her re-schedule the conference. She didn't have time to leave her a note. What would her assistant think when she returned from her run to the post office and found Lauren gone? And what about lunch? Lauren swore silently as she locked the door behind her. Buck had asked her to lunch today. The man was obsessing about a reconciliation. But he would just have to wait, as well.

Lauren's one and only concern right now was Gray Longwalker's return.

GRAY WATCHED the hushed exchange between the Whitmore woman and her lawyer. He vaguely remembered Don Davis. The best he could recall, the man was at least ten years his senior. When Gray had left the small Texas town of Thatcher six years ago, Davis had been practicing law with his father. Gray supposed the older man had retired or passed away since the storefront window now read The Law Office of Don Davis. Gray remembered the elder Davis as a fair man. He only hoped the son would prove as just.

Had it only been six years ago that he had left this godforsaken place? It seemed like a lifetime. Yet nothing had changed. The people in this town would still think of him as nothing more than a half-breed bastard. An outcast. He wasn't blind. He had seen the stares as he walked down the sidewalk to Davis's office. The difference between six years ago and now was that Gray no longer cared. He frowned as the hushed conversation on the other side of the room jerked him back to the present. Whatever Davis was trying to get across to the woman, she didn't seem to be taking it very well.

Lauren Whitmore was a transplant—a northerner, Gray had assumed from her accent even before Davis had mentioned Chicago. From the discussion they'd just had, Gray had learned that she had moved to Thatcher about three years prior and befriended another of the town's outcasts, Sharon Johnson.

Gray closed his eyes and summoned Sharon's image. A slight woman with fiery-red hair and eyes like a clear summer sky. As much as he hated to admit it, he hadn't thought of her in years, though she had been a friend to him for most of his life. Sharon had been the only person who had tried to understand him or the emotions that drove him. Emotions or ghosts? Gray wondered. It had taken him many years to come to terms with what he was and the hand fate had cruelly dealt him.

He and Sharon hadn't been in love with each other, but their feelings had been strong just the same. Those last few weeks before Gray had hit the road and left his sorry past behind, Sharon had been his only source of emotional support. He hadn't meant to make love to her—it had just happened. It grieved him immensely that she hadn't called on him in her time of need. She had died alone, save for the Whitmore woman and the child whom she had kept hidden from Gray.

Gray opened his eyes and forced the painful memories away. He had left Sharon with child, and she obviously hadn't considered him worthy of the knowledge. He supposed he couldn't really blame her. He had been a bitter, mixed-up hothead back in those days. Still, the fact that she hadn't told him didn't sit right in his gut. He knew Sharon. Or at least he thought he had. Things had gotten a little crazy those last couple of weeks before he left. Leaving Thatcher had been the only thing that had kept him sane and out of trouble with the law—at least the law according to the Buckmasters.

Enough, Longwalker, he ordered. Gray turned his attention back to the Whitmore woman. A thick mane of blond hair fell around her shoulders. Her eyes were the greenest Gray had ever seen. Like jade. She had long, shapely legs to which the navy leggings she wore clung like a second skin. The thigh-length matching sweater did nothing to conceal the lush curves underneath. Gray felt a stirring in his loins and averted his gaze.

She might look like a million bucks, but he already knew that Lauren Whitmore would treat him just the way everybody else in this town did. Not to mention the fact that she stood between him and his child. The child he had only recently learned existed.

Gray set his jaw and willed the rage to retreat. Rehashing the past would serve no purpose, but he would not allow history to repeat itself. Gray had been called a half-breed all his life. No one who wanted to continue breathing would ever call a child of his halfbreed. And no child of his would ever be called a bastard.

He glanced at the Whitmore woman again. No one would stop him from claiming his child.

No one.

Since Gray's whereabouts had been unknown, an ad announcing the Whitmore woman's intent to adopt the daughter of Sharon Johnson and Gray Longwalker had been placed in the local newspaper of his last-known city of residence.

Gray knew without a doubt that no real effort had been made to find him. Davis had merely fulfilled the necessary legal technicalities to proceed with the adoption. Neither he nor Lauren intended for Gray to find out about Sarah. If they had known that Gray still had connections in Laredo, the ad would never have been placed in a newspaper there. Still, he'd had to give her the benefit of the doubt. But when he had gone to Lauren's door, her attitude had told him she wasn't interested. And now, here they were, sitting in her attorney's office getting nowhere.

Lauren and Davis had apparently reached some sort of decision and both returned to their seats. Davis settled behind the big oak desk and Lauren sat in the chair adjacent to Gray. She kept her gaze fixed firmly on Davis, not giving Gray so much as a sideways glance.

Gray's pulse picked up. Now he would find out just how serious Lauren Whitmore was about keeping his daughter from him.

"Mr. Longwalker," Davis began, "the law clearly gives you the right to demand custody of your child—"

Lauren gasped, but quickly cleared her throat and clasped her hands in her lap. Gray saw the tremendous effort she required to compose herself once more. She evidently didn't want to hear what her attorney had to say now any more than she had a few moments ago.

"As I was saying," Davis continued. "If you are,

in fact, Sarah's biological father, then you have every right to petition the court for custody.''

"Is there any question that I'm the father?" Gray straightened in his chair and leveled his full attention on the round face of the stocky attorney. "I thought Sharon named me as the father on the birth certificate." And with his Navajo heritage there couldn't be much question as to whether the child had inherited his Native American features. That part would be obvious. With her Irish-American background, Sharon certainly couldn't have passed those traits onto the child.

"That's true. Ms. Johnson did name you as the father, however, that alone won't stand up in court.''

Gray's hackles rose at the implication. "Sharon Johnson might not have been one of Thatcher's more prominent citizens, but she would never have lied about something like this." Gray had no intention of sitting here and allowing some spit-polished, college-educated snob to sully Sharon's name, even though she hadn't seen fit to let Gray know about his child.

"I didn't mean to imply otherwise," Davis clarified quickly.

"Good," Gray said, and glared at the man behind the desk. He forced his fury back to a manageable level. He had worked long and hard to learn to control his temper, but this new turn of events was testing those limits.

"Ms. Whitmore was given full custody of the child by the biological mother. If you choose to contend her adoption proceedings, then it's up to you to prove your right to do so in a court of law.''

Gray shrugged. "I have no problem with that. Just tell me where to go and what to do.''

Davis eyed him skeptically. "The test and court costs will be quite expensive, Mr. Longwalker. Since it is up to you to prove paternity, then the burden of cost for both you and the child will fall on your shoulders."

"Whatever it takes," Gray responded without hesitation. His own attorney had warned him to expect this stall tactic.

Lauren darted a nervous glance in his direction. Gray smiled to himself. He may have left Thatcher as poor as dirt, but he hadn't been as dumb as dirt. Don Davis would probably faint dead away if he knew just how much money Gray had growing interest in a Dallas bank account.

"Well, then." Davis jotted a few notes on his legal pad before looking up again. "I'll see that the arrangements for the test are made as soon as possible. Leave a contact number with my secretary and I'll be in touch. Once the paternity issue is resolved in the eyes of the law, Mr. Longwalker, you may petition the court for custody."

Gray had a bad feeling about the custody part. Lauren Whitmore probably had the whole town on her side—including the judge. "How long will the test results take?"

"Two weeks at least," Davis answered smoothly. "The custody battle, however, could go on for months—" he peered self-righteously at Gray over his wire-rimmed bifocals "—or years even," he finished smugly.

Gray restrained the anger that skyrocketed inside him. He didn't care how long it took. Sarah was his child, and he fully intended to have her. "Fine," he relented, his patience holding on by a thin thread. "When can I see Sarah?"

"Don," Lauren protested. She clutched the arms of her chair, her knuckles white with the effort.

"We won't discuss visitation until after paternity has been established," Davis stated, as if the issue was closed to further discussion.

Gray rose to his full height of six feet two inches. He leaned over and placed his hands palm down on Davis's gleaming desktop and settled a gaze Gray hoped communicated the seriousness of his words to the man staring up at him. "Discuss visitation or don't discuss it, it makes no difference to me. But I will see my daughter. Is that clear?"

"You will have absolutely no contact with Lauren unless it comes through me, Mr. Longwalker. I hope that's clear," he said cautiously. "And threatening me won't do you any good," he added carefully.

"It's not a threat," Gray offered without apology. He straightened and picked up his hat from the table that separated his chair from Lauren's. "It's a promise." He met Lauren Whitmore's gaze for the space of two heartbeats before turning away.

Gray strode out of the office without a backward glance. As angry as he was, he knew one thing for sure—he would never be able to forget the look on Lauren Whitmore's face. As pale as a ghost, her eyes full of fear, she had looked ready to break down and cry.

He hardened his heart against the sympathy that arose immediately. It wasn't as if he hadn't given her the opportunity to resolve this thing between the two of them. But she wanted no part of a negotiation. She had made up her mind long before laying eyes on

Gray. She intended to keep his daughter from him, that much was evident. Gray clenched his jaw. He had no doubt that the woman cared deeply for his daughter. Lauren Whitmore would suffer as this battle played out. But her pain was inconsequential, Gray reminded himself. His only concern was claiming his daughter—Sarah.

Chapter Two

Gray stood in the middle of Thatcher's only cemetery. The March wind whipped around him and through the branches of the old oak trees, the sound breaking the deathly silence. He felt cold and uncharacteristically lost inside. In the distance the small town that was supposed to be his home sprawled across the flat landscape that seemed to go on forever. The place had never actually felt like home to him, not even when he was a small child. No pleasant memories sprang to mind, no old friends he longed to visit. Nothing remained for him but pain and bitterness, and enough anger to last three lifetimes. But he'd been born and raised here.

And that made this place home.

Gray had always been an outcast. A half-breed bastard who worked like two men for half the pay of one. Gray swallowed the anger that accompanied that memory. Old man Jennings had at least given him a place to sleep, and three meals a day. No one else would have taken him in after his mother died, leaving him alone at sixteen, with no money or place to go. Gray drew in a deep breath and scanned the wide-open blue sky. It was during that eight-year stint on Jennings's ranch that Gray had discovered his God-given talent with horses and how to use it. But it wasn't until he left this hate-filled place that he had learned to utilize his skills to their fullest extent.

Horse training required great patience and the ability to open himself completely to reach the animals, and before Gray could do that he'd had to learn to control the rage that had driven him from the age of ten. Self-discipline had been hard earned and long in coming. But he had mastered the art four years ago. Oh, he had the occasional relapse, like today in Davis's office, but he'd grabbed back control swiftly enough. He wasn't the same man who left here all those years ago. Despite the indifference and taunting he had suffered growing up, he held no true grudges, except one.

Gray glanced beyond the rows of typical headstones until he found the one of the man who had sired him. A massive monument loomed over the family plot. He gritted his teeth and tamped down the churning emotions that threatened now, even after all this time. His *father*—the word turned his stomach—had taken advantage of Gray's mother, turning her into his mistress. Then he'd killed her one inch at a time. Never once had the man spared one iota of concern for the illegitimate child born of their infidelity. By the time Gray had reached school age, the man had turned his back on both of them. Covered up his wrong doing, making their lives miserable in the process.

Determined not to be undone by his past, Gray shifted his gaze back to the small headstone that marked Sharon Johnson's final resting place. Tiny blue flowers blanketed the year-old grave. A frown furrowed his brow as he tried to think why Sharon would hide the existence of his child from him. They had been friends. It was true that he'd made a mistake by taking her to bed that last night, but she seemed to need him as much as he needed her.

Gray blew out a weary breath. There was no point in wasting energy trying to analyze her motivation. The fact was she hadn't wanted him to know, and she had made the Whitmore woman promise to keep the child from him. He could not bring himself to hold that mistake against Sharon. God knows he'd made his share. What was done was done.

The sound of a vehicle pulling to a stop next to his truck tugged Gray's attention in that direction. It was an older model sedan, its dark-blue paint dusty from the gravel road. He squinted to make out the face of the driver. The door opened and an elderly woman slowly emerged from behind the steering wheel.

Mrs. Jennings.

Gray removed his hat and waited silently as the old woman approached the cemetery gate.

She hesitated when she noticed him. Gray saw the instant recognition flare. She eyed him another long moment. Then, using her cane for assistance, she closed the distance that separated them.

"I'd heard you were back," she said in a voice rusty with age. Faded-blue eyes studied him with surprising sharpness. "Causing trouble already, too, they say," she added, pointedly.

"Is that what *they* say?" A smile tugged at the corners of his mouth. Maybe he did have one good memory or two. Marilee Jennings was one little old lady who had a stubborn streak herself. She liked nothing better than to put a cocky young man with a smart mouth in his place. No fifth-grader ever dared defy her authority. Not even Gray.

She nodded sagely. "Of course I set them straight about that." She leveled her gaze on his and thrust out her thin chin for emphasis. "I told them that to my knowledge Gray Longwalker never started any trouble in his entire life, but he sure as blazes would end it if anyone started it with him."

The smile won the tug of war with his lips. "It might not be so easy to end this time."

She lifted a sparse gray brow. "You may be right on that one. That city gal's mighty sweet and extra good to that little girl of yours." Mrs. Jennings leaned on her cane for support. "She'll give you a run for your money. Have you got yourself one of those fancy lawyers?"

"Yes, ma'am," Gray assured her. "The best. I had hoped it wouldn't come to that though."

The old woman shook her head. "Don't count on it, Gray."

Gray glanced back at the sedan she had arrived in. "How is Mr. Jennings?"

She pointed to the far side of the cemetery with her cane. "He passed on last year." Tears glistened in her eyes. "The ranch hasn't been the same without him." She glanced back up at Gray. "You should stop by while you're in town. I still put dinner on the table at the same time every day."

"I'll try to do that," he promised. It was probably the only place in the whole county where he was half-way welcome.

"You paid your respects to your momma yet?" she demanded in that once-a-schoolteacher-always-a-schoolteacher tone.

"I was about to do that." It was a lie. He had no desire to visit his mother's grave. He didn't want to be reminded of her final days. But Mrs. Jennings still wielded an unexplainable power over him. Since fifth grade some deeply entrenched habit took over whenever she rattled off an order, and he found himself responding positively.

"Well come along, then, and we'll see my Fred, too."

Gray stepped back for her to lead the way. "Do you know Lauren Whitmore well?" he asked as he followed Mrs. Jennings's slow progress down the long center aisle that separated the two sides of the cemetery.

"I know she won't give up that little girl without a fight." Mrs. Jennings turned back to Gray, her gaze connecting with his once more. "She loves the child like her own. She's done a fine job since Sharon, God rest her soul, passed on."

Though he appreciated what the Whitmore woman had done for his daughter, renewed anger twisted inside him that she somehow thought a few months of baby-sitting made the child hers. "That may be, but Sarah is my daughter, not hers."

"Watch your step, Longwalker," she warned. "Things are not always as cut-and-dried as they seem. Lauren isn't the only citizen of Thatcher who has an interest in little Sarah."

Gray considered her words for a long moment. "Sharon had no living relatives," he countered. There was no one, except him, that would be related by blood to Sarah.

"Let's just say that blood isn't always thicker than water. Buckmaster himself told me just before he left this world that he intended to make things right with you. I doubt his boys liked that idea very much."

"They can rest easy," Gray told her. "I never heard from the old man."

LAUREN PACED the long entry hall that separated her living room and dining room, then peeked out the window for the umpteenth time. Nothing, only pastures quickly turning a rich-green spread out as far as the eye could see. Bluebonnets added a punch of color to the sea of green. Though Lauren's small ranch only included fifty acres, she loved every square foot of it. Five years ago she would have laughed had anyone told her that very soon she would be living in the middle of nowhere on a former horse ranch. Lauren had loved the energy of the city. Loved the hectic pace of her job. But things changed.

Pushing the thoughts of the past away, she paced in the other direction, her fuzzy pink house slippers soundless on the polished oak floor. Otherwise Sarah would have wondered why her mommy was behaving so nervously.

Fluffy, Sarah's huge black-and-white Persian, sauntered to the door and yowled. Lauren smiled and reached down to scratch the feline's furry head. Like Spinner, the old horse left on the ranch she had inherited from her aunt, Fluffy had come with the place. It hadn't taken Lauren long to realize that life on a ranch wouldn't be complete without at least one cat and one horse. While most folks around here felt lost without a dog sleeping on the porch, Lauren had yet to make a trip to the pound in Dallas to adopt one. Something always came up. But she had her heart set on a big old Labrador. Fluffy voiced her irritation with Lauren's slow reactions.

"Okay, girl, you can go outside even if the rest of us are stuck in the house." Lauren opened the door just far enough for an impatient Fluffy to squeeze out, then closed and locked it. She immediately resumed her pacing.

This is ridiculous, she fumed silently. She couldn't keep worrying that Gray Longwalker would show up at her door again. Don's parting words echoed inside her head. *You need a restraining order.*

"Yeah, right," Lauren huffed to the empty hall. She knew all about Longwalker's reputation. If he wanted to drop by, it would take more than a legal document saying he couldn't to stop him.

"Mommy!" The shrill little voice pierced the tense gloom shrouding Lauren, bringing a smile instantly to her lips despite her worries.

Lauren stepped into the living room to see what Sarah wanted this time. Five minutes ago, she thought, affection widening her smile, it had been Leah. Sarah hadn't been able to find the special doll she'd had since the day Lauren brought her home to live with her. After searching every nook and cranny of the house, they had finally found the doll under the dining table.

"What's wrong, sweetie?" Lauren crooned to the little girl, who was gazing expectantly at her.

"Can I have a cookie, please?" The child smiled angelically, her expression hopeful as well as pleading. "Pretty, pretty, please? With sugar on top?"

Sarah's big gray eyes mocked Lauren, reminding her of the man poised to shatter both their lives.

Lauren tamped down the sudden urge to grab the

little girl and run as far away as possible—maybe even back to Chicago. But Lauren knew that her life was here now, and Thatcher was the only home Sarah had ever known. And she had made that promise. She had to trust Sharon's reasons, though she had not expounded upon them in depth, for not wanting the child to be raised by her father. If he was half as bad as the people in this town insinuated, he had no business raising a child.

Whatever happened the next few weeks, Lauren had to act as if everything were normal until the problem of Gray Longwalker could be resolved. Hard as it might prove to be, she would keep a happy face in place for Sarah's sake. Her daughter was particularly adept at picking up on Lauren's feelings.

Lauren forced her usual disciplinary expression, which was not nearly effective enough, and said, "You know better than to ask, Sarah, it's only four-thirty. You've had your after-school snack already." She gestured toward the television. "Watch cartoons. Dinner will be ready in a little while."

Sarah groaned and pulled her knees up under her chin. She shifted her doleful gaze back to the animated antics on the television screen. In a matter of seconds she had forgotten the denied request and was giggling at *Bugs Bunny*.

A long curtain of silky black hair slid around her thin little shoulders. Other than her skin being a shade or so lighter, the child looked exactly like her father. Lauren shivered at the memory of that haunting gaze of Gray Longwalker's.

Exactly.

Lauren's chest felt unbearably heavy. She couldn't lose this child—not now, not after she had fallen head over heels in love with her and made Sarah her own. Her breath caught at the memory that Lauren had at first refused Sharon's deathbed request to take the child. After losing the only man she had ever loved four years ago, Lauren had resigned herself about never having children. She couldn't possibly ever love another man; the risk of losing was too great. Thus, there would be no children. She had turned off those emotions. Though she loved children, she had simply disassociated herself with the concept of ever having any of her own. The thought of a child without marriage first had never entered her mind.

She closed her eyes and allowed the memories she would just as soon forget to flood her mind. She and Kevin were both ambitious and career oriented. They planned to marry and someday in the distant future they would have had children. They had been happy. Until the accident. And then he was gone. Lauren opened her eyes and clenched her jaw. It was bad enough that she lost the man she loved that dark, rainy night, but fate had also thrown her one final blow— the headaches. Life-altering headaches. Headaches that kept her from participating in life as she once had. That sent her scurrying away from the stress and noise of big-city living. That kept her working from a home office to reduce her stress even further. She'd even had to hire an assistant to help her do a job she had once accomplished by herself without thought.

Lauren sighed wearily and shuffled back to the hall. But she had survived, moved to Thatcher and made two very good friends, Rosemary and Sharon. Just over one year later, and at Sharon's perpetual insistence, Lauren had started spending large chunks of time with Sarah. The knowledge that the little girl would very soon be completely alone in the world had worn away at Lauren's resolve not to grow attached to her. Slowly but surely, the child had stolen Lauren's heart. And now Sarah belonged to her in every sense of the word. Nothing, not even Gray Longwalker was going to change that. He would not take her away, Lauren would see to that if it was the last thing she ever did.

She took one final peek out the window before going to the kitchen. Don was a good attorney. If anyone could prevent Longwalker from breezing back into town and taking Sarah, Don could. Lauren had to trust that, otherwise she would have a heck of a time maintaining her sanity.

A pleasant aroma met Lauren when she entered the kitchen. The roast she had planned for dinner simmered in the oven. Lauren smiled and double-checked the temperature setting. She loved to cook, even if it was only for the two of them. When she had remodeled this old ranch house, Lauren had designed a large, gourmet-style kitchen. Though she rarely entertained guests, she had wanted this big, airy kitchen and she had gotten it, guests or no.

Well, there had been those few dinners with Buck. Lauren shook her head. How could she ever have believed that she would be happy with him? She couldn't love him, she was too gun-shy to give her heart away again. Lauren threaded her fingers through her hair. Lack of confidence in herself in her new role as mother and plain old fear of the unknown had made her vulnerable to Buck's relentless pursuit. After Sharon's death, Lauren had somehow gotten it into her head that Sarah needed a father figure in her life. And, she admitted ruefully, she had been desperate to ensure she raised the little girl properly. After all, what did she know about raising children? She was an only child.

Thankfully, Lauren had realized in time that she didn't need Buck or anyone else to help her love and care for Sarah. Lauren was plenty capable of doing so on her own. Buck hadn't given up completely, though. He still called her from time to time. In fact, now that she thought about it, his efforts seemed to have increased lately.

Just what she needed, Lauren mused, another man disrupting her life. She shivered. Gray Longwalker looked man enough for two lifetimes. That strange awareness pricked Lauren at the thought of just how much man Longwalker was. So very tall, dark and...dangerous. And it wasn't just his rumored reputation, either. There was something about him...something Lauren couldn't quite label that made her uneasy, restless even.

She shook off the ridiculous feeling and turned her attention to the bread rising on the counter near the sink. She did not need anyone except Sarah to make her life complete. They were a family. And Lauren's parents were thrilled about having a grandchild. Both college professors, they would be coming for a visit at spring break. Lauren smiled when she suddenly remembered Sarah's glee at seeing snow in Chicago this past Christmas.

A wave of dizziness broadsided Lauren. She clutched the counter to steady herself, belatedly realizing she hadn't eaten since breakfast. The dizziness passed, but the deep, heavy ache that settled on the right side of her head didn't.

"Geez, you know better than this, Whitmore," she

grumbled. Lauren reached for the medication she kept
by the sink. She hoped she hadn't waited too late for
the drug to be effective. Everything around her had
spun out of control, the last thing she needed to do
was let this monster rear its ugly head.

A loud knock at the front door startled Lauren. She
jumped, and a few of the pills scattered across the
counter. She hastily scooped up the runaway pills and
dropped all but one back into the bottle.

She blew out a breath and willed herself to calm.
She was letting her imagination run away with her.
Lauren popped the single pill into her mouth and
washed it down with the last sip of cold coffee left in
her favorite mug. She grimaced at the bitter dregs, set
the mug that said I Love You, Mommy down and
headed into the hall to answer the door. Lord, there
was nothing in the world that tasted worse than cold
coffee.

She prayed it wasn't Longwalker. Don had mentioned calling this evening, maybe he had decided to
drop by instead. Lauren could use a little more of his
reassuring to shore up her waning resolve. She had
spent the entire afternoon pacing the floor and worrying about the situation.

"Pull yourself together, Lauren," she chided aloud.
"Falling apart isn't going to help." Another knock
echoed down the long hall.

"I'll get it!" Sarah squealed.

"No!" Lauren shouted as she bolted for the door.
She caught Sarah just before she opened it. "I'll get
the door. You go right back into the living room and
play or watch cartoons."

"Mom-mee," Sarah whined. Her big eyes darkened
with disappointment. As they had so few callers, the

child loved answering the door when the occasion presented itself.

"Do as I say, young lady," Lauren told her firmly. The little girl dropped her chin to her chest and trudged back into the living room. Not wanting Sarah to overhear any conversation regarding the present situation, Lauren closed the French doors behind her.

She chastised herself for being so hard on the child. They usually played games after school or watched Sarah's favorite cartoons together, but today had been different, and Gray Longwalker was to blame. None of this was Sarah's fault, yet the effects were already filtering down, changing Sarah's routine. No matter how things turned out in the long run, Lauren knew that Sarah would be the one to suffer and not understand why.

The pounding came at the door again, louder this time, more insistent.

Lauren exhaled and braced herself for the worst. Surely Longwalker wouldn't show up again today. Don had told him that all contact with her was to be made through him. But she knew deep in her heart that it was most likely him. Don wouldn't pound on her door like that. Outside of calling the sheriff, who would be a good twenty minutes responding, she felt she had no choice but to answer the door. If it was Longwalker, she doubted he would simply go away if she didn't answer.

The knock rattled the hinges this time. Lauren muttered an unladylike curse. What was she so worried about? Don was convinced that Longwalker couldn't possibly *really* want Sarah. Once he'd had a chance to think the whole thing over, he'd surely realize that fighting over a child he didn't even know would be far more trouble than he wanted. Once his indignation cooled, he would likely be on his way.

He was a drifter, what would he do with a child?

Feeling a boost in her confidence, Lauren pulled the door open and looked up into the very face she did not want to see. Gray Longwalker stared down at her with equal measures of wariness and impatience. She tried without success to blink away the black spots that suddenly floated before her eyes. A bolt of pain shot through her head, and she almost winced.

"Is my daughter here?" Gray asked quietly, his gaze steady from beneath the wide, black brim of his hat.

"Mr. Longwalker, this is my home, you have no right to be here." Lauren kept her voice low so as not to draw Sarah's attention. "I didn't extend an invitation, so please leave." She took several slow, deep breaths to counter the intense pain sizzling around the edges of her consciousness. She had waited too long before taking her medicine and now she would pay the price. She blocked the doorway with her weakening body. Please God, she prayed, let him leave before—

"I only want to see her," he persisted. "You can't keep her from me."

"You can't just show up like this," she argued with the last of her waning strength. Nausea rose in the back of her throat. She needed to lie down. Her body trembled. "Please go away. Talk to my attorney."

That silvery gaze settled fully onto hers, the weight almost buckling her knees. "I can't do that."

Lauren opened her mouth to protest, but a blinding flash of light obscured his image. Her knees gave way beneath her.

No, she willed silently, *not now. This can't happen now.*

Lauren struggled to hang on to consciousness. Darkness swallowed her as the pain exploded inside her head.

As if from some place far away, Lauren heard Sarah's cry…*Mommy.*

Chapter Three

Gray caught Lauren Whitmore just before she hit the floor. He held her limp body in his arms and dropped down to his knees.

God in Heaven, what am I supposed to do now?

"Mommy!" a shrill voice screamed.

Gray jerked his head up at the terrified sound. What he saw sucked the air right out of his lungs.

A little girl stood stock-still in the middle of the entrance hall. The terror in her eyes far exceeded what he had heard in her voice. Big, tear-filled eyes stared back at him...*gray eyes*. Black hair draped her trembling shoulders and fell all the way to her waist. Hair so black it looked blue wherever the light reflected against it.

The drumming of Gray's heart blocked all other sound. An emotion so foreign he couldn't possibly hope to identify it rushed through him.

This was his child.

Gray didn't need a test. He couldn't have denied this child even if he had wanted to. *This* was why Lauren Whitmore's eyes had widened so when he had first appeared at her door this morning. Gray had assumed she had recognized him by old photographs Sharon had left behind, but that wasn't the case at all.

Lauren Whitmore had seen Sarah in him.

"What's wrong with my mommy?"

The question jerked Gray from his intense reverie. He looked from the frightened child to the woman in his arms and relaxed the overtight hold he'd only just realized he had on Lauren. She was out cold.

"I don't know," he said, and then lifted his gaze back to the child's. She watched him with a wary but expectant gaze. "We were talking and she passed out."

The little girl sniffed and eased closer. "Mommy says if nobody's home 'cept me when she gets sick, I should call 911 like she showed me." She gave him another wary look as she took one more small step closer.

Gray exhaled heavily. He looked down at Lauren Whitmore, who still hadn't moved a muscle. He checked her pulse at the side of her throat. "Well, she's breathing and her pulse is strong and steady." He looked back at the child, hoping to appease her. "I don't think we need to call 911, Sarah."

The child's eyes grew wide at his use of her name. "How'd you know my name? You're a stranger."

Holding Lauren against his chest, he stuck out his free hand. "Gray Longwalker."

Sarah stared at his outstretched hand, her dark eyebrows knit in worry. "Are you a friend of my mommy's?"

Gray hesitated, then nodded. It was a flat-out lie, but he knew the child needed reassuring.

Sarah didn't take his hand. "Are you gonna help my mommy, mister?"

"Just call me Gray," he offered, letting his hand drop.

Sarah didn't respond, she simply stood there and stared at him—clearly fearful of what might happen.

"How about we lay your mom down somewhere and then I'll call her doctor? She has a doctor, doesn't she?"

The child nodded and gestured for Gray to follow her down the hall. Gray took off his Stetson, tossing it on the hall table. He adjusted his hold on Lauren and got to his feet. He followed Sarah to the far end of the hall, into a darkened bedroom. She turned on the bedside lamp and climbed onto the bed. Silently she waited while Gray laid Lauren beside her.

"Dr. Bill's number is by the phone in the kitchen," she said quietly, never taking her eyes from the still form next to her.

"I'll go call, then."

Sarah didn't answer or even look up. She caressed Lauren's cheek with small, trembling fingers.

Gray forced the haunting image from his mind as he retraced his steps down the hall until he found the dining room. He skirted the already-set table and passed through an open doorway into the kitchen. After locating the phone, he punched in the posted number for Dr. Bill Prescott. Gray didn't recognize the name, obviously another newcomer to Thatcher.

Gray inhaled the mouthwatering aroma that filled the kitchen. His stomach rumbled. How long had it been since he'd had a home-cooked meal? Too long to remember, he thought with uncharacteristic longing.

While he listened to the receptionist's greeting, Gray turned the oven off. Whatever Lauren Whitmore had on tonight's menu would have to wait. He noticed the open medicine bottle by the sink and picked it up to read the label.

Gray gave the receptionist a quick summary of what had taken place. After a brief wait on hold, a man answered and identified himself as the doctor.

"Tell me exactly what happened," Prescott ordered, concern in his voice.

"One minute we were talking and the next she was out like a light." Gray rotated the bottle in his hand to verify the name when the doctor asked about medication. "Yes, the open bottle was next to the sink, but I have no idea if she took a tablet."

"This is the first episode Lauren has had in quite some time," Prescott said, and then hesitated as if considering the best course of action. "She'll sleep for several hours. When she wakes up she'll be weak, and the pain will likely come again. Just keep her comfortable and have her call me as soon as she's up and around again. I can come by tonight if she needs me."

"If you don't mind my asking, what's wrong with her?" Gray ventured, and then quickly added, "I haven't known her very long."

There was a long pause before Prescott responded. "She has cluster headaches," he finally explained. "They're similar to migraines, but the cluster effect makes them more intense. She doesn't have them often anymore, but when they strike they're debilitating. It's not as bad as it sounds, Mr....what did you say your name was?"

"Longwalker. Gray Longwalker."

"Mr. Longwalker, Lauren's headaches appear to be mainly related to stress. As long as she stays clear of any major stress she doesn't have any problems. I have no idea of your relationship with Lauren, but I sincerely hope you won't let this incident color your opinion of her. Lauren's a terrific young woman. Obviously, though, there's something stressful going on in her life right now.''

Gray assured the doctor he would have Lauren call him. He pushed the off button and placed the cordless receiver back in its cradle. He swallowed hard as he considered Dr. Prescott's words.

Stress.

He had done this to Lauren Whitmore. Gray shook off the regret and forced away the guilt. The woman had chosen to come between him and his child. She had, in effect, brought this particular stress upon herself, he rationalized, but it didn't relieve the guilt nagging at him.

When Gray returned to the bedroom, Sarah sat in the exact same place he had left her, still stroking Lauren's cheek. Gray eased down on the edge of the bed feeling sorely out of place in the role of caretaker to anyone but himself.

"Is my mommy gonna be okay?" She looked up at Gray with a worried gaze that squeezed his heart.

"Yes." He smiled and awkwardly patted her shoulder. "She'll sleep for a while, but the doctor says she's going to be fine." He quashed the renewed rush of guilt that crowded his chest.

"Good." Sarah frowned then, her whole face puckered in the process. "I don't want my new mommy to go to Heaven like my old mommy did."

Gray swallowed back the emotion that pushed up into his throat. He'd never in his life been an emotional man. He didn't quite understand his reaction. Maybe he was tired from the trip and all the anger he had felt at life these past two days.

"Don't worry, Sarah. She'll be fine."

"You promise?" She stared up at him, tears brimming.

"I promise," he said, his voice strained, almost harsh.

Gray had wished for many things since he had learned of his child's existence, not the least of which was the blackest curse he knew to fall upon the person's head responsible for trying to keep his child from him.

Right now, though, he prayed with his entire being that Lauren Whitmore would be okay.

For Sarah's sake.

LAUREN DRIFTED somewhere between asleep and awake well before her eyes would obey the command to open. Wherever she was, darkness surrounded her. No glimmer of light shone through her closed lids. She could hear something...the sound vaguely familiar.

She tried to reach out, to feel and maybe identify her surroundings despite the darkness, but her arms were so heavy that she couldn't move. Her head hurt.

The sound was louder now.

Water.

Water was filling the car. Lauren was trapped. She couldn't move, couldn't breathe...

Fear crowded her throat and robbed her of rational thought. She struggled against the seat belt, but couldn't quite free herself. The water continued to rise around her.

Air...she needed air.

Hold your breath, Lauren, hold your breath. Kevin... She reached for him...

Lauren sat straight up in bed, gasping for air.

A dream. *It was only a dream,* she realized. The accident was a long time ago. It was over now. She was safe.

Weak as a kitten she cradled her head in her hands and willed the lingering remnants of pain to retreat. She massaged her forehead and then pressed the tips of her fingers against her temples in an effort to keep the raging beast at bay.

Slowly, very slowly, the perception of time and place returned.

She was home. And she was okay.

Just a headache and a nightmare. It had been a long time since she'd had either. Not since Sharon's death.

She should get up and check on Sarah....

The memory of what had taken place just prior to her blackout slammed into Lauren's head. She threw back the coverlet, dropped her feet to the floor and forced herself to stand. A wave of nausea washed over her when she took a step, but she ignored it and forced another step and then another after that.

She had to find Sarah.

Lauren had no idea how long she had been out. Longwalker could have taken Sarah anywhere by now. She swallowed back the metallic taste of fear. Goose bumps skittered across her skin as adrenaline surged through her body, giving her the strength she needed to stagger across the room.

Once in the dark hall, her hopes plummeted. The house was entirely too quiet and dark.

No playing-child noises. No television sounds. Nothing.

Lauren moved down the hall, her heart racing, urging her to hurry. She tried to breathe more slowly, but failed. Her hold on composure thin at best, she kept one shaky hand against the wall for balance.

God...Sarah has to be here. She just has to be here.

Lauren blinked back the tears threatening and tried to recall the details of Longwalker's truck. The police would need that information. She frowned with the effort of concentration. Her head felt like a bomb that had already exploded once and was prepared to do so again.

Think, Lauren, think. Black, she knew it had been black and new looking. But that's all she remembered.

She should never have opened the door. Never have allowed him inside. Why hadn't she called the sheriff?

Now he had Sarah.

Oh, God. How would she ever find her? If Gray Longwalker disappeared again, she'd never find Sarah.

The night's full moon had pitched the dimly lit living room into long shadows. The television taunted her with its black screen. Panic rushed anew through Lauren then.

They were gone.

She pivoted unsteadily and propelled herself in the direction of the kitchen. She had to call the police *now*.

And Don. She should call Don, too.

Lauren banged her hip against the dining table as she passed, a chair clattered to the floor behind her. She knew she would have a huge bruise by morning, but at the moment she didn't feel the discomfort. She clenched her teeth and refused to give in to the storm steadily building inside her head.

Lauren snatched the phone from its cradle and sagged against the wall. She squeezed her eyes shut at the fierce stab of pain that knifed through the right side of her skull.

The light...the overhead light was so bright. Had she turned it on? She didn't remember.

Unable to stand any longer, Lauren slid down the wall to the floor. A sob tore past her lips at the next rush of pain and she clenched her teeth to prevent the scream that wanted to follow. Biological parents stole their children back from adoptive parents all the time. Ultimately the law was on the side of the matching DNA. Getting Sarah back would be next to impossible.

Lauren had to make that call—now—before she lost herself to the pain. She clutched the receiver and forced her eyes open. The numbers on the keypad blurred. She blinked and tried again to focus. The overhead fluorescent light sent black spots floating before her bleary vision. She couldn't do it.

Another sob escaped her as she momentarily yielded to the anguish. "No," she whispered hoarsely. Lauren sucked in a ragged breath and peered at the numbers through the haze of pain. She had to do it. She had to call.

Seemingly out of nowhere, strong fingers grasped her arm. Lauren screamed and tried to jerk free of the powerful hand holding her so firmly. Her heart thundered in her chest. The beast inside her skull roared, breaking the fragile barrier between her and the pain.

"What are you doing?" a deep, raspy voice demanded.

Ignoring the torturous light, Lauren looked up.

Him. It was him. Gray Longwalker was still here.

"Where's Sarah?" she choked out, her throat almost closed with fear and anguish.

If he was here, then...Sarah must still be here, too. Lauren clutched the cordless receiver and struggled to get to her feet. Her stomach churned violently, followed so closely by a stab of agony that she almost blacked out. She moaned despite her best efforts not to.

She sank back to the floor and squeezed her eyes shut. God, it hurt so badly she could hardly draw in a breath. "Sarah," she murmured.

"Sarah is asleep in her room," Longwalker said quietly, as if he knew not to speak too loudly.

But how could he know?

Lauren forced her eyes open to see his face, and immediately regretted doing so. The light inflicted more of its pain. Could he be telling her the truth? She had to be certain. She had to see Sarah with her own eyes. She commanded her body to move…but nothing happened.

"What can I do to help?" He knelt beside her now. The slightest hint of concern in his voice.

"The light," Lauren whispered. "Please turn off the light."

The light was out before she realized he had even moved.

"Do you need the medicine on the counter? Your doctor asked if you'd taken it."

His words registered in her brain, but didn't quite make sense. Had he called her doctor? Why would he do that for her? Why hadn't he taken Sarah and gotten as far away as he could before Lauren regained consciousness? Maybe he still intended to do just that.

"Sarah…I have to go to her," Lauren whispered as she waged a war with her unwilling body to stand. She opened her eyes, immensely thankful for the answering darkness.

"Let me help you." His strong arm slid around her waist, and he lifted Lauren to her feet with ease.

Why would he help her? Suspicious, Lauren jerked free of his grasp, almost falling as another wave of pain slashed through her. The silent figure towering over her steadied her with sure hands.

"Don't touch me," she warned and backed away, the wall stopped her.

"It's okay, I won't touch you."

Lauren couldn't see his eyes in the dark room. It was impossible to guess what he might be thinking. She didn't care. She only knew that she had to get to Sarah.

She drew in a deep breath and focused on blocking out the pain. She got a slight measure of temporary relief.

Still holding the phone, Lauren groped her way along the wall for balance as she moved down the dark hall toward Sarah's room. Uninvited, Gray followed.

When Lauren finally reached Sarah's door and opened it, the dim night-light gave off enough illumination for her to see that her child was, as he had said, tucked safely into bed. Sarah slept soundly, totally unaware of the threat that lurked just outside her room.

And what had he told Sarah while Lauren had lain unconscious?

She backed out of Sarah's room and quietly closed the door. Lauren turned to the man waiting in the darkness behind her, his silent presence more unnerving than the pain radiating beneath her scalp.

"If you said anything to upset her—"

"I told her I was a friend, nothing more," he said, his voice cautious, unreadable. "You should take more of your medication and lie back down. I'll help you. Dr. Prescott said—"

"I want you to leave, *now*," Lauren said with as much bravado as she could muster. How dare he speak with her personal physician. Had he asked questions about her? If he had, surely Bill hadn't answered. Longwalker already knew more about her than she wanted him to know—she wasn't about to tell him anything else. He would no doubt look for anything to use against her in the custody battle.

"I'm not leaving," he stated flatly. "You're in no condition to be left alone with a child to care for."

The sudden blast of outrage Lauren felt almost cloaked the fierce pain. "I appreciate that you stayed," she said, her voice strained, "but I have *real* friends I can call for help, Mr. Longwalker."

"You'd better call someone, then, because I'm not leaving until you do."

Lauren held her anger in check, knowing the emotion would ultimately only add to her misery. Somehow she had to stay in control until she could get this man out of her house. There was no way of knowing why he had decided to be nice to her. Or why he hadn't taken Sarah and gotten as far away as possible. But she wasn't about to risk a sudden change of heart. Lauren concentrated on the task of locating the correct numbers without the aid of sight. Much calmer than before, she was able to visualize mentally their location and punch the necessary numbers without much trouble.

Rosemary, Lauren's friend and assistant, answered after the second ring. "It's Lauren," she said without preamble. "I need you to come over and—" she glanced up at the brooding figure next to her "—stay with me tonight.'' Rosemary agreed without hesitation, Lauren thanked her and disconnected.

''Satisfied?'' Her breathing had become shallow with the increasing difficulty of keeping the mounting pain at bay.

''All right,'' he said roughly and turned away.

Relieved, Lauren followed him toward the front of the house. Gray snatched his hat off the hall table, opened the door and turned back to face her. A golden glow pooled around him from the porch light. Lauren could see the rigid set of his shoulders, the grim line of his mouth. Her heart thudded in response, sending a quickening of panic through her weary body, which only served to add to her suffering.

''I will be back,'' he warned.

''You know what my attorney said,'' she argued, ''you have to wait for the test results.''

His taunting smile was slow, bitter, involving only one corner of his mouth. ''I don't need a test and *you* know it. Sarah is my child and I *will* be back.''

Lauren braced herself against the wall for support. She was close to losing control again. ''Why don't you go back to wherever you came from and leave us alone?'' She hated the desperate sound in her voice, hated her weakness in front of this man.

''Get used to it, Ms. Whitmore. I'm not going anywhere.'' He turned and disappeared into the dark night without a backward glance.

Lauren closed and locked the door behind him. Rosemary had a key. She could let herself in when she arrived. Lauren pressed her forehead against the hard surface of the door and slowly yielded to the agony that would be postponed no longer.

The threat of Gray Longwalker would have to be

shoved to the back burner until tomorrow or maybe even the day after. Right now Lauren had to deal with the pain. She sank to the floor and curled into a ball, surrendering to the pain and the blackness that would soon follow.

Gray Longwalker would just have to wait his turn to make her life unbearable.

SHE WAS DOING the right thing, Lauren told herself two days later when she took Sarah to the lab appointment Don had scheduled. It was a necessary evil that should have been done yesterday, but the bout of headaches had kept Lauren in bed for nearly forty-eight hours. This morning was the first time she had been out of the house since the episode with Longwalker. She forced the memory away. She didn't want to think about that right now. She wanted this business over.

Sarah held Lauren's hand as they followed the lab technician down the long, white corridor. Lauren could almost hear the pounding of her own heart; the sound seemed to echo in the stifling silence around them. The steady tap of her low-heeled pumps countered the squeak of the lab tech's rubber-soled shoes against the polished tile floor. Both kept time with the pounding in her chest. *I'm doing the right thing*, Lauren told herself once more.

She glanced down at her daughter, who was busy taking in everything she saw. Sarah hugged Leah close to her side. Lauren had dressed Sarah in her favorite pink overalls. Her long black braid hung down her back with a pink satin ribbon tied at the end. The plain white blouse looked stark against her dark skin.

Lauren shivered when Gray came immediately to mind, despite her best intentions not to think about him. This was all his fault. If Gray Longwalker had stayed away, she and Sarah wouldn't be here right now. Lauren moistened her dry lips and swallowed hard. But he has rights, she reminded herself. She just prayed those rights didn't allow him to take Sarah away and prevent Lauren from seeing the child again.

Frank, her boss, was nearing a cardiac episode with her work delays. An architect at the growing Dallas firm, Lauren was very lucky that Frank allowed her to work from home. He was very sympathetic to her needs. But this thing with Longwalker only made matters worse. Though he understood, Lauren knew the last few days had put him seriously behind. The rest of the world didn't stop just because hers was crashing down around her. Contractors needed their new specs for design changes, clients wanted their architectural drawings now. No one wanted to wait. Except Lauren. She wanted time to stop right now, before fate tore her heart out yet again.

The lab tech she and Sarah followed down the endless corridor would take the necessary blood and saliva samples for the DNA test.

Lauren shuddered inwardly but smiled down at Sarah's upturned face. She had to be strong. She had to. "It'll be okay, sweetie," she assured her quietly. Sarah blinked and managed a hesitant smile.

"Right in here, Ms. Whitmore," the lab tech announced and gestured toward an open door.

"Thank you," Lauren said automatically, though she felt far from thankful. Every instinct told her to grab Sarah and run. Her stomach twisted itself into a thousand knots as she led her innocent, unsuspecting child into the small room. Sarah had no way of knowing that what was about to happen would forever change her life.

Lauren had struggled with the decision the entire journey to Dallas. If she opted not to submit Sarah to the test, Gray would no doubt make a legal move. By taking the test, Lauren had a couple of weeks to figure out some way to fight him. Two weeks, three tops. It was no time at all.

"You may hold Sarah in your lap if you'd like," the tech suggested, nodding toward the beige molded-plastic chair against the wall.

Numbly, Lauren sat down and pulled Sarah onto her lap. She pressed a kiss to the top of her head and gave her a hug. Her chest ached with the fierce pounding of her heart.

"Mommy, if I'm a good girl, do I get a present?" Sarah looked up at Lauren, her big gray eyes hopeful.

Please let this be the right thing.

"Sure, baby," Lauren said softly.

"And I want a Little Mermaid Band-Aid," Sarah piped up.

"I think I can handle that." The tech smiled.

Lauren fought the burn of tears behind her eyes. Even the medicinal smell of the place made her stomach churn. She had to do this. They needed the time before Gray made a move. But Lauren knew how this test would turn out.

"Now," the tech began, "this won't hurt a bit."

Chapter Four

Time crawled at a snail's pace for Gray. Three days had passed since he had arrived in town...since he had seen Sarah. He had been in Thatcher only seventy-two hours and it felt like a year.

He hated this god-awful place. Sarah was the only reason he had come back. Yesterday afternoon he had driven to Dallas and parted with the required samples for the DNA test. He supposed that Lauren had taken Sarah, as well. But, of course, he had no way of knowing because no one told him anything.

Gray blew out a disgusted breath as his surroundings came back into focus. He sat alone in the diner. The booth's red vinyl seats were faded and cracked with age. Nothing had changed about the place. Same scarred counter. Same black-and-white tile floor, coated with years of wax and buffed to a high, slightly yellowed sheen. Booths and tables, some mismatched and all worn from decades of use, filled the surprisingly clean diner.

A waitress placed his breakfast in front of him, freshened his coffee and smiled flirtatiously. Gray nodded, but didn't return the smile.

He knew what people thought of him in this town.

He'd stopped caring long ago. The quick, nervous glances and periodic murmuring told him that, like the diner's decorating scheme, the people hadn't changed, either.

Gray stared at the bacon, eggs and toast on his plate with complete disinterest. He really wasn't hungry. He hadn't been for days.

Not since he had seen his child...*Sarah.*

Gray closed his eyes and envisioned the little girl. His heart squeezed in his chest. When he'd first learned of her existence, he had tried to imagine what she looked like but hadn't been able to put a mental image with his expectations.

Now he knew.

He opened his eyes and surveyed the small crowd in the diner. These people knew Sarah was his daughter, as well—they would have to be blind not to know. Mrs. Jennings had known.

Had anyone in this pathetic excuse for a town ever treated Sarah as they had treated him? Anger rose with such swiftness that he balled his fists.

Gray forced back the anger, shuddering with the effort. He would not allow it to consume him. He picked up his fork and stabbed at the food. His stomach turned. He couldn't eat. Even the invitation for dinner at the Jennings ranch held no appeal for him. The fork clattered against the heavy white plate, earning Gray another round of suspicious looks and renewed murmuring.

Gray clenched his jaw and met each look with a fierce stare of his own. *Let them say something,* he mused. His fingers itched for an excuse—any excuse—to pound someone senseless.

He dragged in a long, deep breath and forced his

attention to the wall of windows and the street outside. The last thing he needed was a fight. The law in this town would love an excuse to send him packing, or worse.

Gray hadn't been in a brawl in more than four years. He walked away from conflict now. He had made peace with himself, if no one else. He had chosen his path and never looked back. There hadn't been any reason to look back, until now.

The idea that his blood ran through that little girl's veins shifted something—some sort of balance—deep inside him. Gray didn't quite understand the feeling. He didn't exactly love Sarah.... How could he? He didn't even know her. The sensation was something much more primal than love. A sense of responsibility or protectiveness maybe.

Whatever it was, it grew with each breath he took.

When he had tucked Sarah into bed the other night, he had sat on the floor for a long while and watched her sleep. He had never before experienced such a driving desire to possess something. He wanted this child. *His child.*

Gray pushed his plate away and finished off his coffee. He hadn't heard anything from Lauren Whitmore's attorney other than the time and place for the lab appointment. Davis had until five o'clock today to contact Gray, after that his own attorney would start legal proceedings. He would not waste any more time waiting or analyzing Mrs. Jennings's comment about someone else having an interest in Sarah. No one would keep him from claiming his daughter.

Gray had stayed away from Lauren since the episode on Monday night. He had struggled ever since with guilt he shouldn't even be feeling. He didn't know much about headaches, other than he'd had his share, but he had never seen anyone suffer the way Lauren had. But he had to set his sympathy aside. Lauren Whitmore was an obstacle he intended to remove from his path—one way or another.

Gray stood, ignoring the wary looks his every move earned him. He dropped the cash on the table for his meal and headed for the door. He'd had about all the Thatcher social life he could stand for one morning.

A bell jingled as he pushed the door open and stepped outside. Gray closed his eyes and raised his face to the warmth the sun offered against the cool March wind. He drew in a deep breath, settled his hat on his head and wondered how he could occupy himself today. He had visited a few of his old haunts the last couple of nights. What little night life Thatcher had to offer hadn't changed much since he left, either.

Maybe he would go out to Manning's ranch and take a look at that stallion the old man was having such a hard time with. He had heard the stories at the tavern last night about the demon horse Manning owned. The animal had injured the half dozen or so men who had tried to work with him already. Gray had a gut feeling that the horse had probably paid dearly for his rebellion, and that bothered him far more than what the men who had tried to break him had suffered.

Gray walked in the direction of the hotel where he had taken a room and left his truck. Thatcher was always quiet at this time of the morning. The kids were in school, and most of the other folks were at work, except those who made a career out of hanging out in Sid's Diner or Dilbert's General Store.

The same old storefronts lined the sidewalk, with

only a fresh coat of paint here and there to mark any progress. The wind slashed down the straight line called Main Street that cut smack through the middle of the two-horse town.

Gray shook his head in disgust. Thatcher only reminded him of the things he had worked hard to forget. The longer he stayed the harder it became to maintain the discipline he had struggled to achieve.

A mane of blond hair fluttering in the wind caught Gray's eye. His gaze traveled the length of the female whose back was turned to him. His attention riveted to the firm, round derriere encased in snug-fitting jeans. Maybe there was a thing or two in this town worth a second look. The sound of the woman's almost musical voice wafted to his ears. Gray stopped dead in his tracks. Every muscle in his body tensed.

Lauren Whitmore.

Gray headed in her direction. No time like the present to find out just what was going on with the visitation arrangements. He had no intention of taking no for an answer.

Lauren shifted, providing an unobstructed view of the man who had her attention.

Gray's step faltered, and his gut clenched. His fingers curled into tight fists.

James Buckmaster, Jr. *Buck.*

Gray swore hotly. The very sight of the man resurrected a lifetime of bone-deep hatred. Gray set his jaw hard against a long string of vulgarities lined up on the tip of his tongue.

The annoyingly pleasant sound of Lauren Whitmore's laughter floated across the breeze. Buck smiled and leaned down to drop a kiss on her waiting cheek.

Something inside Gray broke lose and threatened to

explode. Rage like he had not allowed himself to feel in a very long time washed over him.

Whether Lauren Whitmore knew it or not, the stakes had just been upped.

LAUREN MANAGED a polite but strained smile for Buck. The man was incorrigible. No matter how often she said no he still asked again. Would he never get the message? She just wasn't interested in resuming their relationship. She would never allow herself to fall in love again, and a loveless marriage held no appeal whatsoever. Besides, her plate was full with taking care of Sarah and work. Frank had faxed her two more designs for which he wanted immediate changes. Rosemary could do many things for Lauren, but architectural design wasn't among her talents. She was way behind schedule.

"It's just a fund-raiser, sugar," Buck persisted with a charming smile. "You remember last month when the Conroy place burned?"

"Of course I remember. Elly, their youngest, is in Sarah's kindergarten class." How could she forget such a horrible event? Though no one had been injured, the family had lost everything.

"Then how can you say no to such a good cause?"

Lauren sighed. How could she say no? But how did she get the point across to the man that he was barking up the wrong tree? She had nothing to offer him.

"Okay, Buck. I'll go to the dance with you." She relented, faced with the alternative of having him suggest a cozy dinner for two or, worse, a night out at the movies. He wasn't going to let it go with her usual brush-off.

"Well, gosh, Lauren." He pushed his wide-brimmed hat a little farther up his forehead and set one hand on his hip. "Don't make it sound so bad."

"Personally, I can't think of anything worse."

Lauren whirled at the sound of Gray Longwalker's smoky voice. She found herself face-to-face with his tall, muscular frame. His cool gray eyes fixed on hers and her heart stumbled. A slow heat simmered inside her when his gaze slid slowly down her body. Nerves, she decided. The man made her seriously nervous. His full lips tightened into a grim line as if he disapproved of what he'd found.

"Mr. Longwalker," she managed despite the sudden dryness in her throat.

The wind shifted his long raven-black hair over those impossibly broad shoulders. When his gaze met hers again, Lauren saw the faintest flicker of something akin to desire, but it vanished so quickly that she thought she must have imagined it. She had to have imagined it.

"Well, well," Buck piped up, an edge in his voice. "I'd heard you were back in town, Longwalker."

Gray shifted his intimidating attention from Lauren to Buck. Barely checked anger sent a warning. Buck reacted instantly. Only the slightest change in his posture, but Lauren noticed.

"And no welcome-home party?" Gray returned haughtily.

Lauren stepped back from the anger generated by both men. Whatever the story with these two, it wasn't good. Maybe if she just walked away neither would notice.

"Why, heck, Longwalker, me and the boys heard you were dead."

An evil gleam sprang to life in Buck's eyes taking

Lauren by surprise. She had never seen this slightly sinister side of him. He had always come off as the good-old boy type to her—easygoing and happy-go-lucky. But his complete dislike, if not total hatred, for Gray Longwalker was more than obvious.

Gray cocked one dark brow. His stance remained relaxed and confident despite Buck's fierce glare. His mouth curled into a contemptuous half smile. "Wishful thinking, eh?"

Buck laughed, but the sound held no trace of amusement. "Yeah, maybe so."

Lauren retreated another step. The tension was too thick for comfort. She didn't need to hear this, and she certainly didn't want a confrontation with Gray Longwalker. It had taken her forty-eight hours to recover from his last visit.

Dr. Prescott had chastised her repeatedly for not taking care of herself above all else. *Take your medication, Lauren. Don't let the stress get to you,* he had said.

Easy for him to say, Lauren mused. He didn't have Gray Longwalker to worry about. Or Buck Buckmaster for that matter. She knew if Gray gave her a hard time, Buck would react with his usual "this one's mine" mentality.

"I'll pick you up at seven, Lauren."

Startled, Lauren jerked to attention. She had lost the thread of conversation in her attempt to escape. "Sure, Buck, that'll be fine."

His usual pleasant smile slid back into place and he acknowledged her acceptance with a tip of his hat.

Gray continued his lethal stare long after Buck had turned and walked away. Lauren didn't think she had ever seen that much hatred in a man's eyes, not even in Buck's just moments ago.

Seeing her chance, she swung around and started in the other direction. This was one encounter she had every intention of avoiding.

"In case no one's told you, that man is a snake."

His words brought her up short. "Excuse me?"

Gray closed the distance between them in two long strides. When he stopped, he was too close. Lauren looked up into his steely gray eyes. *Way too close.*

"Buckmaster is a low-life bloodsucker who would sell his own mother if the price was right."

"Buck's mother died two years ago, Mr. Longwalker," Lauren said curtly, though she had no idea why she felt compelled to stick up for Buck. He was certainly capable of taking up for himself. "Not to mention that his father died just three months ago."

"I guess we're even then," he said without remorse.

Lauren shook her head in disbelief. "What's that supposed to mean?" Appalled, she wondered how anyone could be so callous.

"You wouldn't understand," he assured her.

"I'm sure I wouldn't. If you'll excuse me, Mr. Longwalker, I have things to do."

His hand was on her arm before she took her next step. Gray swung her back around to face him, his hold restraining but not overly forceful.

"Let go of me," Lauren insisted, scanning the sidewalk in both directions. The last thing she wanted to do was give the gossipmongers anything to talk about. She could imagine the curious faces pressed against the glass in the shops on either side of the street.

Since he didn't appear ready to release her, Lauren had no choice but to hear him out.

"I've warned you that patience is not one of my strong points. I will see my daughter before the results of the test we both know is unnecessary."

Lauren jerked her arm free of his hold. "I'm headed to Don's office right now. I'll ask him to call you."

"No, thanks," he said. "I'll just go with you."

"This is a private meeting, Mr. Longwalker, between me and *my* attorney."

He stared at Lauren for a long moment, seeming to weigh her words. "All right, then," he said slowly. "I'll call you at noon for an update."

"Fine." Lauren squared her shoulders and turned to go. She prayed Don would have good news for her. Some revelation that would rid her of Gray Longwalker once and for all.

"Lauren."

The sound vibrated through her, caressed her…hinting at future intimacy. An emotion she didn't quite recognize swirled quickly and then died. She didn't like it. She didn't like it at all. Lauren released a heavy breath and faced him once more. His eyes were softer now, almost kind.

"Don't let Buck fool you. He can't be trusted," he said quietly.

"But you can be?"

"Don't doubt my word, Lauren." His piercing metallic gaze latched on to hers with an intensity that shook her. "I never say anything I don't mean. *Never*," he added.

"You can't be serious," Lauren demanded as she dropped into the chair opposite Don's desk. He had lost his mind completely, of that she felt certain.

"We have to think of Sarah," Don reminded gently.

Lauren tamped down the anger that wanted to surface and massaged her right temple with trembling fingers. "I've thought of nothing else since this whole mess began."

"Does the name Thornton mean anything to you, Lauren?" Don rested his elbows on his desk and tented his fingers, keeping his gaze steady on hers.

Lauren shook her head. "Should it?"

"Victor Thornton is our new nightmare."

Lauren only stared at him...afraid to ask. The name meant nothing to her, but Don's tone spoke volumes.

"Thornton is the attorney who handled the Bradshaw case."

Lauren felt the blood drain from her face as the reality of Don's words hit her. The Bradshaw case represented a fight between adoptive parents and the biological father of a three-year-old boy in Houston. The father claimed he'd had no knowledge of the child until the mother had called him in a drunken stupor to tell him that she had given his child up for adoption, some two years after the fact.

"How could Gray Longwalker afford an attorney like that?" she asked in disbelief, remembering with all too much clarity the high-profile case.

Don shook his head tiredly. "I don't know. *I* can't even imagine what kind of retainer fee a man like Thornton would command."

"Wait," Lauren said hopefully. "What about that investigator you've got looking into Longwalker's background?"

"He's as straight as an arrow," Don told her, sounding defeated. "Longwalker hasn't been in any kind of trouble since he left Thatcher. In fact, according to the telephone call I received from Thornton's assistant, there's a long list of character references ready to testify on his behalf.''

"I can't believe it." Lauren breathed the words, her heart sinking with despair. "I thought he was a shiftless drifter."

"So did everyone else," Don muttered, and then added, "He drifts from one place to another all right, but it's because his horseman talents are so highly sought after."

Lauren frowned. "What kind of talents?"

"The explanation is rather vague." Don peered down at what was obviously the Longwalker report on his desk. "He works with horses that no one else can handle." He shrugged. "He's considered to have some sort of gift—one that pays well it seems."

Lauren shook off the strange feeling that stole over her. There was something about Longwalker—about the way he looked into a person's soul. She had noticed it the first time they had met. And that spark of awareness that had gone much deeper than the usual kind. She shivered at the memory.

"What's the bottom line, Don?" Lauren braced herself for the worst.

Don took a deep breath and settled his serious brown gaze on hers. "Lauren, I strongly recommend that you let Sarah get to know Longwalker." He held up both hands to stay her protests. "You know as well as I do how that test is going to turn out. If we back him into a corner he's going to come out fighting. If we work with him—try to compromise, so to speak— perhaps we can reach some sort of amicable agreement."

"No!" Lauren shot to her feet. "I won't let him take Sarah, Don. I won't!" She pointed her finger at him for emphasis, but the shaky gesture fell well below what she had intended. "You're my attorney—figure something out!" A flood of tears threatened to weaken her demand.

Don skirted his desk and drew Lauren into his arms. She resisted at first, but finally gave in to the comfort of his embrace and then the tears. This couldn't be happening. It just couldn't be.

"Lauren, listen to me, please," he said softly. "Leaving Sarah in a stable home in the town where she's lived all her life will go a long way with the judge. But you can't keep the child's father out of her life—without justifiable cause. I know you know that."

"Sharing her life won't ever be enough. He'll want it all. He hates this town, he'll never agree to leave her here." Lauren bit down on her lower lip to quell the sobs. "I can't let him take Sarah. I can't. She's like my own flesh and blood now. I just…" Her voice trailed off as the lump in her throat thickened.

"If we force his hand, you could lose her completely." Don drew back and looked down at her, his gaze sympathetic. "If push comes to shove, the odds are stacked in his favor—Sarah is *his* child."

Lauren shook her head as if to deny his words. "She's my child," she argued, her voice barely above a whisper.

"I understand how you feel, Lauren. We might be able to tie him up in court for a while. But, if we can resolve this without that kind of public spectacle, it would be better for Sarah."

Her mind knew he was right, but her heart didn't want to accept the only feasible alternative. Lauren couldn't imagine her life without Sarah—she refused to even allow the thought to take form. She'd resigned herself to spending her life childless, then suddenly she had Sarah. Nothing could have prepared Lauren for the impact on her heart, her life. Sarah was her child in every sense of the word. Lauren held her when she cried, nursed her when she was sick, helped with her schoolwork. They had bonded on a level that amazed Lauren on a daily basis.

She loved Sarah with all her heart....

"What do I do?" she asked defeatedly.

Don ushered her back into her chair and sat down beside her, in the very chair Gray Longwalker had occupied just three days ago when this nightmare began.

"Be accommodating," Don told her gently. "Let him spend some time with Sarah on the condition that he not rush into telling her who he is. He'll surely see the need for discretion. After all, the child could be traumatized by too much too soon." Don patted the ice-cold hands Lauren had clasped in her lap. "Think about it, Lauren. What would Longwalker do with a child? He moves from place to place, and from all reports, feels some sort of compulsion to do this work of his.

"He'll soon see that Sarah is where she should be, in a fine home and attending a good school. Just maybe, when the burning desire to take what belongs to him subsides, he'll see the reasonableness of leaving Sarah with you and settle for visitation rights."

Lauren wiped the tears from her cheeks with the backs of her hands. Maybe Don was right. Longwalker did seem intelligent enough. If he saw all that it took to care for a five-year-old, he might just decide that leaving Sarah with Lauren was the right thing to do.

"Do you think we have a chance?" She searched Don's eyes for reassurance.

"I think it's our only chance."

Diana Palmer

Chapter Five

"I don't know, Longwalker," Jeremiah Manning muttered as he stroked his stubbled chin. "I don't think there's any hope for that devilish animal."

The skittish black stallion's head shot up at the slightest movement in or around the corral. Gray grimaced as he recalled the threats, taunts and near-torture tactics a couple of Manning's ranch hands had used to usher a reluctant Shadow into the corral. No wonder the animal teetered on the verge of a complete breakdown. Gray could just imagine the fate the horse would have suffered had he not been present to intervene.

"As long as he's alive," Gray replied, never taking his eyes off the wary horse, "there's always hope." Such a beautiful animal, he thought with growing frustration. A fine quarter horse with excellent breeding potential. Manning had a number of horses on his cattle ranch, but none with as much potential as this one. What a waste.

"We've had our differences in the past," Manning offered with reluctance, "but I've heard rumors about what you can do with horses. I'm willing to let you have a try at him." He eyed Gray speculatively. "That is if you're up to the task."

"I'll have a look," Gray agreed. Manning's admission skirted the definition of an apology, but it would do. Gray hadn't come here to mend fences.

He cut a frustrated glance at the group of hands gathered near the barn. So far they had kept their distance and stayed reasonably quiet as he had asked once the horse was corralled. Now, if they would just stay that way until he had finished he would be thankful. Gray opened the gate and stepped into the corral. Shadow shifted backward a halting step.

Gray took another step and so did the horse. He waited until he felt the horse had settled before he moved again. He watched the horse's body language carefully. He had no desire to upset Shadow any more than necessary.

Gray shot another glance at the barn. He hated working with an audience, and the horses usually responded better if there were no distractions. But he wanted to show these cowpokes that all this particular horse needed was a little extra TLC.

After repeating the step-wait-step process until Shadow was backed against the fence, Gray took the first step of what the horse would consider true aggression. Gray held Shadow's gaze and whispered soothing words. Everything and everyone else ceased to exist except the horse and the few feet of dusty ground between them.

Gray could see the horse battling with its own instincts, ears pinned back, tossing its head. Instinct told Shadow to run, but Gray knew his eyes held the horse in a firm grip of curiosity. Shadow wanted to know what Gray was about. That simple curiosity would allow Gray much closer than anyone else had gotten without the use of restraints.

When Gray stood within arm's reach of the horse, he remained still and quiet for a long while. He allowed his eyes and his relaxed posture to speak for him.

The wind kicked up the dust around them, but Gray didn't move a muscle. The next few minutes were crucial. He needed Shadow to understand that he presented no threat.

Gray watched the wariness slip from the horse's big brown eyes. Long minutes elapsed before he felt ready to make the next move. Gray could feel the tension and anticipation of those watching, but he kept his concentration fixed solely on the horse in front of him.

"Shadow," he finally whispered as he slowly extended his right hand. The horse didn't flinch or jerk away, he watched in fascination as Gray reached out. Gray knew the horse still had its doubts, but he waited and watched just the same.

Gray stopped short of touching the horse, but kept his hand steady for Shadow's inspection. Now was the turning point. Gray held his breath and all else faded from his awareness.

Shadow's soft, warm muzzle pushed against Gray's hand and he released the breath he had been holding. Oh, yes, there was definitely hope. He murmured more soothing words as he permitted Shadow to examine both sides of his hand.

Gray gently smoothed his right hand over the horse's face and scratched beneath his forelock. His left hand remained at his side. He wouldn't touch the horse with both hands today. Shadow had to accept and trust him before he could do anything more than what he was doing at the moment. Trust had to be earned.

With one final word of promise to Shadow, Gray turned and strode back to the gate. He closed it behind him and faced Manning.

"Here's the deal," he told the old man. "No one touches this horse while I'm working with him—no one—not even you."

Manning huffed with indignation.

"I don't want any of your hired hands to so much as look at that horse," Gray added before Manning could utter his protests. "I'll feed Shadow myself."

Manning tucked his thumbs into his suspenders. "You don't ask for much, do ya?" he said with a snort of disbelief.

Gray leveled a look of displeasure on Manning. "Your horse, your choice, old man."

"I hear you fetch a handsome wage for breaking horses." Manning visibly measured Gray's worth, his gaze skeptical.

"I don't break horses," he said carefully. "I help them understand."

"What the devil do you expect that dumb animal to understand?" Manning inclined his head toward the stallion. "Danged thing ain't even got the good sense to come when it's feeding time. All I want is for you to make him saleworthy."

"I wouldn't expect you to understand," Gray told the old man and then walked away. He would feed Shadow and put him out to pasture before he left so there would be no excuse for anyone else to go near the troubled animal.

"Hey, wait a minute, Longwalker," Manning called out behind him. "You didn't tell me about your fee."

"This one's for free," Gray answered without looking back. No way would he walk away from this job because an old goat like Manning didn't want to pay the price. Gray looked across the corral and his gaze connected with Shadow's. This horse needed him to come back.

GRAY BRAKED TO A STOP in the parking lot just outside his room at Thatcher's Tumbleweed Hotel. He eased out of his truck and scanned the near-deserted lot for anything that looked out of place. It was an old habit, one that had saved his neck on a number of occasions.

Gray raked a hand through his hair and then settled his hat back into place. He closed his truck door and dug into his jeans pocket for his room key. He needed a shower and change of clothes to rid himself of this layer of dust before he called on Lauren Whitmore. One way or another, he planned to see his daughter today. Three days was too long between visits.

He wouldn't have waited this long if it hadn't been for the ridiculous and uncharacteristic guilt he felt over the possibility that he had caused Lauren that episode of headaches. No matter. Lauren Whitmore would just have to get used to having him around until the custody issue was settled. He was here for the duration.

Gray shoved the key into the lock of the dingy green door and opened it. With the drapes closed the room was as dark as a cave. He dropped his key on the bedside table and sat down to pull his boots off. Gray intended to find a new place to have lunch today. He'd had about all the diner cuisine his stomach could handle for a while. But he wasn't quite ready to go down memory lane with Mrs. Jennings.

Not bothering to turn on a light, Gray shrugged out

of his shirt and then peeled off his jeans. The unbidden recollection of the appetite-teasing aromas in Lauren Whitmore's kitchen made his stomach grumble.

He flipped the bathroom light switch and flooded the small room with a harsh fluorescent glow. Gray turned the shower on and grabbed a clean towel. He clenched his jaw against the memory of how good Lauren had smelled when he had held her in his arms and carried her to her bedroom. Her sweet scent had stirred another kind of hunger inside him. His groin tightened at the thought of touching her body with his mouth.

Steam billowed around him as Gray stepped into the shower's spray of hot water. He forced the unbidden image of Lauren Whitmore from his mind. He refused to like anything about her, yet he couldn't seem to prevent his physical response to her.

But he wouldn't like her. No matter how good she looked or smelled or felt in his arms, he would never like her.

Pushing the wet hair out of his eyes, Gray sighed tiredly. Lauren, tempting though she was, stood for everything he'd had to overcome his lack of: respect, money, family.

He closed his eyes as the water rinsed the soap from his body. He had money now. More than he would ever need. And he was highly respected for his work with horses. He didn't need anything else.

He turned the water off and shoved the shower curtain aside. Truth was, he didn't need friends and he sure didn't need a woman like Lauren Whitmore haunting his thoughts. He had learned the hard way at a very young age that it didn't pay to care about anyone or anything. Caring would only put him in the position to lose.

Gray towel dried his hair and then rubbed the rough material over his skin. A person had to trust to have friends or a relationship with a woman, and Gray didn't trust anyone. Oh, there were a few people he had come across with whom he had reached an understanding of sorts, but he trusted no one. There had been no shortage of willing females, either. But he never went back to the same one twice. Never.

He tossed the towel aside and pulled on a clean pair of jeans. Gray didn't need anyone. He swiped his hand over the mirror to clear away the fog and stared at his reflection. A little girl's image transposed itself alongside his. "Well, nobody but Sarah," he amended aloud. He and Sarah would be a family.

Family. A wave of old pain washed over him as the word echoed inside his head. He'd never had a family. For as long as he could remember it had been just him. Well, his mother had been there for a little while when he was very young. But by the time he was ten she had sunk so deeply into a pit of depression that no one could reach her. Gray had watched the once-vibrant and loving woman wither away for more than half a dozen years before death finally claimed her. Each passing year had hardened his young heart and made him more angry, more cynical until finally the rage had consumed him.

Gray blinked and focused on his reflection once more. "Jesus, Longwalker, get your head out of your past and get on with what you came here to do," he ordered curtly. He would see to it that Sarah never knew that kind of pain or anger. She would have his name if it was the last thing he ever did. He would never ignore her as his father had ignored him.

Gray pulled the door open and stepped out of the steamy bathroom and into the cool darkness of his room.

"You didn't have to get all gussied up on our account," a male voice announced. Someone yanked the drapes open, and light poured into the room.

Gray squinted against the sudden brightness. Four men spread out in an intimidating line across the room. With the blinding afternoon sun to their backs, they closed in on him. "What do you want?" Gray demanded, knowing full well what they had come for.

"You mean you don't know?" another voice taunted.

Gray sized up the young cowboy who seemed to be the leader of the group. All four looked young and capable enough to give him a hard time, but he had faced worse. He didn't recognize any of the men, but he knew who had sent them. "I have no idea what you could possibly want from me, but I'm sure you're going to tell me," he said flatly.

The leader stepped forward. His lips curled into a sneer as he cracked his knuckles. "Consider this your welcome-home party, Longwalker."

LAUREN PUNCHED the off button on the receiver with a vengeance. She had a low tolerance level for people who didn't do what they said they would do, and Gray Longwalker had just put his name at the top of that list.

If he hadn't intended to call her for an update, he shouldn't have made such a point of telling her that he would. Lauren had a sneaking suspicion that, rather than call, he planned to show up at her door about the time Sarah came home from school.

Well, she would just see about that. Lauren snatched up her car keys and headed for the door. He hadn't called, and his phone had been busy for the past thirty minutes. The only thing left to do was give him his update in person, she decided. Lauren locked the door behind her and stalked across the yard, her anger building with each step she took.

''Better at his place than mine,'' she muttered as she slid behind the wheel and started her car.

Lauren spent the better part of the fifteen-minute trip from her ranch to town trying to decide how she would broach the subject of visitation with the man. Her anger had given way to anxiety. She had to choose her words carefully—let him know that he could visit Sarah, without making him feel welcome to drop by any time.

And boundaries. She had to set clear boundaries. Lauren might not be able to prevent him from seeing Sarah, but he would play by her rules whether he liked it or not. At least she would have some sense of control over the situation until a judge told her otherwise.

Lauren parked in front of the hotel's shabby office and was about to go inside to ask for Longwalker's room number when she spotted his fancy black truck. Lauren didn't know much about trucks but she did recognize that the one he owned was an expensive one with all the bells and whistles.

The luxurious truck seemed oddly out of character for the man. Lauren trudged across the parking lot toward the row of rooms that lined the far side of the faded and cracked asphalt.

Lauren glanced down at her watch. One-thirty. It

still rankled her that the man hadn't called as he had said he would. Some father he would make, she fumed, he couldn't even make a simple telephone call. What if Sarah had been counting on his call and he had forgotten? Lauren sighed long and loud at the thought of Sarah being let down by anyone, much less her father.

Her father. God, the words still disturbed her deeply.

And what a fine start he had gotten off to in the fatherhood department. Give the man a break, she chided. Maybe he had taken the telephone off the hook and fallen asleep after lunch. Of course when a grown man needed a nap in the middle of the day, then he evidently wasn't sleeping at night. No telling what a guy like him did after dark.

"Afternoon, ma'am."

Lauren looked up in surprise at the unfamiliar male voice. A rough-and-tumble-looking foursome tipped their hats and grinned in a manner that barely skirted the fringes of being gentlemanly. Lauren forced a polite smile and hurried past. The group looked as if they had only just dragged themselves from the bar in which they'd had an early-morning brawl. Lauren hadn't looked long enough to see which of the group appeared to have gotten the raw end of the deal. They all seemed a bit the worse for wear.

Longwalker's truck was parked in a slot with the number 112 stenciled on the curb. Lauren stepped up onto the walk and located the door with the matching number. She drew in a deep breath and knocked firmly. She frowned when the door swung inward a few inches.

Why was the door open?

Lauren tilted her head to try to see inside the room through the narrow opening. "Mr. Longwalker," she called as she pushed the door open a tad farther.

She gasped at what she found. The room was a wreck. The table and a chair were overturned. Another chair was broken. The bed looked much the way Sarah's did after she and her little friends used it for a trampoline. And there didn't appear to be any sign of the occupant.

"Mr. Longwalker," Lauren called out again, her voice oddly shrill in the too-quiet room. She stepped inside and noticed the telephone on the floor, an irritating high-pitched sound coming from the receiver. Lauren picked up the base and set it back on the night table. No wonder his line had been busy. She placed the receiver back in its cradle and surveyed the room again.

Either there had been a fight or the place had been ransacked by a thief. Longwalker didn't strike her as the type to carry around valuables. In fact, Lauren had him pegged for one of those almost spiritual, back-to-nature types who believed material possessions hampered their oneness with the environment. Except for the truck, of course, she added.

A ripping sound in the bathroom drew Lauren's attention to the closed door. She padded silently across the worn green-and-gold shag carpet. "Mr. Longwalker?" Lauren rapped on the door, then listened and waited for another sound or response of some sort.

After a few moments the door opened and a battered Gray Longwalker glared down at her. "This isn't a good time for me, Ms. Whitmore," he said wearily, a guarded expression in his metallic gaze.

"What happened to you?" Lauren instinctively

reached up to inspect the damage to his face. He staggered out of reach, clutching the porcelain sink to steady himself. The shower curtain hung from one lone silver ring. The thin plastic fabric had evidently proven less than efficient in helping Longwalker to his feet.

"I got my welcome-home party," he said bitterly.

Lauren shook her head. "What are you talking about?"

"What did you come here for?" he countered impatiently.

"Sit down before you fall down," Lauren ordered. She gripped his forearms and guided him toward the toilet seat. Until she touched him, Lauren hadn't noticed that he wasn't fully dressed. His chest was bare and, quite frankly, beautiful.

His long, black hair fell past his mile-wide shoulders and lay against deeply bronzed skin stretched taut over well-developed muscles. Lauren had the sudden and completely ridiculous desire to slide her hand over the smooth contours of that chest. She gave herself a mental shake to dislodge the ludicrous notion. Maybe this new medicine Dr. Prescott had prescribed was having adverse side effects.

"I don't need your help," he warned.

Lauren forced her gaze upward to settle on those fierce gray eyes. She swallowed, her throat inexplicably dry. "Please sit down and let me take a look at you," she said more softly. He stared at her long and hard before he conceded and dropped onto the closed toilet seat.

Lauren grabbed a clean washcloth from the towel bar and dampened it. His wary gaze followed her every move. She pressed the cool, wet cloth to his left eye, which was swollen and rapidly changing colors.

"You need ice for this," she suggested.

"I'll be fine." He shifted from her touch.

"Be still," Lauren told him, impatience making her curt. She eased down on her knees to get a better look at his split lip. The damage was in one corner and didn't appear severe enough to warrant anything other than a cleaning and a little antibiotic ointment which, lucky for him, she always carried in her purse—along with Little Mermaid Band-Aids. Sarah was forever scraping her knees or elbows.

Lauren chewed her lower lip in empathy as she cleaned the cut at the side of his mouth. As she did whenever she worked on Sarah, Lauren focused on the task and not the person. In this instance she couldn't allow herself to consider that she was actually aiding the enemy. Of course, she did kind of owe him one since he had taken care of her the other evening. The thought of owing this man anything terrified her beyond belief.

"Boy, whoever did this certainly intended to make a point," she noted aloud as she surveyed the numerous scrapes and the beginnings of bruises on his chest and arms.

"It took four of them to make that point," he said in defense of his battered appearance.

Four of them. Lauren suddenly recalled the rumpled group she had met in the parking lot. It had taken all four of those men to do this. Gray Longwalker apparently knew how to defend himself. Lauren's gaze locked with his, and she saw the rage simmering just beneath his thin control.

She drew her brows together and wondered why

people in this town hated him so? What had he done to deserve such treatment? Oh, she had heard all the stories about his raging temper, the womanizing and the mega chip on his shoulder. But as far as she could tell, the only person who really had a right to hold a grudge against the man was Sharon Johnson—and now her, of course.

"Why are you staring at me?"

His voice startled Lauren from her worrisome thoughts. "I…I have something for your scrapes." She fumbled behind her for her purse. "Sarah is always scraping her knees—" she hastily dug through the numerous and varied contents of her oversize bag until she fished out the small yellow tube of ointment and small package of Band-Aids "—so I keep this stuff handy." She managed a weak smile despite the severity of his glare. "It really helps to speed up the healing and I…I just thought… Well, anyway." Lauren shook her head as she unscrewed the tiny cap, she was rambling.

"You didn't answer my question," he repeated, his gaze alert to her every move.

Lauren let go a shaky breath and focused on applying the ointment to his scrapes. She started with his chest and arms. The face would have to come later, when she had calmed a bit and could look him in the eye once more.

"What question was that?"

"I don't know why you came here, but I don't need your sympathy, Ms. Whitmore."

Lauren focused on his face now, but avoided actual eye contact. "I don't know what you mean, Mr. Longwalker. I don't recall offering you any sympathy."

Lauren bit the inside of her jaw as she gently

dabbed the ointment onto the cut at the side of his mouth. The knowledge that she knelt between his powerful thighs suddenly slammed into her consciousness. Heat flooded her body. Every cell felt charged, every nerve ending jangled. She would finish what she had started—somehow, she thought as she focused on his mouth. His lips were unusually full, almost feminine. They looked hard, but felt incredibly soft beneath her fingertips.

How would it feel, she wondered fleetingly, to have those lips pressed against her own? Lauren flinched. How could she be thinking such a thing? She definitely had to call Dr. Prescott the instant she got home. She was completely out of control. The pad of her thumb accidentally brushed his chin, tracing the shallow cleft she hadn't really noticed until now. Lauren swallowed hard and stroked his chin once more, her gaze riveted to his beautiful mouth. A need like she had never experienced before shuddered through her.

Gray pulled her hand away and held it firmly. The tube of ointment slipped from her grasp and clattered to the floor. Lauren's errant gaze focused on the contrast of Longwalker's much-darker skin against her pale coloring where their hands were joined. They were completely different in so many ways.

"Look at me, Lauren," he commanded.

There it was again—that strange swirling feeling that swept her each time he said her name. She lifted her gaze to his, her heart pounding faster with the contact. What was happening to her? She felt like a moth fluttering entirely too close to the flames. And, yet, she only wanted to move closer.

"Perhaps you're offering something else?" he suggested in a low, seductive voice.

Lauren shook her head slowly in denial of his words. It was at that precise moment that she knew just how dangerous Gray Longwalker could be. His eyes…his voice were mesmerizing.

His full lips tilted upward into a smile, the first real smile Lauren had seen. The transition was fascinating. With that smile, Gray Longwalker was more than merely handsome, he was breathtaking.

"You've just offered a great deal more than you realize," he murmured, his lips closer than they had been before, though she didn't think he had actually moved—maybe she had.

He stroked the inside of her wrist with the pad of his thumb, and Lauren shivered like a schoolgirl who had never before been touched by a man. She drew in a shallow breath and released it, the sound ragged in the silence that enveloped them.

Gray released her hand and touched her cheek, just the slightest caress of fingertips against her skin. He trailed his fingers down her throat leaving a path of fire that made her tremble. His fingers threaded into her hair, and he pulled her closer—close enough for Lauren to feel his breath on her lips. Her own breath stalled in her lungs.

And then those full, sensuous lips pressed against hers and the explosion of heat that followed made Lauren tremble with gut-wrenching need. He slid his free arm around her waist and pulled her closer between his widespread legs and fully against him. He felt hot and hard. Lauren's hands found their way to his chest, and she reveled in the smooth heat of his skin.

He teased her lips until they parted and swept his tongue into her mouth. Startled by the invasion, Lauren tensed, but his seductive touch soon made her relax. Deeper and deeper she spiraled into a world of pure sensation—sensations she hadn't imagined it possible to feel. Lauren moaned for what she equally wanted and feared. All her defenses had failed against this man. She wanted nothing more than for him to keep doing just what he was doing.

Gray suddenly jerked back, his breath jagged, his eyes glazed. A muscle jumped in his jaw as he set her away from him. "You should go now," he said grimly.

Lauren dragged her hands from his chest and hugged herself against the sudden loss and the embarrassment she felt. She summoned her wayward composure. What on earth had possessed her to allow him to kiss her? Had she lost her mind?

"I'm...I'm sorry. I don't understand what happened.... Why did you do that?" Lauren allowed her gaze to meet his. His eyes were cold and vacant, no longer mesmerizing.

"Because you wanted me to."

"Because I what?" Lauren echoed in disbelief. She pushed to her feet and backed away from him. "I wanted no such thing."

Gray stood, his height and size intimidating enough without the heated glare he focused on her. "Unless my instincts were off—and they seldom are where a woman is concerned—you wanted exactly that."

"Oh, I see," Lauren said, the pitch of her voice rising as resentment and humiliation fueled her anger. "Your special talents extend to women as well as horses?"

"When I choose to allow myself to get that close, yes."

On some level, she had already known that would be his answer. There was something about his eyes— it was as if he could see straight into her soul. Lauren sighed her exasperation and braced her hands at her waist. "I shouldn't have come here. I should have known better than to give you the time of day, much less play nursemaid to your injuries." She whirled to make her exit with at least some amount of dignity, but Longwalker caught her arm and pulled her back around.

He leaned in close and whispered fiercely, "I know what I felt."

"Well, maybe your instincts need a tune-up." She jerked out of his hold and was halfway to the door before she remembered what she had come here for in the first place.

Lauren stopped and faced the brooding figure who stood statue still on the other side of the room. "I came here to work out the ground rules for you to visit Sarah. But obviously you're more concerned with humiliating me than visiting her."

An indiscernible emotion flickered in his unreadable gaze. "Why the change of heart?"

Lauren hesitated. She still hadn't figured out how to explain this part without giving away too much. "I just felt it would be the right thing to do," she told him. Well, at least it was half-true. She really wanted him to go away, but if he insisted on staying, at least they could work out some sort of agreeable terms. "Don suggested that we work something out," she admitted when faced with the look of disbelief on his face.

"When can I see her?"

The anticipatory light that sprang to life in his eyes

made Lauren's heart ache. He was already falling for the child and he had only seen her once. Her hopes of his walking away dashed, Lauren swallowed back the regret. "Give yourself a day or two to heal up. Seeing you like this—" Lauren gestured to his battered face "—might upset her. She wouldn't understand."

Gray nodded. He shoved his hands into his pockets, emphasizing his masculinity. "Would Saturday be okay?"

"Call me Saturday morning and we'll work out a time," she conceded. "But you can't tell Sarah that you're her father until you have a court order giving you permission, and you can only see her at my house."

"Agreed," he said eagerly.

Lauren turned away from his hopeful expression. God, she didn't want to see this...didn't want to know how much Sarah meant to him already.

"Lauren."

The sound washed over her, making her shiver and promising things she prayed he wouldn't try to deliver. "Yes?" She reluctantly turned to face him once more.

"Thank you."

Those two little words shattered the last of Lauren's hopes that she would ever be able to hate Gray Longwalker the way she had expected to—the way she needed to—in order to protect Sarah and herself.

Chapter Six

Gray stopped short of knocking on the door. He squeezed his hand into a fist and then let it drop heavily to his side. Saturday afternoon had come, and he could finally see Sarah again. But that also meant he had to see Lauren Whitmore. He stared at Lauren's closed door and willed his uneasiness to retreat. He had made a mistake by allowing that kiss. He had thought of nothing else since.

Well, that wasn't exactly true—he had thought of Sarah. But he had thought about Lauren entirely too much. Gray didn't usually waste time or energy dwelling on things he couldn't have and sure as heaven didn't need.

He'd had a bad case of running off at the mouth the other day. He'd told Lauren more about himself in those few minutes in that shabby bathroom than he made it a habit of telling anyone. No one ever understood how he could sense their feelings so accurately. Why did he think for one minute that Lauren Whitmore would be any different?

She'd wanted him to touch her. He had felt her desire so strongly that he'd been hard-pressed not to take things further than he had. Gray had realized his error a little late, but he had come to his senses.

Lauren was beautiful—there could be no denying that—and she had a sweetness about her. But no matter how tempting the woman might be, she still stood between him and his daughter. Not to mention that she seemed to be involved on some level with his nemesis.

Gray doubted that her relationship with Buckmaster went very deep. Not after the way she had responded in his arms two days ago. She'd been just as caught up in the heat of the moment as he had. And she had wanted him as much as he had wanted her. Of course, there was always the off chance that his instincts were wrong about Lauren. She could be the type who used her feminine wiles to keep the men in her life in their place.

Gray shook his head. He couldn't be that wrong. But right or wrong, it didn't really matter. Gray had no intention of getting involved with anyone. He didn't believe in that kind of love—responsibility, loyalty, maybe—but not love. Nothing Lauren could do or say would ever change his mind on that score.

Firming his resolve, Gray rapped against the polished oak surface and waited for Lauren to answer the door. When she did, he was totally unprepared.

She had pulled her hair up, but long, wispy, honey-colored strands drifted down around her face and neck. A jolt of awareness surged through him. She gazed up at him through those exotic green eyes, and her rosy lips curled into a tremulous smile. The sight of her made his groin tighten unreasonably. Even the soft flannel blouse and worn denim jeans she wore looked frustratingly feminine. Bright neon-pink toenails caught his eye. Gray almost smiled. He had never considered toes sexy, but Lauren's were.

"Good afternoon, Mr. Longwalker," she said tentatively, drawing his attention back to her expectant gaze. For the first time he noticed the dusting of flour on one cheek. She had been baking. He remembered the unbaked bread rising on the counter in her kitchen the first time he'd been here. Lauren pulled the door open wider and stepped back for him to enter.

"Ms. Whitmore," he returned and stepped inside. Gray took off his hat and deposited it on the hall table. He could feel the doubt and reluctance radiating from Lauren like the heat from a red-hot smithy's iron.

"You're looking much better," she noted after closing the door. Despite her reservations about his presence, she surveyed the healing injuries on his face with genuine concern. "Do the police have any suspects yet?"

Gray made a halfhearted effort at a laugh, which fell well below the mark. "You don't call the police in Thatcher when your name is Gray Longwalker."

"But those men broke into your room and they…they assaulted you," she protested in earnest, a strong sense of injustice emanating from those shimmering jade pools.

Gray sighed. Her naiveté was refreshing. "Trust me on this one."

Lauren's face grew suddenly somber. She bit her lower lip and averted her gaze. "I suppose you want to get right to the point of your visit."

"Yes."

"Would you like me to take that?" She gestured to the package he held.

"It's for Sarah."

"Oh." Lauren nodded but didn't look at him again. Instead she turned and led the way into the living room. Gray's eyes settled immediately on the little girl, and his heart skipped a beat. Sarah sat on the floor surrounded by building blocks. Piles of red, blue, yellow and green shapes lay in no particular order. A doll with long, dark hair sat beside her.

"Sarah," Lauren said, drawing the child's attention from her fierce concentration on one particular pile of blocks. When Sarah looked up, Lauren continued, "You remember Mr. Longwalker who helped out the day I got sick?" Sarah's gaze darted to Gray and she nodded vigorously. "Well he's come to visit us, but Mommy's a little busy in the kitchen with the baking. Would you mind keeping Mr. Longwalker company until I finish?"

"Okay, Mommy," she said without hesitation or particular interest. Instantly her attention returned to the pile of red blocks and she whispered something to her doll.

Lauren quickly turned away. Gray sensed her trepidation. This was very difficult for her, he knew. He found himself wishing that he could somehow make it easier, but he couldn't. His gaze moved back to Sarah. He could allow nothing to stand in the way of claiming his daughter.

Gray joined Sarah on the floor amid the array of colorful blocks. "I brought something for you," he said as he held the package out to the little girl.

She accepted the bag and immediately reached inside. She pulled out the square box and her eyes lit up. "Little Mermaid! I love the Little Mermaid," she squealed gleefully.

Gray smiled. An unfamiliar emotion he recognized

as happiness bloomed in his chest, catching him completely off guard with its intensity. In her hasty departure from his hotel room, Lauren had left a package of Little Mermaid Band-Aids. Gray had assumed that Sarah liked the Disney character and had bought a puzzle they could work on together.

"Can I open it?" she asked hopefully.

"Sure. We can put it together if you'd like."

Sarah jumped up and rushed to the coffee table. She dropped to her knees, opened the box and dumped the contents on the table's polished surface. Gray sat down beside her and surveyed the scattered contents of the box.

"Where would you like to start?" he asked.

"Wait," she said suddenly. Sarah scrambled to her feet and hurried to retrieve her abandoned doll. She set the doll carefully on the table next to the mound of puzzle pieces. "Leah wants to help, too."

Gray's gut clenched, and he stared down at the little girl. "That's a nice name," he told her quietly. He wondered if it could be coincidence or if... No, he argued with himself, it couldn't be anything but a coincidence.

Sarah straightened the doll's yellow dress. "She's named for my grandma," she informed him proudly.

Gray didn't speak for a long moment, he simply watched Sarah fuss over the doll's hair and ribbon. "Do you visit your grandma often?" he ventured finally. Maybe Leah was Lauren's mother's name as well as...

"Nope. She went to Heaven a long time ago, but my first mommy told me all about her." Sarah smiled up at him. His heart skipped another beat. "Grandma

Leah looked just like me. And you,'' she added, touching his hair.

Gray could only nod. His voice had left him. He never dreamed that Sharon would share anything about his mother with the child. Why had she, when she had left him out of the scenario? Gray had resented his mother almost as much as he had the selfish bigot who had fathered him. Sharon evidently had very different memories of Leah Longwalker than those firmly entrenched in Gray's mind.

''I have a picture, wanna see?'' Sarah asked, breaking into his haunted thoughts.

Gray didn't really remember agreeing, but the next thing he knew he was following Sarah to her room. She went over to the many bookshelves lining one wall and retrieved a small silver frame that sat next to a fuzzy white bunny. He had somehow missed seeing it the other night. Maybe because his full attention had been focused on his child.

''See.'' She held the picture out for his inspection.

Gray took the silver frame, his hand shaking slightly. He stared down at the woman in the photograph and a very old, very deep pain stabbed his heart.

Beautiful...she was beautiful. Leah Longwalker had been a stunning woman in her time. She looked young and happy, the picture had been taken before—before she had given up all hope of happily-ever-after. This was the mother he had loved and who had loved him back. But that woman had gone away too many years ago to remember.

He handed the picture back to Sarah. ''She's very beautiful, Sarah.'' He leveled his gaze on the little girl's gray eyes. ''Just like you.''

''I know,'' Sarah chirped as she placed the frame

back in the exact spot from which she had taken it. "Let's put the puzzle together now," she added, her voice containing the same excitement as her step when she skipped out of the room and down the hall, her heels scuffing against the shiny hardwood floor.

Gray followed and settled himself on the braided rug across the table from Sarah as she began the monumental task of picking through the colorful puzzle pieces. Gray watched her little fingers work and her studious concentration as she inspected piece after piece until she found just the one she wanted to use first.

Nothing he could call to mind accurately described the sensation of watching this child…his child. She was part of him—part of his mother—that lived on. Something good and innocent, traits he had lost long ago.

Gray would teach her about her Navajo heritage. He would help her to understand the importance of believing in oneself. And above all else, he would give her his name.

LAUREN TRIED NOT TO HOVER outside the living room door. She told herself over and over that this was the right thing—the only thing—to do.

She had peeked in on Sarah only two times in the last hour. With tremendous effort she forced herself to attend to her bread baking. She loved to bake and it was a great outlet for her stress. Today's baking frenzy was motivated as much by anxiety as by the need for an excuse to stay clear of the visitor in her living room. Lauren had pounded the dough until her arms were weak from it. She had busied herself in the precise process of mix, knead, roll, rise, repeat the last three steps and bake.

Lauren scanned the cluttered counters, the aftermath of her battle to escape the reality of Longwalker's presence. Now she stood in the middle of her homey kitchen with its blue gingham curtains and clay-tiled floor and no longer cared that she had worked so hard to make this room special.

What good would any of this be without Sarah?

Lauren closed her eyes and released a heavy breath. She had spent months designing and overseeing the renovations to this house. She had called it her baby— her special project. Not work, like all the other designing she did, this one had been for her own personal benefit. Her own house. Not long after the renovations were complete, Sarah had come to live with her, and soon Lauren's house had become a home.

At first Lauren had tried desperately to convince Sharon that she wasn't the right person to take care of Sarah. What did she know about children? Lauren had no siblings. She had never baby-sat anyone in her life. She had never been married. The fact was, Lauren had only been involved in one serious relationship. She was a career woman, or had been until the accident. After that, at the ripe old age of twenty-three, she had taken a giant step back from life. Lauren had built a protective wall around herself emotionally.

But Sharon would have none of it. ''Sarah loves you and you love her—I can see it,'' Sharon would say. Lauren had been fond of the child. But… There had been no acceptable buts as far as Sharon was concerned. Eight months after being diagnosed with terminal cancer and proposing that Lauren take Sarah,

Sharon had died, and then there had been no turning back.

Lauren had brought Sarah home to live with her, and in no time at all she had lost her heart to the child.

Her movements on autopilot, Lauren checked the oven and then drifted to her favorite spot in the house—the dining room's huge bay window seat. She dropped onto the cushioned seat and propped on a mound of loose pillows. Fluffy stirred and stretched, but then curled back into a sleeping ball. Lauren stroked the lazy cat as she peered out the window. The view looked out over the acres and acres of pastures that surrounded the house that had once belonged to her great aunt Dorothy. An ancient barn, its siding weathered to a washed gray, stood beyond a hen house, smoke house and bunkhouse.

Lauren had never once visited Thatcher as a child. Her parents had always been too busy, and then Aunt Dorothy had passed away when Lauren was nineteen. Who would have thought, she mused, that a few years later Lauren would be living in Texas on this old ranch in the middle of nowhere. The place was a far cry from the apartment in which she had grown up in Chicago.

Lauren worked now by fax and e-mail. No more power meetings, conferences or business luncheons.

The accident had changed many things in Lauren's life—geography and working conditions being the easiest to accept. Losing Kevin had been the hardest.

Kevin. Lauren closed her eyes and summoned the image of the only man she had ever loved. His blond hair and laughing blue eyes had stopped haunting her dreams a while ago, but the sore place in her heart still ached from time to time. They had both worked at Cutting Edge Architecture after graduating from the same college. She and Kevin had been considered prime recruits and were well on their way up the corporate ladder. Kevin had shared her career-minded attitude. They had agreed that marriage and children could come later. Much later. How could they have guessed that later would never come?

One night had changed everything.

Why had she let him drive that night? She had known he'd had too much to drink, but he had insisted. Rather than have a fight, Lauren had given in. That one mistake had cost her a great deal. She had lost him and gained the devastating headaches. But she had learned a painful lesson—loving anyone was too monumental a risk. Sarah had been the only exception to her hard-and-fast rule. But there would be no others.

Lauren pushed away the thoughts of things best forgotten. Dredging up the past had too often brought on her headaches, and right now she couldn't afford that. At all costs she must stay in control of the situation with Gray Longwalker. He represented a threat to her in too many ways.

The smell of freshly baked bread summoned Lauren back into the kitchen. She smiled as she withdrew first one and then another of the golden-brown loaves. She did love to bake. Cookies, cakes, bread, anything. Maybe she and Sarah would make cookies later.

After placing the hot loaves on cooling racks, Lauren removed her oven mitts and turned the stove off. She swept an errant wisp of hair away from her cheek with the back of her hand and surveyed the less attractive step involved in the baking process—clean up.

Lauren exhaled mightily, set her hands at her waist and tried to decide where to start. The dishes, she supposed. Some she could put into the dishwasher.

Some—like her nonstick baking pans—required a more personal touch.

"Smells good."

Gray Longwalker's dark, irresistibly masculine voice generated an all-too-feminine shudder in Lauren. She whirled around to find him watching her from his relaxed stance in the doorway. He had leaned against the jamb. She wondered briefly how long he had been there. The faded blue shirt and jeans he wore emphasized his bronze coloring. Lauren had never cared much for men with long hair, but there was something sinfully intriguing about all that silky black hair falling over his broad shoulders.

How had he sneaked up on her like that?

"Bread," she said quickly, and gestured toward the cooling loaves. "I just took it out of the oven."

"I know," he said. The hint of a smile twitched one side of his mouth.

He had been watching her. Lauren didn't quite know what to say next. She rubbed the back of her neck with one hand and looked anywhere but at him. That searching gaze never deviated from her. She didn't have to look to know—she could feel it. She could feel him.

"Can I get you tea or…" Lauren's voice trailed off when she at last allowed her gaze to connect with his. All coherent thought ceased, and every part of her being was drawn to the man across the room. She opened her mouth to finish her sentence, then snapped it shut and simply shrugged, hoping he would understand what she intended.

Gray straightened and moved in her direction. For such a tall man, his movements were fluid, sleek—like a cat's. No wonder she hadn't heard him come in. The man could give lessons in stealth. When he stopped and stared down at her, Lauren instinctively stepped back only to be blocked by the counter. Desire shot through her at his nearness, followed immediately by a burst of need so strong it made Lauren weak in the knees. She wasn't supposed to feel this.

"Sarah?" she asked, feeling awkward and nervous under his intense appraisal.

"She fell asleep on the couch."

Lauren glanced at the wall clock and frowned. "It's her nap time. I'm sorry, I should have thought of that this morning when we scheduled your visiting time."

"Sarah showed me the picture of Leah," he said carefully.

Lauren blinked rapidly to conceal her surprise at his announcement. She hadn't considered that he might see the picture of Leah or what kind of impact it would have on him. "Sharon told Sarah stories about her grandmother. She...she thought it would help her to understand why she was...different."

A muscle flexed in his tightly clenched jaw. "You mean a mixed breed—not quite Anglo and not quite Navajo, but something in between."

"No." Lauren shook her head in denial. "That's not what I meant at all."

He looked away, clearly reaching for calm. "I suppose it's not," he relented.

Had it always been this way for him? Had his life growing up been so hurtful that any remark that could even remotely be construed as racist was a personal attack? Lauren scrambled for what to say next. "How about we give this bread a try," she suggested, hoping to lighten the moment.

He met her hopeful gaze, his own still too solemn. "I'd like that."

She gestured to the table. "Have a seat."

But he didn't turn that penetrating gaze away from her. Instead he reached up and touched her cheek with the tips of his fingers. The gesture wasn't threatening. It was simply a touch. The pad of his thumb slid across her skin, the friction sent goose bumps skittering down her neck and across her breasts.

"You have flour—" he swiped her cheek once more with the pad of his thumb "—right there."

Lauren swallowed hard and forced herself to ignore the feelings he evoked with a mere touch. She watched the raw emotions on his handsome face go from solemn pain and frustration to need—a need as strong as the one she felt right now. A need she desperately wanted to deny. Could he possibly know the battle raging inside her? The almost overwhelming desire for his touch warred with the logical knowledge that she should resist. Even over the aroma of home-baked bread, she could smell his earthy essence. The scent beckoned to her on a very elemental level. She wanted to reach across the mere inches that separated them and touch him. To see if the dark skin that lay beneath that faded chambray shirt felt as smooth and warm as she remembered.

And taste him. The thought sent a shiver across her skin. Would he taste as dark and mysterious as he looked? Her own thoughts frightened her more than the man himself.

"Butter," he murmured. "Do you have butter?"

"Yes," she breathed. "I'll get it." Her heart thumped hard in her chest.

He moved away, breaking the spell. Lauren forced

her weak limbs to take the necessary steps to the refrigerator. Gray sat down at the table and waited, but she could feel his gaze on her. He watched her every move. She quickly sliced a slab of warm bread and slathered it with butter. Her heart still raced for some unseen finish line. Her reaction to the man was purely foolish. Flustered, she set the plate down before him and strained for calm.

"Tea?" she all but squeaked, then cleared her throat.

His gaze lingered on hers a little too long. "Sure."

After pouring two glasses of ice tea, Lauren joined him at the table. She watched as he bit into the soft, warm bread, then as he licked the butter from his lips. Heat funneled beneath her belly button, sending desire deeper. Lauren blinked and straightened in her chair.

"So, what exactly is it you do with horses?"

He sipped his tea, his analyzing gaze studying hers so thoroughly she wanted to squirm in her chair. "I'll be glad to answer that question as long as you agree to answer one of mine."

Oops. A tactical error. She hadn't thought of that. But it was too late now. She had already opened her big mouth. "All right," she said slowly. "You answer one question for me and I'll answer one for you."

He nodded his agreement. "I can sense their feelings." He shrugged as if uncomfortable sharing the information. "I communicate with them on some level. I can't explain it, it just is. I haven't met one yet I couldn't reach."

Lauren propped her elbows on the table and rested her chin in her hands. "That's amazing."

"Not amazing," he corrected. "It just is."

"So you travel around the country reaching out to the horses that are labeled as problem animals."

He cocked an eyebrow. "That's two questions."

Lauren smiled. "No it's not, it's a request for a deeper explanation to my first question."

He narrowed his gaze suspiciously. "I think you're making these rules up as you go to suit your purpose."

She laughed then. And he smiled. One of those real smiles that took her breath. "Just answer the question, Longwalker."

"Yes. I travel around the country working with problem horses. I guess you could say it's my calling."

He finished off his slice of bread, then made a sound of approval. "Very good."

"Thank you." A glow bloomed inside her. Why his approval should please her so, Lauren couldn't fathom.

"My turn." He pushed his empty plate away and studied her a moment.

Lauren tried not to squirm under his intense scrutiny.

"Tell me about the headaches," he said quietly.

She looked away. That was a big one. "How about we talk about something else?" she said with a feigned smile.

He shook his head. "You have to answer that one."

Lauren took a deep breath and let it out slowly for courage, but mainly to stall. "Four years ago my fiancé and I were driving home after a party, and we had an accident." She stared at her clasped hands as she continued. "The car went over a railing and into the lake. Kevin, my fiancé, was killed." She felt suddenly cold. "I had a head injury. A man who saw the accident rescued me, but there was nothing he could do for Kevin.'' She blinked back the remembered heartache and met his intent gaze across the table. ''When all was said and done I was left with the headaches.''

He didn't have to say he was sorry, she could see it in his eyes. He felt her pain almost as sharply as she did. Lauren looked away. How could that be? How could he be so keenly aware of her feelings when he barely knew her? *When I choose to allow myself to get that close,* he'd said. She had allowed him too close.

''Why did you ask me about my work?''

Lauren jerked from her intense reverie. ''Trying to slip in a second question?'' she countered, in hopes of closing that line of discussion.

''Why?'' he insisted. Suspicion glimmered in his eyes now, as if he'd only just considered her motivation.

His answer to the question had been no surprise, but she'd wanted to hear the words from his mouth. He would no doubt use her headaches against her in the upcoming custody battle; she had to be prepared with ammunition as well.

''I was curious,'' she hedged.

''You've made up your mind that I'm not the kind of father my daughter needs,'' he suggested.

Lauren swallowed hard. It was almost as if he'd read her mind. ''Sharon warned me about your arrogant anger...your bitterness. She was afraid you'd fill Sarah's head with that same hatred.'' Fear trickled into Lauren's veins. *Had she admitted too much?* She couldn't afford to alienate him at this point.

Stark pain etched itself into his angular features. He stood abruptly, his chair scraping across the floor. ''So you've decided that Sarah would be better off without me."

"I don't know you." Lauren pushed to her feet, putting herself more at his level and feeling far too uneasy in this volatile territory. "Sharon made that decision based on what *she* knew. I'm only following her wishes."

His eyes never left hers, searching, analyzing. "You don't really want me here, do you?"

Lauren folded her arms over her middle, the move proving an ineffective barrier against his all-seeing gaze. He was reading her like an open book. "No, I don't want you here," she admitted, her voice shaky with emotion. "I want you to go away and never come back," she added in all honesty and to her complete surprise. Oh, God, how could she have let that slip out?

"But you know I won't."

She met his penetrating gaze head-on. "I know."

Realization dawned in his eyes. "So Davis told you to humor me until he could figure out some other way to deal with me?"

"No," Lauren denied quickly. She lowered her eyes from his accusing ones and focused on that patch of sleek skin visible at the vee of his shirt. She tried her level best to think of something to say that would convince him she had no hidden agenda, but nothing came.

"Just so you know," he began in a tone that sent shivers up her spine. "I'm not going anywhere until I prove that Sarah is my daughter."

Lauren jerked her head up to meet his lethal glare.

"And when I go, she goes with me," he finished, his expression devoid of any emotion now.

Lauren struggled against the panic that flashed through her. She hugged herself more tightly and stared into those cold, gray eyes, thankful that the table stood between them. "What Sarah needs or wants means nothing to you?" she returned, her own voice oddly emotionless.

"Sarah will learn to want and need me."

Lauren shook her head. "You have no idea what you're proposing."

"Enlighten me," he demanded, his voice low and dangerous.

"Sarah is in school." Lauren moistened her lips and held his gaze, hard as that proved, and continued, "She needs a stable home. She needs to be with her friends. To know where she'll wake up each morning and where she'll sleep at night." The words rushed from her mouth. She had to say it all before she lost the courage. "The road is no place for a child." Lauren's gaze moved to his mouth. Those full lips taunted her with memories of how they felt against hers...how they tasted of mystery and heat. The war between fear and desire intensified, making her weak.

"And only you can give her those things?" The sharp edge of sarcasm added bite to his words.

"You...you move from place to place," Lauren stammered, grasping at the few details she knew, the same ones he had just admitted. "That kind of life wouldn't be fair to any child."

"You think I can't provide a stable home myself? You believe I'm not capable of staying in one place?"

"I don't see how," Lauren told him carefully.

"Don't think you and Davis will be rid of me so easily," he warned. "I won't settle for a few grudging visits with my daughter.'' Gray pushed his chair back to the table. "Good-bye, Ms. Whitmore.''

Lauren watched him walk toward the door and before she could stop herself, she blurted, "And what's to keep me from turning the tables on you, Longwalker? You're not the only one who can push the issue. I could take Sarah and run.'' Her determination grew stronger with every beat of her heart.

He stopped, turned around slowly and leveled his intense gaze steady on hers. "And I would find you,'' he assured her. "No matter where you went, *I would find you.*''

There it was—the bottom line. She and Sarah were stuck with him. No matter what happened in a court of law, Lauren knew she would never be rid of him. Gray Longwalker had staked his claim and he didn't intend to back off.

"But she's my life,'' Lauren whispered. Her vision blurred with the burn of unshed tears. How could she make him understand?

"She's *my* daughter.''

Chapter Seven

Golden light and country music spilled into the night
from the huge barn-like structure Thatcher used as a
community center. When Gray had passed the place
earlier that afternoon it hadn't escaped his attention
that the center had been built and donated to the town
by Buckmaster Brothers Construction.

Buckmaster.

Gray clenched his jaw and stepped out of his truck
and into the parking lot. He settled his hat into place
and walked slowly toward the festivities. When you
had met one Buckmaster you had met them all—
greedy snakes, the whole lot of them. Fortunately there
were only two left—the sons. The old man, sorry piece
of horse dung he was, had finally died. The sudden
heart attack that had taken him out was too easy in
Gray's opinion.

James Buckmaster, Sr., had come from old money.
He, like his father before him and his sons after him,
had enjoyed the many benefits that come with money
and the power it can buy. Land, social position, political ties and women.

Gray stopped short of the wide-open doors leading
into the community center and released a slow, heavy

breath. The Buckmaster men always married well, but it was never enough. They had to have anyone else that appealed to their selfish desires. And when it was over, the woman was always destroyed—if not by her own depression, then by social ostracism.

Leah Longwalker had died long before she'd stopped breathing.

Gray closed his eyes and steadied himself against the rage that once more threatened to consume him. He wouldn't give in. He had worked too long and too hard to separate himself from his past—from the anger. He refused to be drawn back into that vicious cycle of self-destruction.

As soon as the legal matters concerning Sarah were settled, he would leave this godforsaken town and never come back.

"Never," Gray muttered as he sauntered into the benefit dance for the Conroy family.

He scanned the crowded room—for no one in particular, he told himself.

It was a lie.

He knew it.

Gray sighed and pushed through the crowd to find himself an out-of-the-way corner in which to lounge. He wanted to observe Lauren Whitmore with Buck, the elder of the two Buckmaster brothers, to see just what the situation between them amounted to. Not that it was any of his business, but that minor detail had never stopped him before.

Gray ignored the curious glances, hard stares and murmurings his presence elicited. He wondered if it would make any difference to these people that he didn't want to be here any more than they wanted him here? He doubted it.

Occasional laughter and incessant chatter flowed from the throngs milling about. Several couples whirled around the area designated as the dance floor.

Gray made his way past the refreshment tables and finally found a good spot in a corner on the other side of the room. Most of those in attendance had stationed themselves as close to the refreshment tables or the building's entrance as possible; some interested in getting their money's worth in food and drink, while the others focused their attention on who came and went.

Gray didn't acknowledge anyone he met, and they didn't acknowledge him, unless you counted their blatant stares or quickly averted gazes.

Gray swore silently. He had made a hefty donation to the cause, so he had every right to be here.

He leaned back against the paneled wall and hooked his thumbs in his front pockets. He surveyed the crowd twice more before he encountered Lauren…and Buck.

The hair on the back of his neck stood on end, and a sickening sense of dread filled his gut as Gray watched the laughing couple. Buck drew Lauren out onto the dance floor as the band struck up a slow song.

A rich-green dress clung to Lauren's slight curves. With a hem that fell past her knees, long sleeves and a high neckline, the dress left everything to the imagination, and Gray had a very vivid imagination. As she had earlier that day, Lauren wore her hair up, with long, wispy strands falling around her face. Gray didn't have to get an up close look to know that the color of the dress would bring out the exotic green of her eyes.

Need gripped him. Gray shifted and silently cursed his lack of control where Lauren Whitmore was concerned. He hadn't been this easily stirred since he was a teenager. Gray shifted again, bent one knee and pressed his foot against the wall for support.

When Buck pulled Lauren closer into the circle of his arms, Gray's jaw clenched so tight that one corner of his mouth twitched from the tension. He crossed his arms over his chest and forced back the emotion he recognized immediately as envy.

He didn't want Lauren Whitmore.

Fighting for control, Gray turned away from the sight. He would look anywhere else but at her. Buck could have her. The only thing Gray wanted was his daughter.

If his soul weren't already damned to Hades, Gray knew he'd be going for sure, considering all the lies he had told himself since arriving in Thatcher.

His child, he reiterated, was all he had come for and was all he intended to leave with. At least that was the truth.

As if on cue, his eyes found Sarah. She and two other little girls were drinking from colorful disposable cups near the refreshment area. Sarah kept one arm locked securely around her doll, Leah.

The other two girls appeared to be about the same age as Sarah. One was blond and one dark, but not as dark as Sarah. The dark-haired girl also held a doll, similar to Sarah's except with honey-colored hair.

Gray watched the threesome and wondered if Sarah was treated as an equal—something he had never been. The little blond evidently asked the dark-haired girl if she could hold her doll, for the dark-haired girl clutched her doll possessively and turned away. Gray's heart went out to the blond. He wondered if she didn't have a doll of her own or maybe she had just forgotten to bring it.

Pride filled him and a smile eased across his lips when Sarah held her precious Leah out to the little blond girl. Gray couldn't prevent the immediate acknowledgment that Lauren had done a fine job in teaching Sarah to be considerate of others. Sarah showed respect for her elders and obeyed without much fuss. Lauren hadn't failed Sharon.

His smile thinned. He could do the job just as well. He could give Sarah anything she needed or wanted. It didn't take a woman to raise a child. There were lots of single fathers out there bringing up families.

Gray didn't realize the music had changed until Lauren and Buck stepped into his line of vision. The little girls all seemed to be talking at once to Lauren. She smiled and acknowledged each child in turn. She smoothed a hand over Sarah's long dark hair and said something to her. Lauren was a good mother to his daughter, he had to admit. Her smile widened at something Sarah said, and Gray reacted.

A mere smile from the woman—a smile that wasn't even directed at him—sent a jolt of desire thundering through him.

He hated this blasted attraction to the woman, almost as much as he hated—

Gray's thought ended abruptly as Buck swept Sarah into his arms and swung her around. A red-hot, violent rage washed over Gray so fast his next breath failed in his lungs. He had charged halfway across the crowded room before he realized he had taken the first step.

His eyes never leaving Sarah, Gray didn't stop until he stood face-to-face with Buck.

"Put her down," Gray commanded harshly.

LAUREN LOOKED UP just in time to get a good glimpse of the violent rage in Gray Longwalker's eyes. Her heart stumbled, and adrenaline rushed through her veins. He looked ready to kill somebody or at the very least tear someone apart—and that someone appeared to be Buck.

"Well, well, Longwalker," Buck said, his smile widening into a smug grin as his hold tightened on Sarah. "I've never known you to be community oriented."

"I said put her down," Gray repeated, his voice as equally lethal as the look in his eyes.

"Maybe you'd like to try—"

"Let's take a walk with your little friends, Sarah," Lauren said quickly, cutting Buck off. She stepped between the two angry men and plucked Sarah from Buck's arms.

"I played my puzzle again, Mr. Gray," Sarah piped up before Lauren could whisk her away.

Gray shifted his attention to the child in Lauren's arms. He blinked, and all signs of anger disappeared from his angular features; tenderness filled his fierce gray eyes. When he gave the child an uncharacteristic smile, Lauren's heart stumbled a second time.

"All by yourself?" he asked, his deep voice gentle.

Sarah nodded enthusiastically. "All by myself, right, Mommy?"

Lauren pushed a smile into place. "That's right," she agreed, giving her little girl a squeeze. When Lauren's heart skipped again it had nothing to do with the breathtaking smile on Gray Longwalker's lips and everything to do with the deadly glare emitting danger signals from Buck.

"Girls, I think we need to solve the mystery of

missing toilet paper in the ladies' room,'' a feminine voice chimed from behind Lauren.

Rosemary. Lauren felt weak with relief. She passed Sarah to Rosemary and mouthed a thank-you. Rosemary shot Lauren a knowing look of sympathy.

"Come along, girls," Rosemary instructed Elly and Missy, Sarah's friends and schoolmates. Sarah wiggled out of Rosemary's grasp, and all three little girls skipped away with Rosemary's promise of adventure.

Lauren turned her attention back to the two men just in time to hear Buck say vehemently, "That child deserves better than you, Longwalker."

Everything inside Lauren froze in expectation of Gray's retaliation. Fear slammed through her like water pushing through a bursting dam.

"Buck, please," Lauren pleaded. "Don't do this. Not here, not now." She placed a hand on his rigid arm and prayed that he would regain his senses or at least temporary control of his temper. From the top of his blond head to the bottom of his booted feet, Buck looked ready for battle. A muscle jumped in his tense jaw; his fists clenched and unclenched repeatedly at his sides.

"Well that sure disqualifies you, Buckmaster," Gray said in a tone that sounded deceptively calm.

Barely checked rage radiated from Gray Longwalker. Lauren could feel the heat and thickness of it, but unlike Buck there was an utter stillness about Gray. No clenched fists…no rigid stance. Just the absolute calm one could sense during the final, tense moments before a death-dealing storm.

"A smart man would leave about now," Buck warned.

"Leaving yourself out again?" Gray goaded.

A small, curious crowd quickly gathered around them in anticipation of a fight. Lauren scanned the faces for Don or someone else whom she could depend on to intervene, but no one appeared. She had to do something. She couldn't just let this happen.

Buck took a step toward Gray. "Don't think you can waltz back into town and take whatever suits you," he said from between clenched teeth. "Nothing's changed here, Longwalker. People haven't forgotten what you are. You're still a half-breed bastard and you always will be."

All the air rushed out of Lauren's lungs. Fear clenched like a fist in her chest, twisting her heart. How could Buck say such a thing? No matter who or what Gray Longwalker was or had been, he was still Sarah's father. Lauren wasn't about to chance Sarah being exposed to this kind of viciousness.

She turned to Gray, a rebuttal of Buck's hurtful words on the tip of her tongue, but the words died a swift death. Though his face looked impassive, his eyes told the tale. Every instinct warned Lauren to grab Sarah and run from the fury that was no doubt about to descend upon Buck.

"Nothing's ever gonna change here for you," Buck taunted.

Gray still didn't flinch. Save for the darkening storm building in those fierce gray eyes, he remained so motionless that Lauren felt certain he must have turned to stone. All eyes were now focused on the evolving scene. Even the band had stopped playing. *Whatever happened to "and the band played on"?* The words skated across Lauren's mind, making her want to laugh hysterically, but there was no humor in the situation.

Dear God, Lauren prayed, don't let Sarah overhear or see something she shouldn't. Lauren hoped with all her heart that Rosemary would keep Sarah and her little friends occupied out of range of this nightmare.

A sardonic smile suddenly broke Gray's statue-like features. "You should know better than anyone what a bastard I am."

"Why you son of—" Buck exploded into action, taking a furious swing at Gray. Heated shouts burst from the crowd that surrounded them. Everyone stepped back to give the two men room to duke it out.

In one smooth, quick-as-lightning move, Gray caught Buck's arm and halted the blow just before it connected with his jaw. He jerked Buck close and whispered something in his ear. Buck staggered back a step and jerked free of Gray's hold, his face drawn and pale.

"I won't ruin this evening on account of the likes of you," Buck spat vehemently as he took another step back.

Gray held Buck's gaze a heartbeat longer before he turned and walked away. The murmuring crowd parted like the Red Sea for him to pass.

Lauren looked from Gray's retreating form to Buck and back. Two seconds later she was pushing her way through the dispersing crowd. Somehow she had to make this right. She couldn't allow Longwalker to leave angry. He might decide he'd had enough of this town and snatch Sarah and take off tonight.

He had all but disappeared into the shadows on the far side of the parking lot by the time Lauren caught sight of him again. "Gray, wait!" she called out as she hurried after him. She had no idea what to say to the man, but she had to say something...anything to smooth things over.

Gray didn't stop until he had reached his truck. He faced her and waited impatiently.

"What do you want?" he asked when Lauren came to a breathless stop beside him.

"I'm sorry about what happened inside." Lauren swallowed and dragged in another gulp of air before she continued. "Buck had no right to speak to you that way."

The heat from his eyes burned into hers. His mouth had tightened into that firm line he usually wore.

"I don't need your sympathy or your misplaced good intentions," he growled. He gave her his back and reached for the door to his truck.

Lauren stepped quickly between him and the door. "Just tell me one thing before you go," she insisted. Her chest rose and fell rapidly with her pounding heart.

He released an irritated breath and glared at her. "What?"

"What did you say to Buck to put the fear of God in him? I've never seen a man go from battle ready to backpedaling in such a hurry in my entire life." Lauren regarded him steadily and waited for the anger she knew still raged inside him to ease. She had to do this, right? She couldn't just let this situation fester.

His mouth twitched a bit. To hold back a smile Lauren felt sure. She almost smiled herself, but clamped down on her lower lip to prevent it.

"I just asked him if he was ready to meet his Maker tonight, that's all." A wicked gleam sprang to life in his metallic gaze. "Apparently, he wasn't."

Somehow Lauren had a feeling that whatever Gray

Longwalker had said to Buck, it had been more explicit than that.

"Well, whatever you said did the trick, and I'm grateful. I wouldn't have wanted Sarah to witness that kind of scene or the aftermath. Thank you for walking away." Lauren essayed a tremulous smile.

"I didn't come back to Thatcher looking for trouble," he said wearily.

"In this town you are the trouble," Lauren said almost to herself, focusing on the crisp white shirt he wore and the tempting dark skin beneath. She peered up at him. "What's the deal between you and Buck?"

Longwalker gripped the door handle next to her arm. "Why don't you ask your boyfriend," he offered contemptuously.

Oblivious to his comment, Lauren frowned as more details of what had taken place poured into her mind. "And why was everyone so afraid of you? Not a single man in that crowd would have taken you on—at least not alone." Lauren shook her head. "I don't understand why these people hate you so—why they fear you?"

Gray caught her chin between his thumb and forefinger while he moved in dangerously close and then closer still. When his powerful body trapped hers against his sleek black truck, he slowly lowered his head.

Lauren gasped just before his mouth covered hers.

His kiss was hard...punishing...threatening...and yet with a simmering passion neither of them could have denied. The taste of heat and man filled her, renewed the need mushrooming inside her. His left hand threaded into her hair as his right tilted her chin upward to give him better access to her mouth.

That kernel of desire that never seemed to completely go away in his presence burst and flamed. She flattened her palms against his rock-solid chest with every intention of pushing him away, only to find her fingers fisting into his shirt. She could feel his arousal growing against her belly. Heat swirled low and deep inside her, making her ache in secret places.

Lauren's lips parted under his skillful seduction, and he quickly slid his tongue inside her mouth. She tensed at the intrusion, though she had known he would do just that…she had wanted him to do it. Wanted to feel that part of him inside her again.

The harder he kissed her, the more firmly he ground his hips into hers, making Lauren weak and leaving no doubt as to what he wanted.

He broke the kiss, but kept his hard body pressed against hers—a solid reminder of who was in control. His fingers dug into her cheeks as he grasped her chin even tighter. He released a harsh breath that made her shiver when it feathered across her skin.

"Of all the people in this town," he told her, his voice low, husky, dangerous, his eyes brilliant with intense, gray light. "*You* have the most to fear from me."

Lauren was stunned for several seconds. She couldn't move or respond to his threat. Her heart surged into her throat; her blood roared in her ears. Finally she shoved hard at his chest and jerked herself away from him.

Before Lauren could frame the words to respond, he yanked his truck door open, got in and sped away. Lauren could only stare after the twin taillights as they faded in the distance.

"WHAT THE DEVIL did you mean following Longwalker outside? Don't you know the man is not to be trusted?" Buck demanded for the third time since leaving the fund-raiser. "I'm only trying to protect you, Lauren."

Lauren ignored the concerned glances he kept tossing in her direction. She had never been so glad to get out of a place in her life. She had wanted to leave immediately after the incident with Gray, but Buck had insisted on staying to gloat with his cronies. "Longwalker's not going to ruin my night," he had protested. Well it was too late for Lauren, her night— week really—had already been wrecked. Rumors and gossip had been rampant during that last hour she'd had to endure.

Buck had boasted over and over how he had been big enough to back off and not spoil the dance for everyone. If he hadn't been such a gentleman, Longwalker would have gotten his tonight, Buck had bragged. Lauren wondered if the dozen or so times he had repeated that phrase had assuaged the blow Gray had delivered to his ego.

Lauren hadn't worked up the courage to ask Buck what exactly stood between the two men. Surely Sharon would have told her if there was anything significant between them. Lauren sighed. She and Sharon had never really discussed Longwalker in depth. He had always seemed like some nonexistent person to Lauren. She had never concerned herself with him— until now.

"Lauren, I want you to stay away from that man. He's dangerous," Buck ordered.

"Don't talk like that in front of Sarah," she scolded in a hushed voice.

"Dang, sugar, she's dead to the world back there. Besides she doesn't know who Longwalker is, right?"

Lauren peeked over her shoulder at Sarah in the back seat. She slept soundly. But still, Lauren had no intention of discussing Gray Longwalker with Buck in front of Sarah—asleep or not. "It's only a matter of time before she has to know," Lauren whispered with a sigh of defeat.

"I say you don't let the lowlife near Sarah until a judge tells you different."

Lauren closed her eyes and summoned her patience. "I'm only doing what my attorney has advised me to do."

"Well, maybe it's about time you got yourself another attorney. Ewen is the best mouthpiece in the state. I'm sure if I asked him to, he'd be happy to take your case."

Lauren opened her mouth to defend Don, but the sight at the Tumbleweed Hotel stole the words before she could utter them.

Buck slowed only slightly as they neared the place. Two police cars, a fire truck, an ambulance and an assortment of other vehicles filled the parking lot.

"What on earth happened?" An uneasy feeling crept over her as she considered that this was the place Gray Longwalker called home at the moment.

"Nothing we can help with," Buck retorted, and accelerated.

"Wait," Lauren demanded. "I want to stop and see what's happened."

"It's late, Lauren. Sarah is asleep," he offered without slowing down.

"Buck Buckmaster, stop this car immediately," she commanded, her hand already on the door latch.

Buck cursed as he wheeled the car into an adjoining parking lot, then pulled over next to one of the police cruisers. Lauren jumped out before they came to a complete stop. She rushed forward only to be halted by an officer.

"Whoa, ma'am," he said. "I'm afraid you can't go back there."

Lauren could see that four or five rooms had burned to the ground, one of which she recognized immediately from its location as Gray Longwalker's. "Was anyone hurt?" she blurted. She could feel the anxiety building at the back of her throat.

"No, ma'am. Three of the rooms were empty and the occupant of the fourth was out for the evening."

Lauren felt weak with relief. *Thank God.* She closed her eyes and sighed.

"Come to see the show?"

A familiar masculine voice prodded Lauren's eyes open.

"Gray!" she almost shouted. A relieved smile kicked up the corners of her mouth as she rushed past the officer. "Are you all right?"

"I'm fine," he assured her, his voice tense, clipped. Gray's wary regard moved from Lauren to somewhere past her shoulder. "I'm sure that's a big disappointment to you, Buck."

"Why, I have no idea what you're talking about, Longwalker," Buck replied, hatred coloring his tone.

"What happened?" Lauren asked, ignoring the verbal and visual daggers flying between the two men.

Gray leveled his furious glare back on her. "I'm out of a place to stay, that's what happened."

"Surely this hotel has other vacancies," Lauren argued.

"It seems I'm too high a risk for the manager's comfort."

"You mean he kicked you out?"

Gray eyed her for another long moment, some indefinable emotion flickered briefly in his eyes. "That's exactly what I mean," he said slowly, drawing each word out as if she might not understand.

"What will you do?" she pressed. The scenarios that bounced around in her head scared Lauren to death. What if he did decide to take off in the middle of the night with Sarah? What if he pressured his attorney into acting now? What if...

Oh, God. Lauren couldn't deal with much more of this kind of stress. She rubbed at the beginnings of pain in her right temple as she tried to calm her runaway thoughts. She would have to take her medicine the moment she got home or she would be in serious trouble. She glanced at the firemen rolling up their hoses and tried to think what to do. What could she do? Should she even do anything, considering what had happened between them outside the community center?

"Lauren," Gray said, his voice deep and suddenly soft, like rumpled velvet. As always, the sound of her name on his lips seared through her, simultaneously heating her and making her shiver. "I'll find a place to stay."

"This isn't your problem, Lauren," Buck reminded, breaking the shimmering tension, taking it to a different level.

Lauren jumped. She had completely forgotten that Buck was standing behind her.

"Let me take you home. Sarah is still asleep in the car," he added as leverage.

"Go home, Lauren," Gray urged, his eyes softening to match his voice.

Lauren looked from the smoking mass of rubble that used to be room 112, to Gray Longwalker. She couldn't go home and leave him here…homeless. She just couldn't. He was Sarah's father.

"The bunkhouse," she said suddenly.

"What?" both men asked in unison.

"It hasn't been used in years, but it's in good shape." Lauren shrugged. "A little dusting and fresh linens is all it needs."

"Are you inviting me to stay at your place?" Gray asked cautiously.

"Lauren, this is insane!" Buck spouted, pacing back and forth behind her. She had already noted how he kept himself shielded safely behind her.

Lauren hesitated only for a second. "Yes," she said. "That's exactly what I'm doing." Though for the life of her, Lauren couldn't completely understand why she had done it. He was Sarah's father, but he was also her enemy.

"Considering that I don't have any other options without driving forty miles, I accept," Gray said with more reluctance than relief.

"Fine." Lauren nodded resolutely. "I'll go right home and make preparations."

"Fine," he echoed. His eyes searched hers during the brief pause before Lauren turned and walked away. She couldn't read any emotion in his intense scrutiny, but she could feel the heat all the way to the center of her being.

What had she done?

Had she lost her mind?

One brief backward glance confirmed her suspicions. Gray Longwalker watched her walk away with that same hot intensity in his eyes.

She had lost her mind. And if Gray had anything to do with it, she would lose a lot more than that.

Chapter Eight

"I cannot believe you invited the man to stay in your bunkhouse!"

Buck was furious. He paced Lauren's parlor like a caged animal. She stepped back, giving him a wide berth. As soon as he stopped bellowing and left she would see to Longwalker's needs. She refused to question her motivation. She had done the right thing. He was Sarah's father, after all.

"The man is nothing but trash. Can't you understand that?" Buck paused long enough to level his outraged gaze on hers. "He's nothing, Lauren. He doesn't deserve the time of day from you. The man is trying to take your little girl!" he thundered.

"Keep your voice down, you'll wake Sarah," she scolded, her own ire building now. Buck had no right to interfere with her decisions, good or bad. That was just one of the things that she didn't like about the man—he was bossy. And she certainly didn't need anyone to remind her of why Longwalker was back in town.

"Land sakes, woman, don't you see what he's doing?" Buck flung his arms heavenward. "He's playing on your sympathy. There isn't a soul in this town that would spit on him if he was on fire.''

Lauren lifted her chin in defiance. "Why is that, Buck? What did Longwalker do that was so terrible?"

Buck averted his gaze and stalked across the room again. "What didn't he do would be the better question. He's been accused of about everything a man can get into that spells trouble. You and that little girl deserve better than him is all I can say.''

"We'd be better off with someone like you," Lauren suggested pointedly.

Buck pivoted and faced her. "Sugar, that's what I've been trying to tell you for months now. We can work out our differences. I could make you happy, I know I could. I'm the kind of man you need."

Lauren quaked with the revulsion rushing through her. "A rich, white man with the proper pedigree, is that what you mean?"

Realization dawned in Buck's eyes. "That is not what I meant." He swore hotly. "I might as well go. There's no use talking to you when you get like this.''

"I hit the nail on the head, didn't I?" she demanded. He wasn't going to get out of this so easily. A man wasn't trash because he wasn't rich or white or didn't have the right name. Was this the kind of attitude Gray had been subjected to his entire life in Thatcher? Lauren's heart ached for the little boy who must have suffered severely at the hands of those who thought like Buck—which pretty much summed up the whole town's attitude. She closed her eyes against the imagined agony. No wonder he had such a large chip on his shoulder.

"You're making a mistake, Lauren."

Her eyes popped open at the ominous tone in Buck's voice.

"I guarantee you, you don't want to do this."

Outrage flashed like wildfire through Lauren. "Oh, I definitely want to do it." If she'd had any doubts at all, they had just evaporated. "Good night, Buck."

GRAY SAT ON THE TOP STEP leading to the porch that ran the length of Lauren's bunkhouse. He had waited, tension weighing heavily in his stomach, for Lauren to tell Buck good night and send the jerk on his way.

Gray's senses jumped into overdrive when Buck finally huffed out onto the front porch with Lauren trailing. Evidently they still argued. Buck flung his arms upward and spoke much louder than necessary, but not quite loudly enough for Gray to make out his words. The porch light spread a yellow glow around them, like a spotlight on the characters in a play.

Finally, after what felt like an eternity to Gray, Buck turned to stalk away. He froze midturn. Even through the darkness, even across the distance, somehow his eyes met Gray's and locked. Buck suddenly wheeled back around and jerked Lauren into his arms, kissing her hard and fast.

Jealousy swooped down on Gray like a giant hawk, its talons ripping open his chest. He surged to his feet, his breath coming in harsh, ragged spurts. Anger seized him with such strength that he vibrated with its intensity.

And then Buck was gone, his Lexus spewing dust and gravel in its wake. When Gray swung his head back toward the porch, Lauren had vanished into the house. He took long, deep breaths to counter his emotions. He unclenched his fists and willed himself to relax.

What was wrong with him? He had never let a woman get to him like this before. He had never let *anyone* get to him like this. He no longer allowed his emotions to rule him. But since his return to Thatcher, the anger he had banished long ago had resurfaced with a fierceness he continued to find harder to control. And with that anger came these unsettling feelings for Lauren.

He cursed himself for the fool he was. He couldn't prevent his body's need for sexual release, but this obsession with Lauren went well past need and he knew it.

And it scared him like nothing else ever had.

Gray understood that he didn't just want to take her to bed—he wanted to make love to her. Wild, passionate love. And not just once. He wanted to touch her, taste her, over and over again. Already hard and aching at the thought, Gray cursed himself more vehemently.

He scrubbed an unsteady hand over his face. He had lost his control, his perspective. He set his jaw hard and did what he knew he had to, he strode in the direction of his truck. The best thing he could do was leave before he made an even bigger mistake than he already had. Maybe Mrs. Jennings would have an extra bunk at her place.

"I have sheets, towels, soap, everything I think you'll need." The voice of doom called out to him.

Gray stopped dead in his tracks and slowly turned around to find Lauren strolling toward the bunkhouse carrying a huge woven basket brimming with items from her home.

"If I've missed anything, just feel free to knock on the door and ask for it." She smiled timidly when their gazes met, and his resolve died an instant death.

Gray lifted the basket from her arms. Unable to speak, he could only follow her back up the steps to the bunkhouse like a prisoner being led to execution.

Lauren opened the door and flipped on the lights as she entered. "It's nothing fancy. I really didn't have much done out here when I renovated the house, just the electrical and plumbing. I wanted to bring everything up to code, even the barn."

Gray plunked the heavy basket down on the chrome and Formica table that sat in the middle of the long front room. The kitchen and living room spanned the length of the oblong structure. Knotty pine floors and walls looked clean and well maintained. Basic kitchen appliances lined the far wall. Lauren collected the bed and bath linens from the basket and led the way into a bedroom, chattering incessantly about making the place a guest house someday.

The bunkhouse consisted of two bedrooms, one bath and the living-room-kitchen combination. All in all, the place was a big step up from the Tumbleweed. Except for one major problem, Gray reminded himself as he watched her spread a thin cotton blanket over the fresh sheets on the bed.

Lauren Whitmore.

Gray sighed, a little louder than he intended.

Lauren looked up as she smoothed one small hand over the blanket to remove a nonexistent wrinkle. "I'm sorry. You're tired and I'm rambling, aren't I?" She smiled another one of those shy, vulnerable smiles. His gut clenched in reaction.

Lauren straightened and fanned a wisp of silky

blond hair from her face. She drew in a deep breath, the movement drawing Gray's attention to her chest. The size and shape of her breasts were clearly outlined beneath the clinging green fabric. When his gaze collided with hers once more, the shimmering jade of her eyes reminded him that he had been right about the color of the dress highlighting those wide, exotic pools.

At that precise moment he would have paid any price to see her pull the pins from her hair and then watch the long, thick tresses tumble down around her slender shoulders. A wave of desire rose so strongly inside him that it made him weak-kneed. The room grew suddenly tiny with the big, wide bed taunting him. His breath went thin in his lungs, and a strange, unfamiliar emotion ached through him.

With sudden clarity Gray recognized it for what it was, the longing for something beyond his reach— something he could never have. A man like Buck would win the heart of this woman, he reminded himself. Gray didn't have a snowball's chance in Hades of making a woman like this his...even if he wanted to. And he didn't. He was confused, and so was she. A part of her wanted to reach out to him, but another part feared him. Her motivation was unclear. But he could feel her trepidation all the way across the room.

Lauren wrung her hands nervously, as if she'd suddenly sensed the tension in him. Her lips quivered, she blinked and then looked away. "Just flip the breaker to turn on the water heater." She gestured toward the breaker box on the far wall. "If...if you need anything else, you can let me know." She kept her head lowered as she hurried past him.

Like a snake striking an innocent victim, Gray

snagged her by the arm and pulled her around to face him. He was asking for trouble here. He hadn't even gotten his body under control and he further tempted himself by touching her. But he had to know.

"Why are you doing this?" he asked, his voice gruff to his own ears. The question burned inside him like hot, molten steel. He sensed her need to reach out to him even stronger now, he just couldn't understand why. She tried to pull away, but he held her by both arms, his fingers digging into the soft flesh beneath the thin fabric of her dress. "We've already established that you don't want me here."

Lauren moistened her lips, the movement adding to Gray's mounting discomfort. "I—I'm ashamed of the way Buck behaved and...for the way the people here treat you." She peered up at him, her huge green eyes liquid, her lips trembling. "I wanted to try and make it up to you."

Gray's jaw tightened; his desire rechanneled itself into anger. "I don't want your sympathy," he snapped, and then gave her a little shake. Lauren stiffened in his grasp. "These people don't care about me one way or another. They just react the way the Buckmasters want them to. This whole blasted town bows down to the mighty Buckmasters. Don't you know that?" he snarled like a wounded animal.

Lauren moved her head quickly from side to side. "I don't understand. I'm only trying to be nice." A tear slid down her pale cheek, and she trembled in his ruthless hold.

"Don't be nice to me, Lauren. I don't want you to be nice to me," he growled fiercely. The scant inch of air that separated them fairly crackled with tension. Gray wanted more than he had ever wanted anything in his life to take her right here, right now. But instead he released her, looked away and let out a shaky breath. Damn him for feeling this way. Damn her for making him.

"I'll leave in the morning," he told her. "This will never work." Indifference he could deal with. He'd done that his entire life. Anger, hatred he knew how to react to—but *this* he couldn't handle. No one had shown him a moment's consideration since he was ten years old. And right now he couldn't trust himself or this woman who appeared bent on that end.

"I'm just..." she began, her voice halting and trailing off as she backed away from him. "I'm sorry about—"

He glared at her, cutting off her next words. "I'm not," he lashed out, his chest heaving with the anger that boiled inside him.

Something changed in her eyes. Gone was the fear and uncertainty. She balled her small hands into fists at her sides. Outrage etched itself in every feature of her pretty face. Gray watched the transformation with complete fascination.

Lauren advanced the few steps she had retreated. She looked him square in the eye and, before he knew what was happening, had slapped him as hard as she could. His ears rang and his jaw stung from the blow but he didn't move a muscle in reaction. He stood perfectly still and let her have her say.

"You are a bastard, Gray Longwalker, and it doesn't have a thing to do with illegitimacy." She spat the words with a healthy dose of contempt. "You're out of a place to stay and I've offered you one, and you have the nerve to snub my hospitality."

He snatched her wrist before she attempted further

violence. "Why don't you give me the unvarnished truth about why you're being so hospitable," he said from between clenched teeth, his face only inches from hers.

Her bravado wilted. "I've changed my mind," she said, tugging at his hold. "You can leave *now!*"

He tugged back, jerking her soft body against his rock-hard one, lowering his head even closer to hers. "Come on, Lauren, tell me about how you had hoped to be all nice and sweet to me to change my mind about taking Sarah," he goaded, his grip tightening when she would have pulled away. "How far would you go?" He nipped her earlobe with his teeth. She shivered in response. "I can feel the heat between us. Would you go that far? Do you think I'd ride off into the sunset never to be heard from again if you treated me just right? Hmmm?" He buried his face in the curve of her neck and drew in deeply of her sweet scent.

Lauren exploded into action. Screaming like a wild-cat, she kicked him and pulled at his hair. He barely deflected her knee from its most-sensitive target. She sank her teeth into his chest, wrenching forth a howl and several ear-scorching curses. She kicked his shin sending him off balance. They tumbled onto the freshly made bed, a tangle of arms and legs.

"Get off me, you jerk!" She arched upward in an effort to throw him off.

"Forget it," he barked, his breath coming in short, ragged bursts. She arched again. "If you don't stop that, I won't be responsible for what happens next," the hoarse words rumbled from deep within his chest.

She froze, her eyes wide with understanding as his arousal nudged into her pelvis. Lauren gasped, fear flickered in her big, green eyes. "You wouldn't dare," she said on a breath, her rage slipping, the energy diverting to feed her fear.

He cocked one eyebrow and bent his lips into a wicked smile. "Wouldn't I? Haven't you heard about my hot temper and womanizing? Gray Longwalker, the half-breed who'd take another man's woman just to tick him off? The man who doesn't care about anything or anyone. That's me, Lauren, and no one in this town has ever forgotten it—why should you be different?"

She shook her head from side to side. "I don't believe you," she whispered, her eyes shining with unshed tears. She swallowed hard. He watched the delicate muscles of her throat struggle with the effort.

"I've seen you with Sarah." The tears slipped past her long, thick lashes, and her lips quivered before she spoke again. "I'm not afraid of you, Gray Longwalker. I know I should be, but I'm not."

He stared into her eyes and saw the truth of her words. Saw the uncertainty of her own desires, but no fear. "And when I take Sarah away, will you be afraid of me then?"

She shook her head again, slowly, resolutely. "I won't let you take her away," she said with a conviction that knifed through his gut.

"And how would you propose to stop me?" His body hummed with white-hot desire. He lowered his head until his lips almost touched hers and hovered there, allowing the sensation to flow over him, fueling his need.

She sucked in an unsteady breath, her lips brushing his, her breasts rising against his chest. He wanted this woman so much it hurt.

"When the time comes," she said, defying his control, her eyes locked with his. "I believe you'll do the right thing for Sarah."

Her words kicked like a mule, the force jamming into his midsection. He drew back and stared at her, confused and unwilling to believe what he had heard. Everything inside him stilled.

"Then you're a bigger fool than I thought," he said roughly. Gray pushed up from the bed, pulling her up as he went. She moved quickly away from him, adjusting her dress and hair with shaky hands.

Gray stared at the floor willing her to leave. *You'll do the right thing,* still echoed inside his head.

She stopped at the door and turned back to him. "Are you going or are you staying?" she asked, as if none of what had just happened had taken place.

Gray considered her question. Why not? He'd always been a glutton for punishment. Why not stay— it was as good a place as any. Better than some. And he would be close to his daughter.

"I'll stay on one condition."

She tipped her chin up a notch in challenge. "And what would that be?"

"That I pay you room and board."

She huffed indignantly. "I don't want your money."

"Then I go," he said simply.

"This is ridiculous." She planted her hands at her waist and glowered at him.

"I won't accept your charity. I'll earn my keep," he added, giving her body a thorough raking. "In any way you'd like."

She shivered visibly, but then her anxious expression brightened as if an idea had just occurred to her. "What if we compromise?"

Wary, he said, "I'm listening."

"My great-aunt still owned a few horses when she passed away. They've all been sold but one. Spinner was her favorite, and my mother couldn't bear to see him sold. So she paid someone to see after the horse until I moved here." Sadness marred her pretty features. "I suppose all that time running the pastures alone did it. He's as wild as can be now. No one can get close to him. He has to be tranquilized any time he needs attention from the vet."

Gray rubbed the back of his neck and pretended to mull over her offer. He would never turn his back on an animal in need, but she didn't know that. "I suppose I could take a look at him. You're sure no one has abused him?"

"Oh, no. Mr. Burke has taken very good care of him."

Tom Burke. Gray knew him, and if Tom had been responsible for the horse then everything was as it should be. Tom was a good man with a deep love for all animals.

"All right," Gray said slowly and then extended his hand. "It's a deal."

Lauren placed a tentative hand in his to seal their deal. Need flamed anew in Gray's loins. Every carnal act he had ever done or imagined flashed before his eyes, and he wanted nothing more than to do each and every one to and with Lauren.

He had to be crazy or at the very least hell-bent to stay. But stay he would.

Chapter Nine

"Fax this one to Frank right away," Lauren instructed Rosemary as she shuffled through the revised drawings and selected the most urgent one.

"What about the rest?" Rosemary scanned the remaining drawings Lauren had fanned across the desktop like a bad poker hand.

"They can wait." Lauren reshuffled the group. "There are a couple I want to look at one more time." She just hadn't been able to concentrate on her work lately. Big surprise, she thought dryly. With all that was going on in her life she was stunned that she got anything accomplished.

"Sarah told me at church yesterday that Gray had moved into the bunkhouse," Rosemary said a bit too offhandedly.

Lauren paused, midshuffle, and met her friend's gaze. "There was a fire at the hotel. It seemed like the only logical thing to do," she explained.

Rosemary covered Lauren's hand with her own. "I wasn't accusing you of anything, Lauren. I'm just concerned, that's all."

Lauren's gaze narrowed slightly. She trusted Rosemary implicitly, but she wouldn't put anything past Buck. "Did Buck ask you to talk to me?"

Rosemary scoffed. "Are you kidding? You know I'd tell Buck to take a hike if he even proposed such an idea." She squeezed Lauren's hand. "Gray has only been here a week. I've seen what his presence has put you through. Then suddenly he's living on your property. It seems a little strange," she added softly. "Folks talk."

Lauren squeezed her eyes shut and massaged her forehead with trembling fingers. She knew it was strange. But she just couldn't turn him away. The people around town who had nothing better to do would just have to talk. She sighed when she opened her eyes and met Rosemary's worried gaze. "I know it looks—" Lauren grappled for the right word "—odd," she finished. "But what was I supposed to do? You and I both know he's Sarah's father. Could I turn my back on him as if he's a mere stranger?"

Rosemary placed the drawing and the lead sheet she had prepared facedown on the fax machine and pressed the necessary buttons. A busy signal sounded instantly, but the machine would redial until it tapped into an open line. She turned back to Lauren and studied her for a time before she spoke again. "He is a stranger to you and to Sarah," she countered. "But I know you and how you love to take in strays. Fluffy's a prime example of that." She leveled her most serious gaze on Lauren then. "But, Lauren, Gray Longwalker is no stray cat. He's a man...by all accounts, a man to be feared."

Lauren frowned, wondering. "Is that how you remember him?"

Hesitancy claimed Rosemary's features then. She

looked away and forked her fingers through her long brown hair. Before Lauren could apologize for asking such a personal question, Rosemary walked across the room to the wide set of windows and stared out.

"You have to remember that my family left Thatcher for a while when I was a teenager. By the time we moved back, Longwalker was gone and I was in my first year of college. So my memories are really old."

Knowing there was more, Lauren joined her at the window, both staring at nothing at all. "But you do remember him," she pressed.

"I remember him," she murmured, her voice distant.

Silence lengthened between them for one long minute that turned to two. Another dial tone sounded, and the fax machine whirred behind them, carrying on with business despite the heart-stopping anticipation building inside Lauren.

"He was the town bad boy," she began. A hint of a smile pulled at her lips. "All the girls whispered about him. He was so goodlooking." She sighed, reliving long ago memories. "But he had such a reputation." A frown furrowed her brow. "And he was so angry. We were all afraid of him."

Lauren listened without interrupting as Rosemary painted a picture with her words. Gray Longwalker had been an outcast even then.

"The guys all hated him. Buck and his brother especially."

"Why?" Lauren's voice sounded strange, strained with sympathy for a boy she hadn't even known. What was it with Buck and Gray?

Rosemary shrugged. "Who knows? Maybe because

he was poor and illegitimate. You know the Buck-masters, they think God created this earth specially for them. Or maybe it was because the guys knew that all the girls secretly loved Gray.''

''If he was as bad as all that, why did you still like him?''

''Because he wasn't, not really.'' Rosemary glanced at her, then resumed her intent stare out the window. But not before Lauren saw the flicker of remembered emotion in her eyes. ''Well, I mean, at least not to me.

''It was my first date,'' Rosemary continued. ''I was so excited that a tenth-grader had asked me to the ball game. He was on the team, had a letter jacket and all. His name was Wesley. But the ride home wasn't so wonderful. He…he tried to force me to…well, you know.''

Anxiety tightened Lauren's chest. ''What did you do?''

''I got out of his car, determined to walk home.'' She laughed dryly. ''But it was dark, and I was a long way from home.'' She shook her head. ''He just drove off and left me there. Then bragged about it the following day.''

''How did you get home?'' Lauren could imagine the panic that must have overwhelmed her.

''Gray Longwalker came along in his old beat-up truck and offered me a ride.'' She blinked, her eyes suspiciously bright. ''I was afraid at first. But I was desperate.'' She paused, visibly bracing herself. ''He tried to make me feel better by saying what a jerk Wesley was and all that. Then he told me I'd done the right thing. 'You should never let a man take advantage of you,' he said. He even held me while I cried.

Can you imagine?'' Rosemary swiped at her eyes. ''Anyway, when he pulled up in my driveway, my father was sitting on the front porch waiting for me to get home.''

Lauren stilled, knowing what was to come would not be good.

Rosemary slowly shook her head from side to side. ''Daddy pitched an awful fit. Said terrible things to Gray for coming near his daughter. Even told him he'd shoot him if he ever caught him around me again.''

''My God. What did Gray do?''

She shrugged listlessly. ''Nothing. He just took it.''

''What did you do?''

Rosemary drew in a quick breath. ''I didn't do anything. I went inside and to my room just like my father ordered.'' She dabbed at her eyes again. ''I never even thanked Gray.''

Lauren hugged her friend. How that memory must haunt her. ''You were young. You didn't know any better.''

Rosemary drew back and pinned her with the urgency glimmering in her brown eyes. ''Don't you see. It's always been that way. Longwalker never had a chance to be anything but what these people decided he was. And nothing's changed. He's walking around with years of emotional baggage hanging around his neck. Don't let him drag you down with it, Lauren. I'm not sure he can ever escape his past. Even Sharon worried about him passing that same bitterness on to Sarah.''

''But I can't treat him the way these people have treated him. I just can't.'' Promise or no, Lauren couldn't do it.

''Of course you can't,'' Rosemary agreed. ''But be

careful. He walked away from the things he couldn't change six years ago. But I've got a bad feeling that he's through walking away. He intends to have his daughter. I just don't want you to get hurt in the cross fire.''

It was too late, Lauren wanted to say, but held her tongue. She was already in way too deep.

THE BREEZE CHILLED HER SKIN, but the sun shone bright and warm against the green pastures that surrounded Lauren's house. She watched from her secluded spot on the back porch as Gray worked with Spinner. Rosemary had left with a half dozen errands to run for Lauren and a dentist's appointment later in the afternoon. She wouldn't be back today. Lauren closed her eyes and recalled the heart-wrenching story Rosemary had related to her. She shouldn't allow these intense feelings, but she couldn't stop them. Gray was a grown man, he didn't need her foolish sympathy.

Lauren stilled. Was sympathy all there was to it? She had a bad feeling that she was lying to herself. She didn't want to get involved with him on any level. But here she was, determined to help him. And every bit as determined to beat him in the custody battle. The conflicting emotions warred inside her until she felt riddled with confusion.

Lauren firmed her resolve. She had to have a talk with Gray. If he was going to stay, she needed him to understand the ground rules. No more hot searing looks, no more touching, and definitely no more kissing. She had never behaved like a tramp and she wasn't about to start now. Lauren didn't do casual sex. She and Kevin had agreed to wait until their wedding night. But that night never came. She was no longer interested in a relationship with any man. Not now. Not ever. Going to her grave a virgin wasn't such a bad thing.

She hadn't been remotely attracted to any man since Kevin's death, until now. She was only twenty-seven. She supposed it had been foolish to rule out the possibility of ever feeling that way again. But she hadn't wanted to. Still didn't want to. Heat stirred inside her, making a liar out of her.

Lauren had spent her school years concentrating on obtaining the best education possible, and she had gone straight into a high-pressure position after graduating. With no serious dating experience outside her time with Kevin, she felt ill at ease even considering another relationship. The few times she had been out with Buck certainly didn't count. She had never experienced even the slightest pang of desire for him. He was a friend, nothing more.

Falling in love again was too risky. What would happen if she lost someone else she cared about? And it could happen. Fairness didn't have anything to do with it. Lauren shook her head. She couldn't go down that road again. She had already risked her heart to Sarah, she wouldn't risk it any further.

Lauren's attention ventured back to the pasture and settled on Gray. She couldn't deny a powerful physical attraction to him, one that by far surpassed even the one she had felt for Kevin. The feelings confused her. She didn't want to care about him like that. If Lauren ever felt compelled to seek out another relationship, it would be with a marriage-minded man, a family oriented man. And only for Sarah's benefit.

Gray Longwalker fit neither of those categories. Despite the fact that he was the child's father. Like her, fate had dealt him a raw deal. From what she could ascertain, it wasn't his fault that people reacted the way they did to him. It hadn't been in the beginning, anyway. But he had a choice, he could leave it behind or he could drag it around with him. Unfortunately, he chose the latter.

But didn't she do the same thing? She frowned, considering. Losing Kevin and gaining the headaches had heightened her sense of self-preservation. She had given up her life as she knew it, run away to the middle of nowhere and lived like a hermit. She rarely socialized and refused to enter into a real relationship with a man. Was she any better than Gray?

As that thought struck, her errant gaze sought him. Lauren's mouth tugged into a smile as she watched Gray sit patiently waiting for Spinner to come nearer. The horse stood less than a dozen feet away from him. During the twenty minutes or so she had been observing, Spinner had edged forward only two halting steps.

Gray kept a patient vigil. He sat cross-legged in the grass, the breeze shifting long dark strands of hair around his broad shoulders. The sun glinted against the rich highlights in his hair, the result doing strange things to Lauren's insides. She could almost feel the warmth his faded chambray shirt would have absorbed from the sun, heating the skin beneath. The image of what that chest would look like, ridged with hard muscle and covered in smooth bronzed skin, played itself in the private theater of her mind. She had felt the contours and solidity of that chest on more than one occasion.

Despite the brisk breeze, a sheen of perspiration slickened Lauren's skin. Desire sung through her veins. How could she want to touch him so badly?

She barely knew him, and what she did know was far from good. Every instinct warned her to avoid him, but she moved closer with each passing day. Lauren knew perfectly well where the touching and kissing would lead, and she didn't want to go there—did she?

"No," she muttered fiercely. *I don't want that.* But it was more than the physical attraction, it was the man himself. No matter what anyone said about him, Lauren knew he was inherently good and kind. No one who loved animals as much as he did could be bad.

Lauren shivered and pushed the irrational thoughts away. She would not analyze her lapse in judgment any further. She would simply do better from this point on.

Spinner finally took the last steps that separated him from Gray. Lauren held her breath as the horse cautiously reached down to inspect the man sitting like a statue in his grazing territory. Gray remained motionless. His hands were turned palm up on his knees as if in deep meditation. Spinner hesitantly nuzzled each hand in turn. Gray slid one hand slowly over the horse's long face in a reassuring stroke. Man and horse continued for a time to learn each other. His curiosity satisfied, Spinner returned to grazing a few feet from Gray.

When Gray stood, Spinner's head shot up but he didn't bolt. Gray spoke to him, then turned and walked away.

Lauren flattened herself against the wall so Gray wouldn't see her. She watched him walk to the barn and disappear inside. Relieved that she hadn't been caught spying, Lauren hurried back into the house. Over and over she chanted the promise she had made so long ago. She *would not* get emotionally involved with anyone else. Lauren would not fall victim to Gray Longwalker's alluring charms.

An hour and a half later Gray was still in the barn. Lauren had finished her revisions and faxed the rest of the drawings to Frank. Still restless, she had turned to baking. Fresh blueberry muffins cooled on the counter. Sarah loved homemade muffins for her after-school snack.

Lauren drummed her fingers on the counter top as she stretched over the sink to see out the window. What could he be doing in there, she wondered? The barn wasn't that interesting.

"Well," Lauren huffed. "It's my barn, I can certainly go out and see what he's up to if I want." She glanced at the fresh pot of coffee she had just brewed and then at the blueberry muffins. Maybe she would invite him for a snack. A man was always in a better mood for talking when his stomach was full. And she intended to get her point fully across to him. Today.

Besides, there wasn't any food in the bunkhouse. Lauren could at least spare a meal or two until Gray had the opportunity to pick up a few groceries. God, she was hopeless. He was a grown man. He could fend for himself.

Still, Lauren strode out of the house and bounded down the back porch steps. She told herself that she was doing the right thing as she covered the short distance to the barn. She was proving that she could be cooperative. Surely if Gray believed she would allow him to be a part of his daughter's life he would find no reason to take her away. He could still roam around the country and do his job. Sarah would always be here, well taken care of, whenever he wanted to visit. *I'm doing the right thing,* she told herself once more before stepping into the coolness of the barn. She blinked to adjust her eyes to the slightly darker interior after the contrasting brightness of the sun. The sweet scent of hay and horses filled her nostrils. How had she lived all her life and not known the beauty of a country morning or the invigorating smells associated with nature until she moved here?

All thought processes ceased when she caught sight of Gray rearranging what was left of the stack of hay she'd had delivered last winter. He had stripped off his shirt, and sweat glistened on his strong back. His faded jeans hung low on his narrow hips and a red bandanna was tied around his forehead.

Muscles bunched and then flexed with his every move. His shoulders looked a mile wide above his lean, naked waist. Her mouth became parched at the thought of running her hand over all that smooth, dark skin.

Heat surged through her, making her feel flushed and impatient. Her heart pounded traitorously against her sternum. *Coffee, Lauren. Just ask him if he'd like coffee and a muffin.*

Lauren opened her mouth to speak but snapped it shut when he turned around. His gaze locked with hers and then slowly traveled over her. She felt suddenly unprepared for his visual inspection in her oversize Cubs T-shirt and black leggings. Why hadn't she put on a bra this morning? She was accustomed to running around any way she pleased. That was one of the perks of having a home office. If the day didn't include any scheduled reasons to leave the house, she made herself comfortable. It hadn't occurred to her that her manner of dress would need to be altered under the current circumstances.

With tremendous effort she manufactured a smile. She scanned the tidy barn. "Looks as though you've been busy."

He rubbed one wide hand over his flat stomach and surveyed his work. "It was a little disorganized," he said.

Lauren nodded, looking around her again. She hadn't really noticed whether the barn was organized or not. It looked like a barn to her.

"Where's Rosemary?" he asked from right beside her.

Lauren jerked back a step in surprise, banging hard against the weathered plank siding of the barn's wall. "She...she went to run errands," she stammered, struggling to regain her composure.

One corner of his full mouth tilted upward in a wry half smile. "Are you always this jumpy?"

Lauren shook her head. "I'm just not used to having a man around," she added, the words barely crawling out around the lump in her throat.

"Did you come out here to distract me or did you have something on your mind?" he asked, the huskiness in his voice making her nerve endings feel raw, exposed.

"Coffee," she blurted. She ran nervous fingers through her hair and then wrapped her arms around her middle. "I made coffee and blueberry muffins. I thought maybe you'd like some since you don't have any supplies in the bunkhouse yet." She swallowed tightly behind the tangle of words.

He reached for her then, wound his fingers into her hair and let it sift slowly through them. Goose bumps skated across her skin. He watched her intently, those gray depths darkening with desire he made no effort to hide.

"And even after last night, you're still not afraid of me?" he inquired as the last strands slid between his fingers. "You didn't come out here to ask me to leave?"

Lauren shook her head again, not quite able to manage speech.

Gray hummed a note of surprise. "Regular or decaf?"

Her gaze followed the movement as his hand dropped back to his side. "Umm...decaf," she answered breathlessly, allowing her gaze to once more meet the one that threatened to set her on fire. "And, I wanted to talk to you."

He edged closer, braced one hand against the wall next to her head and took her hand in the other, squeezing her fingers. "We do need to talk. I think we have a real problem here, Lauren."

She shivered when he said her name. She wanted to run away but couldn't bring herself to move. "I don't know what you mean." But she did. And he knew it. "I wanted to discuss..."

He pulled her hand up to his mouth and the rest of her thoughts fled. She gasped when he kissed her palm and then rubbed the spot gently with the pad of his thumb, making her pulse erratic.

"We both want the same thing—Sarah," he said. Lauren tried to pull her hand away, but he held it firmly. "That makes us enemies. But even then we can't seem to put out this fire between us," he added, his voice raspy and low.

"There isn't anything between us," Lauren said stiffly.

Gray pressed the palm he had been stroking flat against his bare chest and watched her eyes go wide. He slid his arm around her waist and pulled her closer. "Are you sure?" His lips brushed her temple when he spoke.

Lauren held her breath and squeezed her eyes shut against his nearness and the temptation that hit hard on its heels. "Yes," she lied.

"Then why are you trembling in my arms? Only two things will make a woman tremble like this," Gray said as he teased her ear with his tongue. "Fear or desire. You've already said that you're not afraid of me."

Lauren swallowed tightly and fought the mounting desire to sway into him. *Pull away,* she told herself, but her body would not obey the command. Heat shimmered inside her, focusing on a deep inner core. She felt weak and giddy and shivery and hot all at the same time. She wanted him to keep holding her. To keep talking to her in that slow, sensuous voice.

He planted hot, lingering kisses from her temple to her jaw. He teased her earlobe and then nibbled her neck. Lauren gasped, her free hand going instantly to his chest for support. He cupped her breast gently and then stroked his thumb over her nipple. Her breasts tightened and tingled in reaction. Lauren clutched at him, glorying in the feel of hard muscle beneath her palms.

Gray tightened his hold on her waist and lowered his mouth to the breast he had been stroking. She gasped again. Long and deep he suckled, drawing the nipple into his mouth through the thin, fabric barrier. Lauren moaned as need shot through her, pooling between her thighs.

With one hand he hiked up the hem of her T-shirt, with the other he drew her closer. Lauren shuddered with delight when his mouth closed over her naked breast. Her fingers threaded into his hair and pulled him more firmly against her. His hair felt like raw silk between her fingers. His tongue drew daring circles around her nipple, and then his teeth nipped at the hardened peak. Lauren's heart pounded frantically in her chest.

And then his hand was inside her panties. She tensed. Stop, she told herself, but she couldn't. Sensations exploded inside her, around her. She didn't want him to stop. Lauren had never experienced such need. He could do anything and she wouldn't care, as long as he didn't stop.

Lauren cried out when he touched her. His middle finger slid back and forth, slowly, delicately along the part of her most secret place. She pressed her back against the wall, afraid to move, afraid to even breathe while he tortured her with his mouth and hands.

Gray shifted his attention to Lauren's other breast and at the same time cautiously parted her feminine folds. His touch turned more urgent as he massaged that aching part of her until she thought she would die of it.

Heat and sensation…sensation and heat kept building and building. Light pulsed behind her closed lids. She couldn't breathe. "Gray. Stop, please," she cried. Before she went insane, she didn't add.

Instantly his hand stilled. His glazed eyes focused on hers. "Stop?" he asked, his own breath ragged.

A groan of protest rose hard and swift in her throat. A mind-bending ache wrenched through her. Her knees were weak with want. "No," she murmured. "Don't stop."

"Hold on, baby, you're almost there."

Harder, faster he stroked her, drawing on the well of desire she hadn't even known existed inside her. Tension built until her inner muscles clenched tight. Lauren cried out and instinctively arched against his hand, seeking, needing relief. Relentlessly he sucked her breasts, one and then the other.

"Oh, please," she moaned, the words barely audible.

Gray made a feral sound in his throat as he pushed one finger inside her. Lauren gasped, and everything exploded at once. Her body ached and throbbed, sensations pulsing inward, deeper and deeper. Her feminine muscles clenched hard on a second finger that pushed inside, stretched her and then penetrated slightly deeper. A savage groan tore past Gray's lips against her skin. He snatched his hand from her panties and then rubbed her through the double layers of fabric, bringing the spiraling sensations to completion. Lauren's whole body went tense and then suddenly too liquid to stand.

Gray settled onto the hard-packed dirt floor and pulled Lauren's weak, trembling body onto his lap. He held her close and stroked her hair. She pushed her arms around his neck and nestled against his solid chest. He smelled so good, like clean male sweat and the remnants of this morning's aftershave. His heart hammered behind the wall of muscle. Lauren could feel the stiff arousal in his jeans pressing against her bottom. Tears welled in her eyes and she fought hard to hold them back, but they fell anyway, slipping down her cheeks and onto his sleek, dark skin.

Why did he stop? Why didn't he...? Why did she let him do what he did?

"I didn't know," he told her in a voice so soft she hardly recognized it as his.

Her tears turned into sobs and Lauren shook in his arms. She tried hard not to. *What had she done?* She squeezed her eyes shut and tried to ignore the lingering desire still strumming through her body. How far would she have let him go if he had decided to pleasure himself while she was so caught up in her own world of sensation and pleasure. This wasn't supposed to happen. She wasn't supposed to feel this way about anyone...most especially about him.

Gray drew back and tilted her chin up to look into her eyes. He swiped the tears from one cheek with the back of his hand. "I should have stopped." Concern creased his brow as his eyes searched her face.

Lauren shook her head. She kept one hand against his chest for support, to feel the heat that still radiated from his hard body. "I shouldn't have come out here. I only wanted to talk to you and..." She couldn't finish. She couldn't repeat the unbelievable stupidity she had just allowed to happen.

A long breath slipped past his lips. He opened his mouth to speak, but then hesitated. His eyes were so amazingly beautiful, Lauren realized, momentarily forgetting all else. She shivered at the mesmerizing power there. His arms tightened around her.

"Why have you never allowed a man to make love to you?"

Lauren looked into his worried face and wondered how she could be having *this* conversation with *this* man. How could she have let Gray Longwalker touch her as no one else had?

"There hasn't been anyone since—" She didn't want to talk about Kevin or the decision they had made to wait until they were married. Her cheeks heated with shame.

"I should have stopped," Gray repeated quietly. "I didn't know until—"

Lauren scrambled out of his lap. "I have work to do." She righted her clothes with nervous hands, looking anywhere but at him. "We can talk later."

Gray rose in one fluid move, his too-observant gaze remaining steady on her.

"Help yourself to the coffee. I'll be in my office upstairs." Lauren spun around and walked away as fast as she could without actually breaking into a sprint.

GRAY SAT on Lauren's front porch with his second cup of coffee and cursed himself again for being the fool he was. How could he not have known?

Her startled response the first time he kissed her and slipped his tongue inside her mouth. The way she had held herself in his arms.

The signs were there. He had just been too full of himself to notice. At least he hadn't actually made love to her. If he'd…

He couldn't even complete the thought. Lauren Whitmore was a twenty-seven-year-old virgin. And he had seduced her.

Gray had thought virgins didn't exist anymore in women past the age of fourteen. And what would he know about virgins anyway? He had never had one. His first experience at fifteen was with a woman ten years his senior.

Gray liked his women experienced and aggressive.

Normally he wouldn't have even been attracted to a woman like Lauren.

He blew out a disgusted breath. And now she was all he thought about. His blood had been boiling in his veins before he had even touched her. He had wanted her so badly that nothing could have stopped him—except the undeniable barrier of her virginity. That sudden realization had stunned him.

Guilt gnawed at his gut. He'd sworn he wouldn't get involved with her, and look at him. Gray shook his head in defeat. A man didn't take a virgin to bed and then just walk away. Lauren Whitmore was strictly off-limits.

The sound of gravel crunching jerked his attention back to the here and now to find a white Lexus braking to a stop in Lauren's drive.

Buck.

Gray set his coffee cup aside and stood. This was all he needed right now.

"Where's Lauren?" Buck growled, striding in Gray's direction.

"In her office."

Buck started up the steps as Gray started down. They met midway.

Buck faced him, his expression hard. "Just so you understand the situation, Longwalker, Lauren's my woman."

Gray stared back at him without a word. Anger knotted inside him, but he refused to show it. He raised one skeptical eyebrow and asked, "Is that a fact?"

"It's a fact. Don't you forget it, either," Buck warned.

"Oh, I'll remember that," Gray replied easily. His

lips curled into a smirk as Buck strolled across the porch and rapped against the door. ''I'll be sure to remember that,'' he repeated, then turned to walk away. *Next time she falls apart in my arms,* he added silently.

Chapter Ten

"Sarah, find your shoes. Quickly! We're going to be late." Lauren tucked her shirt into her jeans, then tugged on her own shoes and made fast work of tying them. She rushed to the dresser and ran a brush through her hair. God, she was late. She never overslept.

"I can't reach them, Mommy!" Sarah called from her room.

Lauren huffed a defeated sigh. Just what she needed. She rushed to Sarah's room and found her daughter sitting in the middle of the floor waiting.

She pointed to the bed. "They're under there." Her eyes rounded. "Real far away."

Lauren dropped to her hands and knees and stuck her head under the bed. "Is your backpack ready to go?"

"Yep. I told you they were far away."

Flattened on the floor, Lauren reached for the scattered sneakers. She pulled one out and pitched it to Sarah. "There's one." She did the same with the second one. While Sarah pulled on the left shoe, Lauren tied the right.

"Ready now?" She pushed to her feet.

''Gotta get my backpack! And the dollar Uncle Buck gave me.'' Sarah scrambled up and dashed out the door.

Lauren absolutely refused to think about Buck's little visit yesterday. The man was still furious with her for allowing Gray to take up residence in the bunkhouse. He pushed her again to consider reconciliation. How would she ever make him see that she wasn't interested in a relationship with him or anyone else? Gray's image immediately loomed large in her mind, contradicting her determination.

The memory of how he had touched her made her tremble. Her first climax. And he had been the one to awaken that side of her. Her body longed for him now, on a level she had never known existed. And he had stopped, when Lauren knew he wanted more. That reality only served to strengthen her growing respect for the man.

A shaky breath slipped past her lips. How could her heart long so to know him completely when he stood ready to rip it from her chest? He was her enemy in the strongest sense of the word. He, and only he, held the power to take from her the one thing she loved more than life itself.

The ringing of the telephone shattered her worrisome thoughts. A loud rap at the door snapped her gaze in that direction before she could reach the telephone.

''I'll get the door!'' Sarah shouted.

Frowning, Lauren hurried to the kitchen and snagged the cordless receiver from its base. ''Hello.'' She made her way quickly back to the front hall as she listened to Don's urgent request that she come into his office this morning. "Well, sure, if you need me to."

Gray Longwalker stood in her doorway talking to Sarah. She was showing him the shiny gold dollar Buck had given her. Great, Lauren mused.

Another frown tugged at Lauren's expression when Don repeated the urgency of his request. "I'll be there. Thanks." Lauren pushed the disconnect button, her thoughts reeling. What could have Don in such a tizzy? Surely nothing new had come up. Her gaze traveled to Gray. Her defenses instantly melted when his gaze connected with hers. The smile that tilted his lips paralyzed her thoughts.

The telephone in her office rang, snapping Lauren from the trance of Gray's smile. She swore under her breath. She didn't have time for all this. Sarah was going to be late for school. The telephone in her hand rang, startling her.

"It looks as if you're a little busy," Gray commented. Sarah was now wearing his hat and galloping down the hall on her make-believe pony. Where was her backpack?

Lauren shrugged and pressed the talk button on the phone in her hand. "Hello," she snapped.

"Lauren?" It was Rosemary. "Are you all right?"

"I'm fine, just running behind."

Rosemary groaned. "I'm about to make things worse. I've got to take Erin to the doctor this morning. We've been up all night with a bellyache."

The telephone upstairs rang again. Lauren massaged her forehead and tried to ignore the sound. "It's okay. I'll manage. Take care of Erin, and I'll see you tomorrow." They exchanged goodbyes and Lauren disconnected. This was not going to be a good day.

"I suppose this isn't a good time to talk to you about getting a companion for Spinner."

Lauren tried unsuccessfully to block the effect of his voice on her traitorous body. She shivered in spite of her best efforts. Knowing it would only make things worse, she met his gaze. "I'm really late right now, could we talk about it another time? Sarah's going to be late for school, and that darn phone won't stop ringing." Lauren closed her eyes for a second to drag herself back under control. Her office line upstairs continued its insistent ringing.

"Look." Gray moved closer to her, soothing her frazzled nerves with his nearness. "You go upstairs and answer the phone. I'll take Sarah to school."

How did he do that? He hadn't even touched her and already she felt tremendously better just hearing his voice, just having him near. God, she was pathetic. His words penetrated the frenzy in her brain. She frowned "I...I don't know about that."

"Trust me, Lauren." He did touch her then. His fingers trailed down her arm, squeezed her hand, then released her. "I'll take her straight to school. She can even call you from there if you'd like."

"I want Mr. Gray to take me to school!" Sarah chimed in, rushing to his side. "I wanna wear his hat, too."

"I don't think your teacher would be too happy about that." Gray plucked the hat off her head and smiled down at her.

Sarah raced to the door. "Come on, I'm gonna be late!"

Gray looked back to Lauren for approval.

"Fine," she relented. "But you have to give me a kiss first," she said to her exuberant daughter. Lauren leaned down, her hands braced on her knees. Sarah dashed back and pecked her cheek.

"Bye, Mommy."

"Bye, sweetie." The child disappeared out the door. She was probably excited about the prospect of riding in Gray's truck.

"I'll be back soon." His gaze lingered on hers a moment longer, before he turned away.

Promise or threat, she wondered suddenly. The telephone in her hand rang again, echoing the renewed ringing upstairs. Lauren shook herself from her disturbing thoughts. She had to get to Don's office. Something must be up.

I TOLD YOU I'D BE BACK, Gray reminded the horse with his eyes. He slipped through the rails and stepped into the corral where Shadow waited, his gaze tracking Gray's every move. Gray shifted the coil of rope in his hands, allowing it to come to rest in plain sight against his thigh. Suspicious, Shadow sidled away, bumping up against the fence.

Ignoring his small audience, Gray stood in the middle of the corral for a time, the sun warming him against the cool spring breeze. Standing stock-still, Shadow eyed Gray warily. Then, as if he'd made his decision, the animal turned his rump in disinterest.

Gray smiled. "So that's the way of it," he murmured softly. Shadow might be curious, but he wasn't about to allow Gray too close with the rope in his hand. Someone had no doubt used the rope on the horse before, leaving him frightened and possibly even hurt.

Never taking his eyes off Shadow, Gray prepared a loop, purposely keeping his movements slow, methodical. Shadow reacted to the gesture as Gray began to swing the loop around. The horse moved, at first slowly, then into a trot around the outer circle hoping to escape the inevitable. Gray turned more slowly, never changing the rhythm of the swirling lasso. Now would begin the intricate dance of communication. Gray needed Shadow to hook-on, to trust him. But that kind of trust didn't come easy when an animal feared humans.

Gray swung the loop, then snugged it up around Shadow's neck. The horse reared, showing the whites of his eyes, baring his teeth, then bolted. Gray held fast, his hands steady and his voice smoothing as he spoke to the animal trotting around the corral. Manning and one of his men stumbled away from the corral when Shadow stalled, bucked, then tried to leap over the fence. Gray pulled hard on the rope in a display of control. Shadow bolted toward him. Gray sidestepped the horse's path, drawing the rope taut once more when he passed. Still snorting his displeasure and annoyed that his act of aggression had failed, Shadow galloped around the circle for several more minutes before he finally quieted. Gray immediately allowed the rope to go slack, an unspoken reward.

The gallop slowed to a trot, then a walk as Shadow grew accustomed to the feel of the rope around his neck. Gray kept his reassuring gaze steady on the animal's. When the rope had stayed slack for a time, Shadow stopped his pacing. Gray moved slowly closer to him, maintaining that steady eye contact and a smoothing tone in his voice. When Gray was only a few feet away, Shadow faced him in anticipation of his next reward. Gray moved in the final steps and lifted his hand to smooth it over the horse's forehead.

Gray stroked Shadow's neck for a time, earning more of the animal's trust. Then, in slow motion, he drew the loop from the animal's neck.

"Good, boy," Gray said softly. "I knew you had it in you." The horse turned his muzzle into Gray's caress. "Next time," he promised, "we'll take a little ride."

Right now Gray had to get back to Lauren. Shadow wasn't the only one who needed a little extra TLC today. He wasn't sure he could bear to see her suffer through another episode of those headaches. That thought disturbed Gray more than he was willing to admit. A great deal more than it should.

LAUREN SAT FACING DON, her mouth gaping at the absurdity of his suggestion. "This is your plan?"

Don stared at his desk a moment, his palms flattened on the polished surface. When he lifted his gaze to hers once more, she saw the seriousness there.

"Lauren, I'm trying to help you." He cleared his throat. "I spoke with Judge Madison personally. He insists that being a single mother is not going to be to your advantage."

Lauren made a sound of disbelief. "Longwalker is single! What's the difference?"

Don sighed patiently. "He has biology on his side."

"Oh, God." Lauren shook her head. "I can't believe this."

"You hired me to advise you. You don't have to take my advice, but I would be negligent if I didn't tell you this. You're a single mother who works and has debilitating headaches from time to time." Lauren started to protest but he stopped her with an upraised palm. "Don't think Longwalker's attorney won't use those things against you. He will."

"This is ridiculous."

"Be that as it may, the judge will look more favorably upon your side of things if you have a husband who can support you and Sarah in the event you become incapacitated by your headaches. A complete family unit will go a long ways, Lauren."

"So where am I supposed to find myself a husband?" she demanded, frustrated.

"Is there any chance of a reconciliation between you and Buck?" he ventured.

Buck. "I have to go." Lauren stood. She wasn't going to listen to any more of this. No way.

Don quickly skirted his desk and walked her to the door. "Just think about it, Lauren. I wouldn't give you this advice if I didn't think it was extremely important to your case."

Lauren paused and looked back at him. "I'll think about it."

He nodded. "Good. It might mean the difference between winning and losing. And we both know you don't want to lose Sarah."

GRAY STEPPED through Lauren's open door and listened intently for any sound. A heated curse echoed from upstairs. "Lauren?" He closed the door and moved closer to the foot of the stairs. "Is everything all right."

"Everything's just peachy," she called back crossly.

He climbed the stairs cautiously. "Where are you?"

"In my office."

On the second-story landing, he paused. The upstairs was one large room filled with office equipment, drawing tables and desks. Lauren sat in the middle of the floor, attempting to untangle a mass of wires. She looked like a child, her hair falling around her face from its upswept do. A frown marring her pretty face.

A very adult curse hissed past her full lips. Gray bit back a smile. "What are you trying to do."

She glowered at him. "I'm trying to untangle this stupid phone wire so I can hook up this blasted answering machine."

The answering machine lay at her feet. The wad of wires knotted in her fingers. There was no sign of a box, the machine was obviously one she already owned. At least he hoped the accompanying wires didn't come out of the box looking like that.

"Would you like me to hook it up for you?" He crouched in front of her.

Another glare arrowed his way. "I can hook it up. I've done it before."

He raised a skeptical eyebrow. "Are you the one who—"

She cut him off with a seething look. "Is there something you want, Longwalker?"

He did smile then. There were a great many things he wanted, but he would take none. The way her eyes sparkled when she was angry did strange things to his insides. He held her gaze steady as he took the mass of wires from her hands. "I thought we'd play the question game again," he suggested as he made himself more comfortable by bracing one knee on the floor.

She fanned a wisp of hair from her face. "One for you and one for me?"

"You can start." He deliberately slowed the movements of his hands. He twisted and looped, looped and twisted, slowly methodically, drawing her attention to the repetitive moves. She was seriously flustered. Gray remembered Dr. Prescott's warning that stress brought on the headaches. Gray had to defuse the stress that had obviously been building all morning. Just like he'd done with Shadow this morning.

She blinked, but kept her gaze glued to his hands. "You go first."

Another loop, another twist, even slower this time. "Why are you still single?"

Her startled gaze connected with his. He shifted, drawing her attention back to his hands. She pulled her knees to her chest and rested her chin there.

"I don't know. Just haven't met the right guy, I guess."

Gray twisted his right hand in the last yard of wire and slowly looped it around the bundle in his left. "Buck seems willing enough." Jealousy knifed through him at the suggestion.

Much calmer now, her gaze shifted back to his. "Buck and I are nothing but friends."

There was more. "But he wants to be more than friends?" The subtle change in her eyes answered him before her lips could form the word.

"Yes."

He placed the wire on a nearby table and set the answering machine beside it. "He's got everything the average woman looks for in a man."

Lauren giggled, then clamped her lips together.

Gray grinned. "You don't think good old Buck's got it all?"

"Everything except personality maybe."

Gray settled down on the floor in front of her. "That still doesn't answer my question."

She studied him for a time before she responded. "You can't lose anything if you don't invest in the first place."

They had much more in common than Gray first thought. "True," he agreed. "But you don't gain anything, either."

She sighed. "And you would be the expert in that area," she offered.

He looked away. "Yes, I would."

"My turn."

Gray draped his arm over his knee and feigned nonchalance. "Hit me."

"What's the story between you and Buck."

"Let's just say we have a common, unresolvable issue."

"And you're not going to tell me."

He shook his head. "But I will entertain another question."

Lauren smiled, relaxed now. "Okay." She thought for a minute. "What about your mother? What happened to her?"

This one was almost as complicated as the first. "It's a very sad story, you're sure you want to hear it?"

She nodded, her wide green eyes expectant.

Gray leaned against the table behind him. "She was never married to my father." He banished the emotions that wanted to surface and summoned the indifference that had carried him through the worst of times. "She was his mistress for more than a decade. But it was enough for her. She kept a roof over our heads, barely, by cleaning houses and doing laundry for the half dozen or so wealthy families in town.''

Pain threatened to break through his defenses. Why was he putting himself through this? Lauren Whitmore didn't need to know any of this. Yet he continued. ''She developed crippling arthritis, and by the time I was ten, she knew she had to make a stand for my sake. So she confronted my father and demanded that he provide for me. He laughed in her face, and we were forced to live on the charity of the state until I was old enough to work.''

Gray swallowed the bitterness that welled in his throat. ''She was never the same after that. I don't know if it was all the pain medications or the depression, but the woman who had raised me to that point went away. It wasn't enough that my father turned his back on us, but he made sure everybody in town turned on us, too. My mother was devastated. A few years later she ended her misery by taking too many pain pills and never waking up.''

Lauren's hand slipped into his. She squeezed. ''How awful for you. How old were you?''

''I was sixteen.'' Gray turned away from the sympathy shining in her eyes. ''It took me a long time to forgive her for that.'' He blew out a defeated breath. ''Maybe I still haven't.''

''I'm sorry, Gray.''

His gaze moved back to hers. Why did she care? But she did. He could see it in her eyes. No one else had ever looked at him that way. And here was this woman he hardly knew, who had every reason to despise him, looking at him that way.

''I can't imagine how you managed to survive.''

''Mr. and Mrs. Jennings offered me a place to stay

and a job. We do what we have to, Lauren. Your *have-tos* were just different from mine. You had more options. I plan to make sure Sarah is never left without plenty of options.''

She blinked, then scrambled to her feet. ''I should get this answering machine hooked up.''

Gray pushed to his feet. ''Need some help?''

She shook her head. ''I can manage, but thank you.''

Gray turned his back on what he saw in her eyes and walked away. Lauren's desperation was growing. She wanted so much to reach out to him, but in the same instance wanted to push him away. She'd backed herself into a no-win situation.

And, dammit, so had he.

LAUREN CLIMBED onto the bottom rail of the old wooden fence and propped her elbows on the top rail. She shaded her eyes against the sun with her hand and peered out across the pasture. She smiled when she spotted Spinner coming around the thicket of trees on the far side. Sarah sat in the saddle in front of Gray's tall, lean frame. The horse was like a different animal already, gentle and friendly. She couldn't believe how much progress Gray had made so quickly. It would be a while before Sarah could ride the horse alone. He was still a little edgy.

Lauren sighed as the animal loped toward the barn and her perch on the fence. Sarah resembled Gray so much that it was almost unnerving. Long jet-black hair and copper-colored skin set them apart from anyone else in Thatcher. On horseback the two looked like characters out of an old Western movie. How could anyone doubt that they were father and daughter?

Lauren focused on Gray as he guided the horse and chatted with Sarah. He smiled down at the child, the tenderness on his face was more than she could bear to see. She looked away. She had to protect herself…to protect Sarah. Lauren couldn't allow any more sympathetic feelings for the man. But how could she not? The man's life had been one tragedy after the other. How could anyone endure so much pain? But he still represented a serious threat to her and to the child she loved with all her heart.

Some small part of Lauren that was totally unrelated to reason believed Gray would do the right thing, that he wouldn't take Sarah away. But she would not allow that small part to override her good sense or her fear of what he could do. He had a good heart, Lauren felt sure of that, but it was buried under so much anger and bitterness that no one could touch it.

Except Sarah. She reached him in a place that, by all accounts, no one else ever had.

Lauren knew by his actions that Gray had feelings for Sarah that he didn't even understand yet. When he looked at the little girl, Lauren could see it in his eyes; she could hear it in his voice when he spoke to her. Gray Longwalker loved Sarah with whatever heart he had, and that scared Lauren more than any high-priced attorney ever could. Love knew no boundaries. Love could make a man do things he would not otherwise do. Would it make Gray Longwalker do the right thing or the wrong thing for Sarah?

Lauren braced herself as they neared. She swallowed hard and produced a smile for her daughter.

"Mommy! Mommy! Did you see me?" Her small face glowed with pride and excitement.

"I sure did, sweetie." Lauren met Gray's eyes only

briefly. Even that momentary contact sent an unwanted tingle up her spine.

Gray dismounted and lifted Sarah off the saddle and onto the fence next to Lauren. Lauren wrapped her arms around her daughter and gave her a hug. "Looks like you were having fun on old Spinner," she said lightly, and brushed Sarah's hair back from her cheek to place a kiss there.

"I had this much fun!" Sarah exclaimed holding her arms open wide. "I want you to ride him, too!" She looked expectantly from Lauren to Gray.

"I don't know about that, sweetie. Mommy hasn't been on a horse in a very long time."

Gray's eyes twinkled mischievously, but to his credit he remained silent.

"Please, Mommy?" Sarah's eyes glittered with hope. "Mr. Gray will ride with you."

"I'd be happy to take you for a ride," he offered generously.

Lauren glowered at him, which only made him grin. Her heart did a funny little flip-flop at the gesture.

"Mommy, you have to do it!"

Gray shrugged, and Sarah wiggled enthusiastically.

"All right, all right." She shot Gray a pointed glare. "But only for a few minutes, and really, really slowly."

Lauren slipped through the fence and strode purposefully up to Spinner. She could do this. If her five-year-old daughter could do it, she surely could. She approached the horse and took a deep, resolute breath. Lauren grabbed the saddle with both hands and lifted her left foot into the stirrup. Gray's hands settled on her waist, and he gave her a boost.

She removed her foot from the stirrup and eased

forward as far as possible as he slid onto the horse behind her. Before she could protest, he pulled her against his body, one arm holding her in place while he guided the horse with the other.

"Remember, I said slowly," she reminded crossly.

"Relax, Lauren," he murmured against her hair, she shivered as usual at the sound of her name on his lips. "Anytime I'm in the saddle it's always slow and easy."

His palm flattened on her abdomen and pressed her closer to his hard, male body. Heat rushed through her, making her tremble at the feel of him. His fingers knotted in the soft cotton of her T-shirt, then relaxed. He felt it, too, she realized. Gray Longwalker might like to pretend he was in control, but when it came to this attraction between them he was as defenseless as she was.

LAUREN STABBED the start button on her heavy-duty mixer, and it buzzed to life—*in high gear*. Chocolate frosting flew in every direction before she could poke the off button. She swore at the mixer, then cursed herself for not paying attention. She knew better than to start the thing without first checking the setting. Lauren swiped her cheek with the back of her hand and surveyed the disaster she had single-handedly created. A dusting of flour coated the island worktop and the area of floor between it and the sink. The array of utensils she had used for mixing and baking the yellow layer cake filled the sink.

And now, the grand finale, she mused dryly. Drops of chocolate frosting had splattered the cabinets, the countertop, the coffeemaker. Lauren looked down at herself and continued her inventory. Her chef's apron and nightshirt were speckled, and no doubt her face and hair were, as well.

Lauren sighed and wiped her hands on the closest towel. She was exhausted. But the distraction had worked—until now. The clock in the hallway chimed its ancient tune and then counted the hour as midnight. Sundry fears and worries assaulted Lauren once more as she emerged from her baking trance.

Gray Longwalker wouldn't get out of her head.

"I don't want to think about you," Lauren muttered. "I can't think about you." She squeezed her eyes shut against her thoughts. Instantly her too-vivid imagination painted a picture of Gray's handsome face. He made Lauren feel things that threatened her sense of self. She no longer felt satisfied, or understood why or what she wanted. And he was responsible for those unsettling feelings.

Lauren felt torn between hating him and wanting somehow to make him believe again in all that was good. Her heart yearned to reach out to him. To make him feel just once in his life what she had known for all of hers. But she couldn't allow herself to be that vulnerable to him. He was the enemy, she reminded herself without much conviction.

A possibility occurred to Lauren, and she stilled. She bit down on her lower lip and let the concept take form. What if they could *share* Sarah? The notion had crossed her mind more than once. What if Lauren could somehow convince Gray to allow her to stay in Thatcher? His work kept him on the road most of the time, anyway. He could as easily travel from here as he could anywhere else. Between jobs he could spend time with Sarah.

That could work, couldn't it?

But how would she ever convince him to stay? Lauren recalled the intensity of the desire she had seen in his eyes more than once, and the way his body responded to hers. She reacted instantly; heat flowed through her, rushing to her center. He wanted her, on a physical level at least. And, though she knew she shouldn't, she wanted him.

Lauren swallowed tightly. She did, she wanted him. She had never played this kind of game before. She didn't know if she knew how to seduce a man. But if she could make him fall for her, maybe he would stay. She and Sarah could continue on as they had, and Gray could visit whenever he wanted. It made sense to her, except for two little details. He hated Thatcher and the people who lived here, and he didn't trust anyone. Why on earth would he ever entrust his heart to her?

"You're crazy, Lauren," she mumbled as she massaged her temples. She needed sleep. She had tried to lose herself in sleep earlier, but it wouldn't come. She had even paced the floors for a while, which had only heightened her anxiety. Anxiety was a sure precursor to her headaches—and she could definitely do without the headaches. She thought about the way Gray had defused her mounting anxiety earlier today in her office. There was something about the way he moved, the way he looked at her, and the sound of his voice that calmed her.

But tonight she'd had to immerse herself in flour and sugar and vanilla and all the other smells and textures that always provided swift and certain stress relief. Now the fears and worries came tumbling back, the situation only magnified by the clutter surrounding her.

A soft knock at her back door startled Lauren into near cardiac failure. She pressed her hand to her chest and blew out a breath. Who would be at her door at this time of night? She wondered, frowning. Who else? The man she didn't need to see for fear of behaving foolishly. The man who threatened all that was dear to her heart.

Hastily swabbing her cheeks with the backs of her hands for any residue of chocolate, Lauren padded to the door. She pulled in a deep breath and asked, "Who is it?" *As if she didn't know.* Well, she told herself in her own defense, it was better to be safe than sorry.

"Gray," came the answer she had expected.

Lauren chewed her lip and for all of one second considered not opening the door, but some force beyond her control took over and she flipped the dead bolt and opened the door wide. Her breath fled her lungs and she immediately lost all decorum. Her wayward gaze traveled slowly over his amazing body.

He'd obviously had a sleepless night, as well. His hair was mussed and those silvery eyes looked a bit red-rimmed. He seemed to have made a hasty departure, since his shirt hung open, revealing that broad, muscular chest. Lauren's heart bumped into an erratic rhythm as she visually memorized every ridge and contour. When her gaze settled on his navel and the open button beneath it, her knees tried to give way. His carelessly donned jeans fit every inch of his lower body as if they had been tailored especially for him. And he was barefoot, she realized suddenly.

"Is everything all right?"

The sound of his voice jerked her attention to his face. Concern softened his features, but did nothing to quell the heat she saw in his eyes. Heat she knew had been building since the day they met when that first tiny spark of awareness had ignited a fire between them.

"Everything's fine," she managed to say. Her throat had gone so dry that her words were hardly more than a croak. "I was making frosting and I had a little—" she gestured at her apron "—accident."

He combed the fingers of both hands through his hair, the movement revealing more of his magnificent chest. "I couldn't sleep," he explained. "I saw the light and thought maybe something was wrong."

Lauren reminded herself to breathe. "Everything's fine," she repeated. Her voice climbed as her nerves frayed, threatening her flimsy composure.

He stepped inside and closed the door against the cool night air. Gray scrutinized the tremendous mess she had made. "You're sure you're okay?"

Lauren nodded vigorously. "I know it looks like a disaster, but I'm fine…everything's fine."

Another step disappeared between them. He smiled, and Lauren's heart stopped beating completely. "You have chocolate," he rubbed her cheek and then licked the sweet dollop from his thumb, "all over you."

He licked his full lips then, and Lauren felt suddenly dizzy, she braced one hand against the nearest counter and found him a weak smile. "The mixer. I didn't know it was on high and…" His gaze locked on her mouth, and Lauren knew all holds had just been unbarred—he was going to kiss her, and she was going to let him. Slowly he lowered his head. His lips parted, moved closer, but didn't connect with hers; instead he licked her chin and groaned with pleasure.

More chocolate, she realized.

Next he tasted her temple, then her throat. His hot

tongue laved and tortured each spot he selected. She tentatively pressed her hands to his chest to steady herself. The feel of his sleek skin beneath her palms unraveled her nerves further. Heat coursed through her veins, making her body hot from head to toe. The sound of his breathing filled her with want. Finally his mouth found hers. He pried her lips apart with his tongue, and the taste of chocolate and man filled her. His tongue probed her mouth, gently at first, then more thoroughly as he deepened the mind-bending kiss. Lauren melted against his strong body, her softness molding to his every hard contour.

Without breaking the contact of his mouth on hers, he reached around Lauren's waist, then around her neck, and untied her apron and tossed it aside. Gray lifted her with one arm and moved away from the door. He shoved aside the clutter and settled her onto the flour-dusted counter. He parted her legs with one lean hip and nestled himself in the cradle of her thighs. Lauren moaned at the feel of denim against her tender flesh.

His lips withdrew from hers, and the whisper of his breath on her mouth almost sent Lauren into orbit. He dipped his head lower and kissed her throat, then the vee of her nightshirt, just before he released the first button. His skillful mouth followed his equally masterful hands. Finally he drew her shirt open and revealed her tight, aching breasts. He ran a long finger over one taut tip. Lauren gasped at the sensation that sent liquid heat to her core.

She clutched helplessly at his shirt and watched as he dipped that finger into the frosting and traced slow circles around her nipples. His mouth descended and followed that sweet path with the same painstaking slowness. Lauren closed her eyes and restrained her cry of need. She buried her fingers in the rich, dark silk of his hair and encouraged his ministrations.

His hands slid up her thighs, the coarseness of his palms creating a delicious friction. Gray's arms wound around her waist and pulled Lauren more firmly against him. Instinctively she wrapped her legs around his lean hips and pressed into him. His mouth reclaimed hers, his kiss was demanding, and Lauren quivered beneath his possession. She knew what he'd come for—what he wanted. What they both wanted.

He stopped suddenly and pressed his forehead against hers. His ragged breath fanned her lips, making them tingle, making them ache for his.

"Gray?"

He drew back, looked deeply into her eyes. "I had to come. I had to touch you." He tugged her shirtfront back together. "But I shouldn't have. It was a mistake."

"No." Lauren pulled him close again. "I want you to stay." He knew what she wanted, she could see it in his eyes.

He released a heavy breath. "I've done a lot of things in my life that I'm not proud of." He caressed her cheek with the back of his hand. "I'm not going to add this to the list." He shook his head in denial of the desire that was clearly in his gaze. "When I leave this time, I don't want anyone to have any regrets."

He left without looking back.

Chapter Eleven

"Sarah, be careful in that tree," Lauren warned.

"Okay, Mommy."

Lauren watched a bit longer with growing concern. Sarah was too high for comfort. As Lauren watched, Sarah moved lower. Lauren knew she couldn't keep Sarah cooped up in the house all the time. She was a child; she was supposed to run and jump and even climb trees. But her activities tested the strength of Lauren's heart on a daily basis.

Forcing her attention back to the flower bed, Lauren turned the rich soil with a vengeance. With a plentiful supply of bread, cookies and muffins on hand, there had been no excuse to bake today. But she could prepare for spring planting. Thankfully, Gray had been gone all day. Lauren's hands stilled in their work. She closed her eyes and relived the overpowering sensations that accompanied his kisses, his every touch. He had made the decision to go last night. Had it been up to her, he would have stayed. Lauren released a long, slow breath.

Gray Longwalker was not at all what she had expected. Sharon had led her to believe that there was no goodness in him whatsoever. But that was far from the truth. She wondered briefly why Sharon would have lied so vehemently. Perhaps it was the hurt of knowing he had left her behind and never came back. But why punish Sarah? Especially when her death had been imminent. Gray was most likely wondering the same thing, but he never once said anything negative regarding Sharon.

He was immensely patient with Sarah. And the progress he'd made with that old horse was nothing short of amazing. There was something magical in his touch, Lauren was convinced. He could calm her runaway emotions with those skilled hands and silver gray eyes in a completely nonsexual manner. It was a tremendous gift. The fact that he had survived his tragic upbringing and was still able to use that special talent to help others was nothing short of miraculous. Lauren had a great deal of respect for him. The bottom line was…she cared a great deal for the man, in spite of the anger and bitterness he radiated at times.

Lauren assured herself that her feelings were simply a result of his being Sarah's father. Her love for Sarah had somehow spilled over to him. But it wasn't true. Gray was a good man, an honorable man even, there was no denying that. But he still represented a major threat to Lauren and Sarah and their future together. No matter that he seemed to like Lauren and was definitely attracted to her, he was still determined to walk away with his daughter.

How many men would have done what he did last night? She'd been prepared to cross the line, but he'd put the brakes on. She knew he wanted her, there'd been no way to hide his desire for her. But he knew it wasn't the right thing to do and he had resisted. Lauren shook her head at her foolish delusions that he might actually fall in love with her and want to stay. Happy endings only happened in fairy tales. And this was no fairy tale. Gray Longwalker wanted his child and he wanted no part of this town. And he trusted no one. He would leave. Lauren had best prepare herself for the fight of her life.

"Look, Mommy! No hands!"

Lauren looked up just in time to see Sarah lose her balance and plummet to the ground. Lauren's heart dropped to her stomach. She was at her child's side with no recall of how she had gotten there.

Sarah cradled her left arm and howled with pain.

"Okay, sweetie, it's okay." Lauren surveyed her little body for injuries. She hadn't fallen so very far, and she'd landed on her side. No bleeding, no protruding bones.

"Let me see your arm, baby."

"No! No! It hurts!"

Lauren prayed it wasn't broken, but she had a strong feeling that it was. "Let's go see Dr. Bill," Lauren urged softly as she tried to pick Sarah up. Her cries increased with every move. Panic tightened Lauren's chest. She needed help. She needed the phone. But how could she leave her baby lying here?

The sound of a vehicle arriving jerked Lauren's gaze in that direction. *Gray.* Thank God.

He was running across the yard before Lauren could call his name. He knelt on the other side of Sarah.

"Hey, chickadee, what happened?"

"She fell out of the tree," Lauren said in a rush. Her heart was pounding so hard now she could hardly breathe.

"It hurts," Sarah cried, tears flowing down her cheeks.

Gray glanced at Lauren and she saw the absolute fear in his eyes. "We need to get her to the doctor."

Lauren nodded. "I tried to move her, but—"

"Get in the truck. I'll bring her to you."

Lauren knew he was sending her away so she wouldn't have to see the pain he was going to cause Sarah by moving her. Listening to the cries was enough. Lauren jerked the passenger side door open and flung herself onto the seat. Gray spoke softly to Sarah, the sound of his voice calming her. Lauren watched, bewildered, as he moved slowly toward her. By the time he reached her, Sarah was sobbing quietly.

She whimpered when he lowered her into Lauren's lap, but she didn't cry out as she had before when Lauren tried to move her. Tears streamed down Lauren's cheeks. She closed her eyes and fought to hold them back.

"She's going to be fine."

Lauren met his now-serene gaze, and somehow she knew he was right. As long as he was here, everything would be fine.

But when he left, Lauren's whole life would fall apart.

LAUREN STOOD in the doorway of Sarah's room and watched as Gray covered the sleeping child. She had a fracture, but it wasn't so bad. The neon-green cast would come off in a few weeks. Pain medication had her sleeping like a baby now. Lauren closed her eyes and relived the heart-wrenching moments at the hospital. She had watched Gray mesmerize his child while the doctor and nurse did what they had to do. He'd kept her calm the entire time while Lauren had stood in the background sobbing silently.

He had done what Lauren could not. She could never have comforted Sarah the way he had. The two connected on a level that went far beyond the typical. She was his child. There was no way to deny that. No way to make it untrue. Whatever happened in the courts, Lauren would never be able to put the scene she had witnessed today out of her mind. Gray Longwalker loved his child, would take good care of her in every way. Lauren no longer doubted his capability.

But, God help her, she wanted to pretend it wasn't real. She wanted things to be the way they used to be…before he came into their lives. She wanted her baby back. A sob escaped her and Lauren clamped her hand over her mouth.

His arms went around her and he pulled her into the protection of his warm body. "Shhh. Sarah's fine," he murmured. He ushered Lauren into the hall far enough to close the bedroom door.

He brushed the tears from her cheeks and smiled reassuringly. "It's not so bad. She'll be as good as new in a couple of weeks."

But will she still be mine? Another tear trickled past her lashes.

Still holding her close, Gray kissed that lone tear away. "There's no need to cry," he murmured against her skin.

"I should have been watching her more closely. I—"

"Don't do this to yourself." The fingers of one hand threaded into her hair and pressed her against his chest. "You didn't do anything wrong."

Lauren relaxed in his protective embrace. The sound of his voice made her want to crawl inside his skin and stay there forever. His bare skin felt hot beneath her cheek where his shirt opened at the throat. His scent made her light-headed. She inhaled deeply, then turned her hungry mouth to that patch of sleek skin. She kissed him, her lips lingering on the smooth flesh. He stilled, save for the thundering of his heart. She kissed the pulse pounding at the base of his throat, then moved up that corded column, her lips tasting, teasing.

She kissed his chin, then the shallow cleft there. His fingers tightened in her hair, not holding her back, but poised to do just that. The fingers of his right hand were splayed over her back, unmoving. He wanted to resist. Lauren could feel the battle raging inside his tense body.

"You're upset," he said raggedly. "You don't know what you're doing." He groaned when she touched her lips to his jaw.

Her hands slid up his sculpted chest, then around his neck. "I know exactly what I'm doing," she murmured. Tiptoeing she tasted his mouth, taking her time to enjoy the fullness of it. She pressed firmly into his arousal and his breath shuddered. He held her back, her face only an inch or so from his. His eyes were fixed on her mouth. Slowly, seductively, Lauren licked her lips. She felt his tension escalate. His restraint was crumbling. Hers was already gone.

He moved closer, his lips almost touching hers now. A fierce stab of desire made her breath hitch; his echoed the sound. Then his mouth covered hers. He kissed her deeply, thoroughly. Fire raced through her veins, heating her from the inside out. Her body melded with his, his arms strong around her, and Lauren knew there would be no stopping this time.

Lauren felt herself being lifted, knew they were

moving down the dark hall, but she cared only that he kept touching her with his mouth...with his hands.

Gray shouldered open her bedroom door, stepped inside and then pushed it shut with one foot. He settled Lauren on her feet next to the bed. The bedside lamp cast a soft glow over and around them. His fingers tugged her shirt from the waistband of her jeans. He stopped kissing her only long enough to pull the shirt over her head. It fell to the floor. One callused palm glided over her rib cage, then to the closure of her bra. It joined her shirt on the floor. Lauren shivered when he knelt and those same hands slowly removed her sandals and jeans. Feeling vulnerable, she quickly crossed her arms over her breasts.

"Don't be shy, Lauren," he urged softly. "You're beautiful. Let me look at you." His eyes spoke of fierce need, but he made no move to touch her. He waited patiently for her to relax.

She moistened her lips and shoved aside the second thoughts surfacing in the far corners of her mind. She resisted the urge to tremble as she slowly lowered her arms to her side.

His beautiful smile and the awe in his eyes shattered the last of her trepidation. Lauren had never been looked at quite like that, as if she were some rare and delicate treasure. Without taking his eyes off hers, Gray unbuttoned, then shrugged out of his shirt. He stood, the heat in his gaze searing straight through to her soul.

Lauren wanted him as she had never wanted any other man in her life. She wanted to make him feel. She wanted to make him believe...to make him love...her. The realization made her want to weep. How could she have fallen for this man?

"I want you, Lauren Whitmore." His declaration was blunt, guttural and punctuated by the sound of his lowering zipper.

Desire shot through her at the primal quality of his voice. "I want you, too," she said, her own voice little more than a whisper. *She did want him.* Whatever the future held for her, Lauren knew without a doubt that she wanted Gray Longwalker to be her lover. She wanted to give him something no one else ever had, her innocence...her complete trust, if only for the moment. She had never wanted this before, not even with Kevin, not like this.

Never taking her eyes off his mesmerizing movements, Lauren sat down on the edge of the bed, then eased back onto the mound of pillows. Unable to help herself, she openly admired his undeniably male body. She didn't want to wait anymore. In her heart of hearts Lauren knew that if she didn't seize this moment, it would pass, and something precious would always be missing in her life as a result. All that made her who she was warned her not to make that mistake.

He toed off his boots, then stripped off his jeans and briefs in one smooth motion. Next he stretched out on the bed beside her. He was beautiful, strong and sleek. His wide hand moved over her abdomen, then down to her bikini panties, evoking tremors in her heated flesh. Without hesitation Lauren lifted her hips for him to push away the final barrier between them. He nudged one knee between her thighs and rested his weight against her. His heavy arousal pressed her with its urgency. Anticipation thrilled through Lauren with the heady feeling of naked male flesh against hers. All thought fled with the first brush of his lips.

His first touch to her femininity sent sensations so hot, so incredibly wild spiraling through her body that Lauren shuddered and writhed uncontrollably. Gray suckled each breast in turn as he stroked her until she felt ready to explode.

"Gray, please," she whimpered. She couldn't think, she could only react to the wonderful feelings he awakened in her body. Lauren had no idea how to tell him what she wanted, only that she needed... something.

He shifted more fully onto her and captured her mouth with his own. His hands slid over her body, both soothing and inciting her frenzy. He parted her lips and teased her tongue, thrusting and retreating repeatedly, inviting her to join the dance. Tentatively, Lauren touched her tongue to his and then followed into his mouth. His unique flavor tantalized her. His tongue stroked against hers, making every part of her body long for all of him.

Lauren smoothed her hands over his strong back, reveling in the amazing contours of his masculine flesh. His scent, leather and sandalwood, made her crazy with want. Unable to resist any longer, she followed her body's instinct and arched against him. He groaned in response.

As if sensing her urgency, Gray moved his other leg between hers and pressed his length against her center. Lauren clung to him then, hopelessly lost to new and dizzying sensations.

Slowly he began to move against her, tantalizing but not penetrating. Fire flamed to life inside her, and the mounting tension twisted tighter. She wanted to scream with need, to beg for something she couldn't name.

He drew back slightly, then nudged her entrance. Lauren cried out at the feel of him.

"Look at me, Lauren." It was a command, pure and simple.

Lauren obeyed, her gaze connecting with his dark, glittering gray one.

"I want you to remember the man who takes you for the first time."

Lauren gasped at the first sensation of penetration. By slow degrees he entered her. The stretching, burning pleasure-pain sent shock waves quaking through her entire body. He stopped all too soon, and Lauren made tiny sounds of protest. She struggled to arch into him, to force him deeper, but his strong thighs pinned her to the mattress. His face was taut with restraint.

"Easy, baby," he murmured, his gray eyes still searing into hers. With slow, sinuous strokes he began to move shallowly inside her. He shivered with his own tenuous grip on control.

Tighter and tighter the tension coiled at her core. Lauren strained toward release, but Gray would not relent. He continued the slow shallow strokes until colored lights danced before her eyes. Lauren pressed against his spine, wanting, needing him to mate fully with her—to complete his possession. He groaned and defied her attempts to push him over the edge of control.

The first clutch of climax seized Lauren and she cried out his name. She sucked in a sharp breath as he moved a fraction deeper and her feminine muscles tightened painfully around him. She couldn't wait...she would die if this delightful torture continued.

His rigid control crumbled as Lauren surged upward

and forced him past the thin barrier. Gray uttered an agonized, primal sound. Pain sliced through Lauren, followed immediately by a crashing climax. Her cries of release ignited his fury, and he buried himself fully inside her. Gray held absolutely still while the waves of completion shattered through her, his eyes held that same tenderness she always saw when he looked at Sarah. The depth of need that accompanied that tenderness made her weak. In that instant Lauren knew that she loved him. And she had shown him, in the only way he would understand. A man like Gray Longwalker would never accept pretty words or trust promises. So she had given him the most precious thing that belonged solely to her—her body.

His eyes frantically searched hers before he took her mouth with abandon. He flexed his hips and sealed their bodies as one, held and then retreated. Gray pressed his forehead against hers and pounded into her with long, solid thrusts. She watched the kaleidoscope of emotions move across his handsome face as climax claimed him with a fierceness that both frightened and fascinated her.

He groaned, and his heavy body relaxed against hers. Gray brushed his lips over hers and rolled to her side, pulling Lauren close and holding her tightly. She blinked back the tears that threatened, too overwhelmed by her own emotions to speak. Gray stroked her hair, and Lauren sensed that he wanted to say something but was reluctant to begin.

Long, pensive moments later he broke the silence. "I will always treasure what we just shared," he said softly.

Lauren closed her eyes and allowed his uncharacteristically sweet words to echo inside her. She could face the consequences tomorrow, but tonight she wanted to relish the afterglow of their lovemaking.

Gray closed his eyes against the emotions raging inside him and held Lauren close to his heart. From the very beginning he had known there was something between them…something that pulled at him like nothing else ever had. He had never known this feeling before, a kind of tenderness that made him want to hold her forever, the emotion almost suffocating with its intensity. And with that came the same kind of protective instincts that Sarah evoked in him…but his feelings for Lauren were infused with raw lust.

He released a long, ragged breath. Gray had come to Thatcher to claim his child, to give her his name, but he had given her something he had no idea he could…his heart. The first time he held Sarah something moved inside him, and that tiny stir started an emotional chain reaction that culminated in feelings he hadn't known he possessed. Each time he looked into his child's eyes the momentum increased, sending Gray hurtling into previously uncharted territory. He had come here to claim Sarah, but she had claimed his heart.

And somehow Lauren had made her mark on that territory, as well.

He pressed a kiss to Lauren's temple. "Sleep," he murmured. "I'll check on Sarah in a little while."

She nuzzled against his body, and he stirred. Making love to Lauren once would never be enough.

LAUREN PARTED THE BLINDS and pecked out to see who had just parked in her drive. *Buck.*

Thank God it wasn't Gray.

She stepped back from the dining room window and

shoved a handful of hair behind her ear. Lauren didn't really feel like company at the moment. But at least if Buck were here when Gray arrived, he'd likely go straight to the bunkhouse without stopping by to see Sarah.

Memories of last night's lovemaking with Gray rushed through her. How would she ever survive this man? She had awakened this morning to find him gone. He hadn't returned yet, and it was nearing dinnertime. She didn't want to wonder where he was or why he'd left without telling her, but she did. She had muddled through the day with Rosemary acting suspicious and Sarah wanting a drink or something else every five minutes.

Lauren tried to rationalize the crazy, mixed-up emotions churning inside her, but she couldn't.

The knock at the door eliminated any further ruminating along that vein. Lauren took a deep, bolstering breath and headed toward the door. Buck probably wanted to rant a little more about Gray's presence on her property. Or maybe he wanted to apologize for being a jerk.

"Yeah, right," she muttered. On her way to the front door, Lauren paused at the living room to see that Sarah was still happily enthralled with her new video game, which had been the price of Lauren's guilt over her fall. Fluffy took one look into the living room, twitched her tail and headed in the opposite direction as if the noise of the video game offended her.

Before unlocking the door and throwing it open, Lauren tried to relax, to ease the tension banded around her skull. Her hands felt clammy, and she was nauseated. She glanced at her watch—still too early to take another dose of her medication. She couldn't let the headaches catch her, she had to stay one step ahead of them. So she focused on remaining calm and thinking serene thoughts. Like making love with the enemy.

Lauren shook off the thought and pulled the door open. She summoned a smile for Buck. His clear gray-blue eyes twinkled and his mouth slid into a charming smile. Something clicked in the back of Lauren's mind, but she couldn't quite grasp the bit of knowledge or recognition.

She shoved away the nagging notion and forced her attention on her visitor. "Buck, hello," she said, offering her cheek before he could plant a kiss on her lips.

"Hey, sugar." Buck stepped inside and dropped his hat on the hall table. "How's our girl? I heard about that nasty fall she had yesterday. I can't believe you didn't call me."

"Sarah's fine. Thanks." Lauren gritted her teeth. There were no secrets in a small town like Thatcher. That was the one unappealing characteristic of small towns. Everybody knew everything. She had never noticed it before, but now with Gray Longwalker being here she felt as if she were the main character in an ongoing soap for all of Thatcher's entertainment.

"I'm sorry. I should have called you."

"Where's that half-breed?"

Lauren scowled at him. "Buck, Sarah is in the living room."

"Sorry, sugar, but we need to talk."

His tone startled Lauren. She met his flat gaze and searched for clues as to what he might be thinking—nothing showed. But if the firm line his mouth had formed was any indication, it wasn't good.

"All right." Lauren led him to the dining room

where Sarah wouldn't overhear their conversation. She indicated the chairs around the table. "Have a seat."

"No, I think I'd rather stand," he said solemnly. He tucked his hands into the back pockets of his starched and pressed Levi's and shifted his weight to one leg.

"Okay." Lauren prepared herself for the worst. She wasn't sure how much more stress she could handle in this lifetime.

"I understand Don passed along the judge's advice as to your best course of action."

"What?" Outraged, Lauren could only stare at him. The discussions between her and her attorney were confidential—even in a small town.

"Don't get all riled up now, sugar. Don didn't tell me anything. I spoke to the judge personally." He smiled his best good-old-boy charmer. "I care about you, Lauren. I don't want that no-account half-breed to come in here and do anything to hurt you or that little girl."

"Well, thank you for your concern, Buck." The words barely edged out past the tangle of tension in her throat. "But I'm perfectly capable of taking care of myself."

"I don't want you to lose Sarah, either," he said with too much sincerity. "Lauren, you know how I feel about you."

She blinked, anxiety pushed ahead of her irritation. "Where are you going with this, Buck?"

Buck took her hands in his and held them tightly. Lauren's heart rate picked up, but it had nothing to do with desire and everything to do with uneasiness.

"I can make this whole thing go away for you."

Everything inside Lauren went very still. "What?"

His right thumb began a steady circle over the back of her hand. "I'm a very wealthy man, Lauren. I have influence."

She nodded, unsure as to why Buck would choose to tell her what was common knowledge around town.

"I have a great many *important* friends," he continued. "I can make things happen."

Lauren shook her head this time. "I don't understand what you're getting at, Buck."

"All I'm saying is that if you need help with this problem, I'm here for you."

Caution slowed her response. "You are?" The uneasy feeling mushroomed inside her.

"I am," he said simply. "I love you, Lauren, and I don't want to see Longwalker hurt you." His wide shoulders squared beneath the crisp white shirt he wore. "I'm willing to marry you today if it'll help resolve your problems."

The shock of his words slammed into Lauren with such force that she swayed from the impact. "Buck—"

"Before you answer—" his hold on her hands tightened "—think long and hard, Lauren. I can help you." He pressed his lips to Lauren's fingers in a light kiss. "I'm a good man, Lauren. I can take care of you and Sarah the way you deserve, *and* I can protect you both from Longwalker. He's a mean, bitter bastard, but I can make sure you never have to see him again."

Confusion ruled. Lauren felt numb. "I don't know what to say," she managed.

He gave her a nod and flashed a sympathetic smile. "I understand. It's a big decision." He draped one arm around her shoulders and guided her back into the hall. "I don't want to pressure you. Take your time. Think about it.'' He released her to open the front door. Buck stood on the threshold and looked back at Lauren. ''I know you'll do what's best for the little girl.''

Lauren closed the door behind him. She didn't say goodbye. She was too shocked, too overcome by something she couldn't even name.

The man had just asked her to marry him. She shook herself; she had to be dreaming. Or maybe she was hallucinating. The recent loss of his father had obviously made him take stock of his life—and hers.

The adrenaline rush receded, leaving Lauren weak. She leaned back against the wall to steady herself and closed her eyes.

Just last night she and Gray had made love. Now, today, Buck asks her to marry him.

Lauren slid down the wall to the floor. She pulled her knees into her chest and rested her forehead against them. She was so tired. Too tired to think straight.

Buck was a wealthy, powerful man. He had connections everywhere—financial and political. He could probably do just what he said he could, but could she?

Lauren squeezed her eyes tighter in an effort to block out the image of Gray Longwalker as he had looked only a few hours ago, his eyes tender with emotion, his body moving over hers.

Buck was offering her the very help Don had advised she needed. If she were married to a man like Buck, would the judge order that Sarah remain in her custody, with mere visitation rights for Gray? Hope soared at the thought but quickly wilted when she considered how that outcome would affect Gray. He would have come back to Thatcher, endured the persecution of these people, relived his haunted past and lost his heart to a child…for mere visitation rights.

But could she *not* accept Buck's help and risk losing her child?

Chapter Twelve

"Hold it like this." Gray held out his right hand, the sugar cube in the center. Spinner gobbled it off his palm, and Sarah giggled.

"Let me try," she demanded from her perch on the middle bar of the old wooden fence. She hung on to the top rail, her neon-green cast dangling over it.

Gray placed a sugar cube in her right hand, and she immediately thrust it in Spinner's direction. He tossed his head at her sudden move. Sarah frowned.

"Be very still and he'll come for it," Gray whispered. A few seconds later the old horse snagged the cube from her palm. Sarah squealed with delight. Spinner didn't take to the piercing sound. He sauntered away.

"I wanna do it again!"

"I think he's had enough today. We'll do it again tomorrow," Gray assured her.

"Time for you to come inside, young lady."

The sound of Lauren's voice warmed Gray. His gaze immediately sought hers. Instantly his body reacted, even before the memories of making love to her played through his mind. The wind tugged at the silky hair she'd piled atop her head. He resisted the urge to pull the pins free and watch the honey-colored stuff fall around her shoulders.

Lauren gifted him with a hesitant smile as she lifted Sarah down from the fence. He had hoped she wouldn't regret what they had shared, but she did—at least a little. And that pained him. He hadn't wanted any regrets this time.

What would she think if she knew he had called his attorney first thing this morning and asked for the swiftest possible court date? As soon as the test results were in, he wanted this over and done with. He averted his gaze from the woman busily adjusting the ribbon in his daughter's hair. When Sarah was his in the eyes of the law, then he would concern himself with whatever remained between him and Lauren. Assuming anything did. He doubted she would want anything else to do with him. Gray had no intention of getting his hopes up where Lauren was concerned. Had it not been for Sarah, Lauren would never have given him a second glance. He wasn't the kind of man women like her looked for in a life's mate.

Last night had been the result of her need for comfort and the physical attraction that had been brewing between them. He knew that then; he knew it now. He should have resisted, but he hadn't. Now it was done. Leaving her bed this morning before she awakened was all that had saved him from complete disgrace.

He had known better than to take what she offered no matter how badly he had wanted her. The foolish feelings he had allowed to take root inside him would only hurt both of them in the end. And still he hadn't been able to turn away from her. Now she was sorry, and he was guilty.

Just like before.

It was the story of his life. Gray let go a heavy breath. Somehow he had to protect Sarah from making the same mistakes.

"Mr. Gray's gonna teach me to be a extragood rider. And he's gonna take me to all the rodeos I want to go to. You wanna go, too, Mommy?"

Lauren's gaze shot to his. He knew in a flash how she had interpreted Sarah's words. He braced himself for her fury.

"You go on in the house, sweetie, and wash up for dinner. I'll be right there."

Sarah skipped off toward the house, not a care in the world. Gray turned to face the wrath he knew would come. Lauren stalked straight up to him.

"What are you doing?" she demanded, fury snapping in her green eyes.

"Making promises I intend to keep." It was that simple.

"You can't do that. You have to wait until—"

"Until what, Lauren?" he growled. "Until you and your lawyer have run out of rocks to turn over in your efforts to find something to use against me?"

She blinked, surprised. Didn't she realize he had known what they were up to from the get-go?

"That was our deal," she said coolly. "You wouldn't tell her anything until a judge gave you permission. You gave me your word."

He shook his head. "I gave you my word that I wouldn't tell her I was her father. And I haven't."

She flung her arms in exasperation. "But you're making her promises—"

"That I fully intend to keep," he finished for her. The image of her face flushed from their lovemaking zoomed into vivid focus. His hands tightened into fists when the spark of desire instantly warmed his blood. He brutally quashed the emotion. He would not allow his feelings for Lauren to get in the way of what he had to do. He knew the deal. He couldn't ever really have her, shouldn't want her and would never in a million years need her. She represented everything that had gone wrong in his life. The perfect childhood with the perfect parents. Friends, money, fancy schools. All the things Gray had never had. A single night of passion hadn't changed the differences between them.

No one had given a damn about him one way or another since he was ten years old. Gray had grown up hard and fast and without any source of support, emotional or otherwise. He had never been in love, and as far as he knew no one had loved him in the past twenty or so years. He and Sharon had been friends but nothing more. Gray supposed that she was the closest thing to family he'd had after his mother's death. Of course, he never really thought about it, because he had stopped caring a long time ago.

He cared now. He wanted more than anything else in this world for Sarah to love him the way she loved Lauren. He wanted her to look at him the way she looked at Lauren. To trust him the way she trusted Lauren.

The only thing of value Gray owned was his truck. He had spent his entire life under someone else's roof, from the old run-down shack his mother had managed to keep over their heads to the hotel rooms he slept in now. The first order of business once the legal matters were squared away was house shopping. Sarah would need a nice house in a nice neighborhood with a nice school.

Just like what she has here, he thought with reluctance. Gray turned away from the woman glaring speechlessly up at him. The same things could be found in another town, maybe even in another state.

"You think it's going to be so simple, don't you?" she demanded, drawing his attention back to her. "You'll take Sarah away and life will be perfect wherever you go."

"Something like that," he explained, though for the life of him he didn't understand why he bothered. She already had the whole scenario planned out in her head. Sure she'd gotten carried away with her mixed-up emotions where he was concerned, but those would clear up quickly enough if the judge leaned in her favor. Gray had made a mistake. Gotten too close. Almost trusted her, but the information his attorney had relayed to him today had cinched his decision. Lauren's attorney had turned Texas upside down trying to find some dirt on him. Even now he was wooing the judge who would most likely hear the case.

"You blow into town staking your claim to a child you've never even seen before—a child I love with all my heart, I might add. And you have the nerve to suggest that what Sarah and I share can be brushed aside so easily?"

She was mad now. Really mad. But so was he. He glared at her with all the anger mounting inside him. "I didn't say that. You did."

"What was last night all about then?" she demanded.

Hurt glimmered in her eyes. Gray suppressed the emotions he refused to feel. "It was about two people needing each other."

Lauren nodded. "I see." She folded her arms across her chest and shot him a withering look. "I've changed my mind, Longwalker, I do want you to explain to Sarah exactly why you're here.''

A muscle flexed rhythmically in his tense jaw. ''Why don't you give me your version of *exactly* what I'm supposed to say.''

Lauren took a step toward him, her renewed rage overriding all else. She lifted her chin and glared at him. ''You tell her that you want to take her away from me.'' She blinked back the tears threatening. ''You tell her that she'll never see me again. That she'll never see her friends again.'' Lauren sucked in an unsteady breath. ''And when you've told her all that, I want you to see if she still wants to go rodeoing with you.''

Gray reached for the calm he knew was somewhere deep inside him before he allowed himself to speak. ''Lauren—'' she trembled when he said her name ''—I haven't done anything wrong. If you're upset about all this, just remember that the DNA test was your idea, not mine. You are the one who demanded that this issue be resolved in court. Your attorney is the one scrambling for loopholes. I only want my daughter.''

''You know exactly why Don ordered that test. Don't pretend you don't.'' She swiped fiercely at the single tear that escaped and slid down her cheek.

''Give it up, Lauren, you won't win. Sarah is my daughter.'' He held her gaze, though he desperately wanted to look away from the tremendous pain he saw there—pain he knew he was causing. He refused to acknowledge the emotions clutching at his chest. She had brought this particular hurt on herself. Her reaction to his plans with Sarah was solid evidence that she hadn't changed her ultimate goal, despite what they had shared. "You can't keep her from me," he added harshly. She didn't care about him. She only wanted his daughter.

She blinked, visibly shaken. "I'm the one who has been a parent to her when she needed one."

Gray jerked with the effort of holding back his anger at her suggestion. How could he be a parent when he didn't know his child existed? He drew in a ragged breath and let it out slowly to try to put the brakes on his out-of-control emotions. "Believe whatever you choose to, but know this," he said in as controlled a tone as he could manage, "it changes nothing. I am Sarah's biological father. You're not her biological mother."

"Semantics, Longwalker." Lauren met his heated glare with lead in her own. "Just because you donated the sperm doesn't make you father material."

"It's all black-and-white for you, isn't it?"

Ready to storm away, she hesitated and snapped, "What's that supposed to mean?"

He shook his head at her naiveté. "Life. It's either good or bad, acceptable or unacceptable. No middle ground. That's how you see it."

"I suppose I'm wrong because I don't see life the jaded way you do?"

"Why would you? You grew up in a close, loving family. Had everything you ever needed handed to you on a silver platter. How could you possibly see things my way?" He met her sarcasm with a hefty dose of bitterness.

"You think you're the only person who has suffered trials in their life? It happens to everyone." Her anger seemed to mushroom with every word she uttered. "I'm sorry about your mother, and I'm truly sorry that the people in this town have treated you so badly. But I'm not sorry enough to roll over and play dead while you take Sarah away."

In two strides he had covered the distance between them. Gray towered over Lauren, every muscle in his body rigid with his building rage. "You don't know anything about how it feels to be me." Uncertainty or maybe even fear flickered in her eyes. "You still had your parents, you had friends. A whole network of people who cared about you. I haven't had anyone who cared about me since I was a kid."

"Don't expect any more sympathy from me, Long-walker," she warned. "I've gone above and beyond."

"I don't want your sympathy, Lauren. I want Sarah."

Her gaze connected with his, her eyes hard and glittering like jewels. "That's one thing I'll never let you have."

"You won't have a choice."

"What Sarah wants doesn't matter," she countered, her voice breaking. "You have to know she loves me. How can you expect to take her away from me?"

There was no denying that fact. Gray hardened his heart to the reality of it. "To put it in the words of your own attorney, 'We'll discuss visitation when paternity has been established.'"

Her lips compressed in a grim line, she spun away from him. Gray watched Lauren stalk across the yard. The emotions he had refused to acknowledge in her presence surfaced with a vengeance. Pain, fear, regret, and other things he wouldn't label, twisted inside him. No matter how hard he tried not to care, he did. He didn't want to hurt Lauren. But how could he not? He would have his daughter, whatever the cost.

"I DON'T UNDERSTAND, Don, what's going on?" Lauren stood in the middle of her attorney's office, dumbfounded. Buck and his attorney from Dallas stood in front of Don's desk.

"Lauren, please have a seat. I called you here for this urgent meeting because there's been a development in Sarah's case."

Numb with the lingering anger from the quarrel with Gray and the new fear Don's words had sent surging through her, Lauren moved to the closest chair. When she'd stormed back into her house after the fight with Gray, Don's message had been on the machine. She had dropped Sarah off at Rosemary's and hurried to Don's office. Now she was even more confused.

"Sugar, Longwalker has made a move," Buck told her solemnly.

"What? I don't understand." She looked from Buck to Don. What were Buck and his attorney doing here? she wondered again.

"Lauren, I received a call from Victor Thorton this evening." Don pushed his glasses higher up the bridge of his nose. "Longwalker has demanded the first available court date following the release of the test results."

"He's pushing for a speedy ruling," Mason Ewen, Buck's attorney, clarified. "That could be disastrous for you, Ms. Whitmore."

Panic exploded inside Lauren. She trembled with the effort of remaining calm and seated in her chair. Gray was going to take Sarah. Deep down, she hadn't really believed he would do it. But he would. He'd said as much today. And his attorney's actions couldn't be ignored. She had to do something.

"What can we do?" Her fearful gaze searched Don's.

"We have to act fast," he suggested.

"Sugar, I've already told you that I have a great deal of influence with a great many important people. With you as my wife, there's not a judge in Texas who would rule against you."

"You...you want me to marry you," she said. "Right away?"

"It will make your case a whole lot stronger," Ewen urged.

"He's right, Lauren," Don put in. "I'm relatively certain that you don't stand a chance under present circumstances."

Lauren looked from one man to the other. How could this have happened so fast? She needed time to think. "I'll have to think about this," she began hesitantly.

"There's not time for that, Ms. Whitmore," Ewen countered. "We can't have your upcoming marriage look in any way related to the trial."

Lauren supposed he was right. Her gaze darted to Buck, then to the floor. But could she marry Buck and be happy? Did it matter in light of what she might lose if she didn't?

"I have an agreement prepared." Ewen picked up a document from the edge of Don's desk. "Don has already looked it over. It's a simple contract really. You agree to marry Buck, he agrees to provide complete support to you and your child, with the usual prenuptial clauses, of course."

"This can't be right," Lauren insisted.

"Is it right for Longwalker to waltz in here and take that little girl?" Buck demanded. "I know you don't want to lose that child. If your own attorney is convinced that our marriage would help your case, how can you hesitate?''

How could she? Lauren felt confused.

''I know you don't feel about me the way you need to,'' Buck urged. ''But in time I believe you'll come to.''

''You're sure this is the only way?'' she asked Don.

''I sincerely believe that it may make all the difference in the world.''

I want Sarah. Gray's words echoed inside her. He was going to take her. Lauren had to do something. Didn't she?

''All right.'' She leveled her gaze on Don's. ''Where do I sign?''

Buck covered her hand with his. ''You won't be sorry, sugar.''

Lauren met his triumphant gaze. She reminded herself again of his assets. Buck was highly respected in the community, he was more than financially stable, and he had always been kind to her and to Sarah. He professed to love Lauren, but could she ever love him? His hair and eyes reminded her somewhat of Kevin, though Buck's eyes were more gray than blue.

''Right here, Lauren.''

Lauren accepted the pen Don offered. She stilled, her hand poised above the signature line as she stared fully into Buck's eyes. *More gray than blue.* Lauren had met his mother once when she first moved to Thatcher, the bluish quality Buck had inherited from her. But the gray...*Buckmaster eyes.* Lauren had met Buck's father on several occasions before his recent death. Buck had gotten the piercing gray from his father. That fleeting sense of recognition exploded into complete clarity.

Gray Longwalker's eyes.

"What's wrong, sugar?" Buck asked, his handsome face marred with concern. "You look like you've seen a ghost. Let me show you the engagement ring I bought to seal the deal."

His words reverberated around Lauren, making her feel as if she were in a well or deep tunnel. She felt sick to her stomach and the room seemed to shift, playing havoc with her equilibrium. Gray and Buck were brothers. That was the thing that festered between them. That meant that Buck's father had been the one to ruin Leah's life.

"Lauren, are you all right?" Don was suddenly beside her. "Would you like me to call Dr. Prescott?"

"I'm okay," she murmured. She met Don's worried gaze and manufactured a faint smile. "I just need to get this done and get home. Too much excitement I suppose."

"Sign the paper, sugar, and I'll take real good care of you."

GRAY STARED AT THE MEAL in front of him with complete disinterest before he shoved it away. He didn't know why he had even bothered to come to the diner this evening, he couldn't eat. The heated words he and Lauren had exchanged twisted inside him, replayed over and over.

But he couldn't go back to her yet. All he could do was think about making love to her. Gray closed his eyes and forced himself to relive once more the gut-wrenching memories of their time together before dawn.

Touching her, tasting her and finally taking her. Gray trembled at the memory of how it felt to be deep inside Lauren, the way her body had gloved him so tightly and responded so completely to his. How could he have ever imagined that making love to her would affect him so deeply? For just a little while during the night, she had given him her complete trust and her body—something she had given no other man.

Gray truly believed that Lauren cared about him to some extent, that she understood him just a little. She had been kind to him, despite the fact that he had dashed her kindness back at her on more than one occasion. *I believe you'll do the right thing,* she had said. And she had spoken the truth. He had seen it in her eyes, felt it in her touch. She did believe.

But no matter how much she wanted to believe in him, she still doubted him when faced with even the vaguest possibility that he would take Sarah away from her. How could she profess to believe in him and then think for one moment that he would take Sarah out of her life completely?

Fear.

The realization sent the air rushing out of him. Tears stung his eyes. He was worse than Buck. Lower than the dust beneath a snake's belly. He had stormed into town and turned Lauren's world upside down. The only thing she had wanted was to keep being Sarah's mother. Lauren loved Sarah, and she didn't want to lose her. And all Gray had been concerned with was claiming the child. Fear of trusting, of giving any small part of his heart had kept him from mentioning an amicable arrangement. The past had blinded him to the future. He hadn't been able to see past his own fears.

Because you're a bitter, selfish fool. Gray cursed himself silently. Lauren had reached out to him as no one else ever had. Maybe she didn't love him, but she had to feel something for him to do all the things she'd done. Gray had just been too busy fighting the past to see it.

Gray had long ago buried his feelings so deep inside himself he had forgotten how to feel. He had spent his entire adult life keeping everyone at arm's length. He had always taken what he wanted from his brief involvements and walked away from the rest. Sarah and Lauren had broken down the barriers he had so carefully constructed over the years. Lauren had forced him to feel again. Forced him to care. Forced him to want her as he had never wanted anyone else.

Maybe he and Lauren could work out some sort of arrangement for sharing Sarah. He did travel a lot, and Sarah needed stability in her life. Sarah's happiness was certainly more important than his grudge against the people in this town. Being separated from Lauren would be hard on Sarah, and deep down Gray didn't want to do anything that would cause her that kind of pain. He could see that now.

Lauren had welcomed him in her home. A big old house filled with the smells of her freshly baked bread, filled with Sarah's musical laughter and filled with the sweetness Lauren had freely given him. *Lauren.* The kind of woman with whom he had never even dreamed of sharing any part of his life. The thought of spending the rest of his life making love to Lauren tugged at a place deep inside him.

Gray eased out of the booth and stood. What a fool he was. He would make this right. Gray tossed the money on the table for his uneaten food and picked up his hat. He would take the chance. He would tell Lauren just what he had in mind and hope for the best. It was all he could do. He didn't know if the unfamiliar emotions stirring inside him were love, but he would give Lauren whatever he had to give. He strode through the crowded diner toward the door. Every instinct told him he could trust Lauren.

"Well, well, if it ain't just the man I've been looking for."

Gray looked up to find Little Willy Buckmaster blocking the exit. The younger of the Buckmaster brothers was a smaller, somewhat-less-intelligent replica of his older brother. Willy was an annoyance Gray could do without at the moment.

"Get out of my way, Willy." Gray met the younger man's belligerent glare with a fierce warning in his own.

"In due time, Longwalker." Little Willy pushed his hat back on his head and hooked his thumbs in his belt loops. "Just wanted to be sure you heard the news about my brother."

"That he's decided to take up residence in the family plot at Thatcher Cemetery, I hope," Gray deadpanned.

"Oh, I think you'll like this even better," Willy sneered. "He's fixin' to marry Miss Lauren Whitmore." Willy leaned closer and added in a stage whisper, "I guess that'll make Buck the daddy to that little dark-haired girl of yours."

A full ten seconds passed before Gray could speak. Something hot and black settled over him, something far beyond rage...beyond hatred. Something he couldn't name. "Move out of my way," he said, his voice so low, so hard, he barely recognized it as his own.

Complete silence had replaced the din around them. Willy held Gray's deadly gaze a heartbeat longer before he grudgingly stepped aside.

The strained silence followed Gray out the door and into the midday sun. He drew in deep, calming breaths. Willy had to be crazy. He wouldn't allow himself to believe what could only be Willy's idea of a sick joke at Gray's expense. Lauren would never do that. He moved quickly to his truck and slid behind the wheel.

Instinct told Gray that he was a fool. Willy had told the truth, Gray knew it with every fiber of his being. He had misjudged Lauren. Gray should have known better than to believe a future with Lauren was possible. He knew better than to believe in anything or anyone but himself. Hadn't life taught him that lesson especially well?

WITH ONE FOOT TUCKED under her, Lauren set the old porch swing into motion with the other. She surveyed the yard and the pastures beyond it. This had been home to her for the past three years, and she hated to leave it. Buck would expect her and Sarah to move into the family mansion on the other side of town. Lauren squeezed her eyes shut and forced the unappealing thoughts away.

Instantly the image of Gray Longwalker leaped to mind. The memory of his raven-black hair caressing her skin as he made love to her sent warmth spreading through Lauren's body. His full mouth had worked in perfect harmony with his talented hands. And those eyes—he had worshipped her with those amazing gray eyes. Even his sweet words had been seductive. Lauren shook her head in denial of what she felt. She couldn't permit herself to nurture the love already growing in her heart for him. Lauren would never again be with Gray Longwalker. In a few short days she would be Mrs. Buckmaster. Facing Gray in the future for his visits with Sarah would be more than simply difficult.

She prayed she had done the right thing. Everything had whirled out of control all at once. But the decision had been made and her fate had been sealed with the signing of the contract.

She squeezed her trembling hands into tight fists in her lap. She didn't want to think about what would happen after the wedding day. She couldn't. One step at a time, one day at a time—that's how Lauren would get through this nightmare. There would be no knight in shining armor to rescue her from her plight. But if this wedding helped her to keep Sarah even part-time, it would be worth the sacrifice.

A frown etched its way across her forehead. Why hadn't Gray told her that he and Buck were brothers? The animosity between them made complete sense now. She shivered when she considered the kind of man she had just tied herself to. Why hadn't anyone ever told her about the secrets lurking in the Buckmaster closets? *These people just react the way the Buckmasters want them to.* Gray's words replayed in her thoughts. How could a whole town stand back and watch one family destroy another?

The sound of a vehicle skidding to a stop in her drive yanked Lauren from her disturbing thoughts.

Gray.

From the murderous look on his face and the rigid

set of his shoulders, Lauren surmised that he had heard the news. She gingerly pushed her weary body out of the swing, muscles she didn't even realize she had were tender from the workout Gray had given her in the wee hours before dawn. Lauren's heart fluttered when she considered one especially tender place. When she had ripped the sheets from her bed this morning, the small bloodstains had served as a grim reminder of the consequences of her actions.

Regardless of what took place from this moment on, Lauren had no regrets. They had shared something truly special and she would hold her time with Gray close to her heart for as long as she lived. Those memories would get her through the nights with Buck.

Gray stopped, less than two feet in front of her, and stared down at Lauren, his gaze cold, brutal. His lips were set in a harsh, tight line and his arms hung at his sides, fists clenched. Lauren braced herself for his fury. She deadened herself against the words she knew he would say. She would not feel any of this and she would not react.

When he finally spoke, his voice was hard and un-naturally controlled. "You have one chance here, Lauren. Just one." He paused for her to consider his words, then continued, "Tell me it isn't true."

Lauren squared her shoulders and lifted her chin. "I can't." Her voice was flat and tired, there was nothing left inside her to provide inflection.

He shuddered briefly, visibly, but quickly grabbed back control. "Then I have one question."

Lauren waited, her heart thundering in her chest. She stood absolutely still.

"Why did you not save your precious virginity for

your future husband?'' The question was laced with biting contempt.

Lauren swallowed back the words that threatened to tumble from her trembling lips. She wanted to scream, ''Because I love you!'' She cleared her throat and forced out the lie she had already composed, ''I had a momentary lapse in judgment.'' She shrugged, or she tried to shrug, but her body responded minimally. ''Buck hounded me for weeks to give him an answer. I guess I got cold feet and...lost my head.'' The lie was bitter on her tongue.

A muscle jerked in his tense jaw. ''So that's all it was, a momentary lapse?''

''That's right,'' she said tightly.

Gray looked away. After a gut-twisting moment, his gaze connected with hers once more. ''You lied to me.''

Tremors shook Lauren's body. She clenched her fists and willed her body to still, but it would not. ''Yes,'' she whispered. Her breath caught, punctuating the single word with a sob. Lauren retreated a step from the rage glittering in his fierce gaze.

''I watched Buck's father destroy my mother by slow, painful degrees. I have no desire to watch Buck do the same to you, but if that's your decision then so be it.''

''That's my decision,'' she said, driving the final nail into her coffin.

''I'll stay out of your way until the hearing, and then I'll leave. And Sarah will go with me.''

Lauren shook her head, slowly, adamantly. ''I'll never let you take her.''

"You won't have a choice. And mark my words," he continued in a low, threatening tone, "as long as you're connected with the Buckmasters, you won't ever see Sarah again."

Chapter Thirteen

"That should do it, Lauren," Dr. Prescott told her with a warm, fatherly smile.

Lauren returned his smile with as much sincerity as she could muster. The past two days had been pure hell. Buck had set their wedding date for one week from today. He had relentlessly pushed Lauren for decisions on each and every detail. Her work had piled up in the process, and Gray Longwalker hovered over Sarah like a brooding shadow. He neither spoke to nor looked at Lauren. The intensity of his resentment and bitterness toward her widened the crack in her heart, but what could she do? Nothing.

"I should have the results of your blood test in a couple of days. If everything is in order, we'll get you started on that new medication pronto. All the experts are singing its praises."

"Good. I could use the relief. The medication I'm taking now just isn't working as well as I'd like," Lauren said tiredly. Maybe if she could sleep she wouldn't be so fatigued all the time.

"Lauren." He took her hand in his. "The biggest problem is all this stress you're under. What with a sudden wedding and that Gray Longwalker business,

I'm surprised you haven't had another episode already."

"It'll be over soon. Don expects the preliminary DNA results later today, then we can set the hearing, and it will be finished."

"And the wedding next week, that's all taken care of?"

Lauren nodded, but she didn't meet his eyes. She didn't want him to see the regret she knew would be there.

"I'll be there with bells on," he teased.

Lauren manufactured a weak smile and thanked him as he hurried away to his next patient. Bill was right about one thing, she thought as she exited Thatcher's small medical clinic, her current medication was only delaying the inevitable. Lauren could feel the pain clawing for release. She wouldn't be able to put off an episode much longer.

Sarah would go home with Rosemary after school this afternoon. Rosemary had a birthday party planned for her youngest daughter. Under normal circumstances Lauren would attend herself, but her current situation was far from normal. She was barely holding the headaches at bay, and Don would be delivering the test results. Not that the results would be a surprise, but she wanted to be available in case he had any other news.

Like Gray Longwalker's sudden change of heart.

GRAY SAT ON THE TOP BAR of the fence and watched the two horses get to know each other. Old Spinner needed company, and Restless had needed a good home. Gray couldn't leave Thatcher knowing Spinner would continue to be lonely. Gray smiled; the sensation felt strange on his lips. He hadn't had a blasted thing to smile about in the past two days. He wouldn't have missed the pleasantness of that particular feeling if Sarah and Lauren hadn't caused him to become familiar with it.

Lauren.

Her betrayal burned in his chest like a brand on his heart. One more scar to add to all the others. How could she marry Buck? She had never given Gray the first indication that Buck's pursuit of her was wanted, much less reciprocated. Each time he saw the two of them together he wanted to kill Buck. The thought of him touching her in any way made Gray's guts twist.

Would she have accepted Buck's proposal if Gray had agreed to share Sarah with her, maybe even take her away with him? Gray gave a small, regretful shake of his head. He just didn't see the connection. What did Buck have to do with any of this? What did Lauren hope to gain by marrying him? Gray had considered the possibilities over and over again and still ended up back at square one. Sure Buck had lots of money and political influence. But the law was the law, and Sarah was Gray's biological child. There was no reasonable explanation for Lauren having turned to Buck. Yet, there had to be one. Lauren was too smart to make a life-altering decision like this without good reason.

But she was desperate, and desperate people took desperate steps. There was always the off chance that Buck had promised to sway the judge's decision. But Gray was ready for that possibility. He would appeal all the way to the Supreme Court if necessary. The Buckmaster influence didn't go that far outside of Texas.

He'd had time to think, and regardless of what Lauren implied, Gray knew she had feelings for him. Her response had been too real, too deep. Every incredible moment of their lovemaking had played itself time and again in his head. His body ached for Lauren. She was his. In the farthest reaches of his soul Gray believed that with complete certainty. But another man would have her. Every instinct told him to fight, not to let her slip away. But how could he?

For years he had fought until he had finally given up and accepted his life for what it was. Gray had found himself an acceptable niche somewhere beyond tolerance, but not quite in the range of happiness. He had spent the past six years of his life turning the other cheek and walking away, until Sarah. When he had learned of his child, nothing on earth could have stopped him from claiming her. And in the process he had grown attached to Lauren.

Gray clenched his jaw hard. How could he stand back and let her marry another man? Was his pride so great that he would cut out his own heart to rid himself of its vulnerability? Pride, bitterness and anger had ruled his life for far too long.

Whatever Buck held over Lauren to sway her decision, Gray felt sure that her desire to stay with Sarah was far greater. If he were to ask her not to marry Buck, would she marry him instead just to be near Sarah? And if she did, would she learn to love him, or grow to resent him for using the child as leverage?

Marriage. The possibility of marrying one day had never even entered his mind. Gray had assumed he would spend the rest of his life alone. But he didn't want that anymore. He wanted Lauren. The admission startled him, but it was true. He had to do something before it was too late.

Gray jumped down from the fence and headed for the water hose near the barn. He was hot, sweaty and dusty. He needed some quick relief, internal as well as external. Somehow he had to cool the rage simmering inside him and think clearly. Gray had to find the right words to say to Lauren to change her mind.

LAUREN PARKED in her drive and stepped out of the car, her gaze riveted to the pasture Spinner called home. A sleek brown horse grazed on the lush green carpet along with Spinner.

"What the devil?" Lauren muttered. Where had that horse come from? She tossed her purse back on the car seat and slammed the door shut. Lauren crossed the yard with quick, determined strides. Gray had to be at the bottom of this. Aloof and hostile, he had spent the past two days watching her world go to hell in a handbasket. And now this! The man had waltzed back into town two weeks ago and destroyed Lauren's life. She had been at his mercy since. But, by God, this was still her ranch, she mused with unreasonable fury. Gray Longwalker had no right to bring a horse onto her property without asking first. Who did he think he was?

Lauren checked the barn but didn't find him. She started in the direction of the bunkhouse, and something in the edge of her vision captured her attention. She stopped and turned back toward the barn. Gray stood, bare from the waist up, hosing himself off at the spigot on the far side of the barn.

Refusing to allow her body's response to extinguish her anger, Lauren stalked straight up to where he stood. The water obviously obscured the sound of her approach, Gray continued his makeshift shower, unaware that she was there. The water sluiced over his face, past his broad shoulders to dampen his dark hair and faded jeans. He dropped the hose and swiped the water from his face, then bent to turn off the spigot. Lauren cleared her throat, and he jerked up to face her.

"Where did that brown horse come from?" she asked sharply. His taut muscular body screamed for her attention. His wide, bronzed chest beckoned to her on an elemental level that almost took her breath, but Lauren willed the desire to retreat.

"I bought Restless from Mrs. Jennings. I thought Spinner could use some company," he offered flatly, his eyes never leaving hers.

Lauren set her hands on her hips and glared at him. "You had no right to buy another horse for me to have to take care of without asking first."

"I tried, but you were too busy that day to listen. Then I forgot. Don't worry, I've already made arrangements with Tom Burke. I'll be paying him to take care of the horse, it won't cost you anything." He pushed his damp hair back and continued his penetrating stare, devouring her with his intense gaze.

"This is my ranch, and if I had wanted another horse I would have bought one myself," she fumed, refusing to get trapped in his hot, searching stare.

"Lauren." He stepped closer, and she shivered before she could stop herself. "Spinner needed a companion. You have plenty of grazing land, what's the big deal? It's not like you'll be living here much longer, anyway," he added bitterly.

"That's not the point," she countered. Her anger blazed hotter at his nonchalance. Lauren took a step closer to him and stabbed her index finger at him accusingly. "You had no right to make that kind of decision."

He swallowed hard, and Lauren found herself suddenly mesmerized by the play of muscles beneath the dark skin of his throat. "I had no right, that's true enough," he admitted, his tone softer now. "If you don't want the horse, I'll find him another home." He let out a heavy breath and stared at the thin strip of ground that stood between them. "But Spinner will be lonesome."

And so would she when Gray left. She would be devastated. Lauren released her own weary sigh. "I don't care if the horse stays, it's the principle of the thing."

He slowly lifted his gaze back to hers; anger glittered there now. "And we both know how principled you are." The words hissed past his clenched teeth.

Lauren flinched at the cutting remark. She opened her mouth to deliver a proper comeback, but conviction deserted her. Instead, she spun around to walk away. She would not do this to herself.

"Lauren." He clasped long fingers around her arm and halted her retreat.

Lauren closed her eyes and held very still. She would not respond to his touch or to the gentle rasp of his voice. Gray moved in close behind her, his body pressed along the length of hers, making her heart thump erratically.

"Do you feel this fire when Buck touches you?" he murmured against her hair.

"Stop," she whispered, though she prayed he would not. Heaven help her, she wanted him to make love to her right now, on the ground, in broad daylight.

"Does he touch you the way I touch you?" He

nuzzled her neck, then planted slow, hot kisses there. "Does his touch make you burn for him as you burn for me even now?"

"No." Had the word been a thought or had she spoken? Lauren didn't know, her mind and body were lost to the man holding her in his firm, sensual grip.

"Do you dream of how we made love over and over again the way I do?" His mouth tortured her shoulder, his words tortured her soul.

Lauren twisted to face him. "Stop," she cried, her desperate gaze colliding with his. The water on his damp skin glistened like diamonds in the afternoon sun. Alarm bells sounded in Lauren's brain. Run, she told herself, but her legs would not obey.

"Do you really want me to stop?" He lowered his head and brushed the promise of a kiss across her lips. Lauren shivered, and Gray folded her into his arms, holding her close against his bare chest. His skin felt cool against her flushed cheek. Gently he kissed the top of her head as if she were a child in need of gentleness.

Lauren closed her eyes and allowed herself this one moment of comfort in the arms of the man she truly loved with all her heart. The past two days had, if nothing else, provided proof positive that she was in love with Gray. She could hardly bear Buck's touch, even in the most innocent way. His kiss repulsed her. And Gray had haunted her every waking moment. Even when she slept, dreams of him taunted her.

"Choose me, Lauren."

Lauren drew back to look into his eyes. They were soft with tender emotion. She blinked. "What did you say?" She had to have heard wrong.

"Don't marry Buck. Marry me, Lauren. *Marry me.*"

She searched his eyes, the emotion there confirming his words. Lauren shook her head, the move hardly a move at all. "It's…it's too late," she breathed. Lauren pulled free of his embrace and backed away. "It's too late," she repeated, her words scarcely a whisper. She turned and ran away from the words that once she would have given anything to hear but that had come too late…much too late.

"Lauren, wait," he called after her.

Lauren didn't stop. She kept running until she had reached her car and grabbed for her purse and keys. She had to get inside and lock the door. She had to take her medicine. She had to hide…to think.

The sound of a car pulling up next to hers jerked Lauren's attention in that direction. *Buck.* Oh, God. She didn't want to see him. She wanted to run away.

"Hey, sugar," he called as he got out of his car.

His expression dimmed when he took a second look at her. Lauren knew she must look rattled. She was rattled. She was crazy. She was a rat caught in her own trap.

"Is something wrong?" He moved to her side just as Gray came around the end of the house still buttoning his shirt. Buck took one look at Gray and immediately sized up the situation. He abandoned his advance toward Lauren and strode in Gray's direction.

"What the blazes did you do to her?" Buck demanded.

Gray fastened the final button on his shirt and leveled a lethal glare on Buck. "What takes place between Lauren and me is none of your business."

"She's going to be my wife, and I'm dang well making it my business!" Buck shouted.

The corners of Gray's mouth hitched up in a mocking smile. "Maybe, maybe not."

"You son of a—" Buck charged at Gray.

Just when Lauren felt sure there would be a fight, Don arrived. The sound of his car braking to a stop halted Buck's advance. Both men focused on Don as he emerged from his vehicle.

Lauren clutched her purse tightly against her middle, her keys in her hand. Don walked toward her, her heart beat wildly as he approached. He had come to make the announcement that Gray would use against her in court. His words would forever change the course of her life, of Sarah's life.

She kept her gaze fixed on Don. She couldn't permit herself to consider Gray's proposal. *Choose me.* Lauren shook herself in denial. *Too late…too late.*

With an unexpected grin, Don threw his arms around Lauren and hugged her close, then whispered, "It's over, Lauren. It's all over."

Lauren choked back the sob rising in her throat. *Marry me, Lauren,* the words echoed. *Marry me. Too late.* Her fate was sealed.

Don drew back and smiled at Lauren. "Everything's going to be fine now." He gave her shoulders one final squeeze and turned toward the two men now standing within arm's reach.

Lauren glanced from Buck to Gray, then back to Don. What did he mean it's over? How was everything going to be fine? Something was wrong.

"Mr. Longwalker, I'm sure your own attorney will be providing you with a copy of the preliminary results, but I will tell you that it wasn't a match."

Gray only stared at him.

"Sarah is not your child," Don added. "Obviously Miss Johnson had another boyfriend of Native American heritage."

Shock settled over Lauren. How could that be? Sharon had told her. The pictures. Sarah looked exactly like Gray. The eyes, everything. Buckmaster eyes. Ice formed in Lauren's stomach. Buck had something to do with this. She knew it as surely as she knew her own name.

"That can't be," Gray said.

No words Lauren could call to mind adequately described the utter desolation that emanated from Gray. A devastation so stark that Lauren could not bear to look at him. She wanted to assure him there was some mistake. That Buck had somehow arranged this. Another revelation struck her before she could speak. She had done this. A wave of nausea washed over her, making her weak. She needed to sit down. By agreeing to marry Buck she had unleashed his machinations.

"This is wrong," Gray said almost to himself. Rage stole across his features and he turned to Buck. "You did this."

"Face it, Longwalker," Buck said sarcastically, "you lost. Once a loser, always a loser. The kid's better off without you."

"Buck!" Lauren lunged forward at the same time Gray moved toward Buck. She absorbed the impact of Gray's rigid body against hers. "Buck, I'd like you to leave now," she said as calmly as she could, considering she stood directly between the two men.

"I want him out of here," Buck commanded, his face red with his own rage.

"Buck, please," Lauren pleaded. "I'll call you tonight. Just go, please."

Buck backed up one step, and Lauren let go the breath she had been holding. He stabbed a finger at Gray. "It's over. I want you out of my town!"

Lauren couldn't see Gray's face, but she felt his body jerk in response though he said nothing. Buck gave Lauren a quick nod before he swaggered off. His car roared to life, and he spun away amid a cloud of dust and spraying gravel.

Spots floated before Lauren's eyes as another bout of weakness claimed her. Her medicine, she had to get to her medicine. She turned around slowly and faced Gray, unable to completely comprehend the emotions on his face.

"I have to go inside now," she managed to say without slurring her words.

"Lauren, perhaps I should stay awhile," Don offered from behind her.

"I'm fine, please, just go," she said without looking back at him. Lauren focused intently on the door as she half stumbled to reach it. Behind her she heard Don's car start up and his slow departure. Lauren paused at the door and summoned her waning willpower. Fight, she ordered herself, don't give in just yet. She reached to unlock the door and dropped the keys. Cautiously she bent down and retrieved them, only to drop them again before she could insert the proper key in the lock.

A dark hand reached out and snatched up the keys before Lauren could react. Gray was at her side, and she hadn't even been aware of him. Lauren closed her eyes against his presence. She heard him unlock the door and push it open. When Lauren would have stepped inside, his words stilled her.

"Tell me how this can be, Lauren."

"I don't know," she murmured without looking at him. "There has to be a mistake. Just please go."

An eternity passed before Lauren heard the heavy thud of his boots across the wood porch. She moved very slowly, very carefully into her house and closed the door behind her. Lauren dropped her purse to the floor and slowly, cautiously made her way to the kitchen. She had left her pills on the counter. Her vision blurred, the beast roared inside her head.

By touch, she located the bottle and twisted the lid with shaky hands. The bottle slipped from her grasp and pills scattered across the counter, the floor. With fierce concentration Lauren managed to capture one between her thumb and forefinger, then popped it into her mouth. She switched on the tap and ducked beneath it for a drink.

Pain exploded inside her head. Lauren groaned. The room shifting and, blackness threatening, she felt her way to the hall. If she could only make it to the bed. The pain roared ferociously, stripping her of the last of her strength. Lauren sagged against the wall and slid to the floor. She pressed her forehead to her knees and prayed for the blackness to swallow her, bringing with it blessed relief. Sarah was in good hands with Rosemary. Lauren willed herself to give in to the pain. Stop fighting, she chanted silently.

"Lauren."

Her name sounded a long way off, though Lauren sensed that it came from right beside her. She didn't dare speak or move her head or even open her eyes; the pain was too great.

"Lauren."

It was Gray's voice. Lauren struggled to lift her head, to open her eyes. She needed to tell him…to tell him…what? She couldn't think.

Suddenly she was moving, he was moving her. It hurt…she didn't want to move. She mumbled a protest, but if he understood he paid no attention. Lauren's heavy lids opened a crack, but she felt more than saw that he had carried her into her bedroom. She sank into the softness of her bed. He covered her and Lauren retreated into the darkness.

Chapter Fourteen

Lauren struggled upward, out of the darkness. *Hurry!* She had to hurry. She pushed through the thick layers smothering her. Sound. She could hear distant sounds. She was getting closer.

Lauren's eyes opened slowly to the semidark room. *Her room,* she was in her room. Long moments passed before the ability to move returned. Lauren felt groggy and heavy against the mattress. She turned the hot, hollow mass that was her head, and her sluggish gaze settled on a familiar face.

Rosemary sat in the chair next to Lauren's bed. Her eyes were closed. Lauren wondered if it was night and Rosemary was asleep. How long had she been out? She remembered waking up several times, but the pain had sent her immediately back into the darkness.

Lauren licked her dry lips. "Rosemary," she mumbled in a rusty voice.

Rosemary jolted to attention. She scrutinized Lauren's face and then smiled. "You're back."

"Sarah?" Lauren asked. She had to know that Sarah was all right.

"Don't worry, honey," Rosemary replied softly. "Sarah is fine."

Lauren smiled faintly. "Good."

Rosemary knelt beside the bed and smoothed Lauren's hair back from her face. Her hands felt cool against Lauren. "Can I get you anything?"

"Gray," she murmured next. "Where's Gray?" She remembered he had been there at least once when she'd surfaced from oblivion.

Rosemary's smile dimmed. "He was really worried about you. He stayed right by your side for most of the night and today, too."

"Where is he?" Lauren insisted. She had to warn him that Buck had done something. The test results had to have been tampered with. She had to tell him...that she loved him.

"He's at the bunkhouse," Rosemary began. "He's leaving, Lauren."

Anguish stabbed Lauren's heart and twisted. "But he can't go. I want him to stay." She struggled to a sitting position.

"Wait, honey, you're still weak." In spite of her scolding, Rosemary helped Lauren to her feet.

"I have to stop him," Lauren said weakly.

"He won't leave without saying goodbye. Take it easy and let me get you something to drink." Rosemary smiled, then hugged Lauren close. "I'm so glad you're not going to make the same mistake I did."

Lauren had made the last mistake she ever intended to where Gray Longwalker was concerned. He may have changed his mind about the unexpected marriage proposal, but she didn't care. Lauren would take a relationship with Gray any way she could get it.

"There's something else," Rosemary said with a sigh.

Lauren's gaze latched on to hers. She wasn't sure she could tolerate any more bad news.

"Buck is fit to be tied." Rosemary shrugged. "I wouldn't let him see you, and he's a little less than pleased with me."

Glee at Buck's displeasure gave Lauren's resolve a shot in the arm. "Don't worry about Buck," she assured her friend. "I intend to take care of him personally."

SARAH TWIRLED GRAY'S HAT in her little hands. Her green cast was now covered in her schoolmates' autographs. He could hardly bear the solemn expression on her face. But he had to go, for the time being. He knew with every fiber of his being that the test results were wrong. But Gray couldn't do anything about that at the moment. That was his attorney's job. Sarah would be safe with Lauren until he could prove his right to his child in the courts. The thought of leaving Sarah was more painful than anything he had ever suffered in his life.

But he couldn't take her with him yet. His chest tightened at the thought of Lauren marrying Buck. Buck was the real bad guy here. Somehow he had convinced Lauren that marrying him was the only way to keep Sarah, and then he'd had the test results altered. Gray knew the Buckmasters well enough to know that they would stoop to any means to get what they wanted. He just couldn't figure out why Buck would want Sarah. Did he believe she was the key to possessing Lauren? Was this what Mrs. Jennings had tried to warn him about the day he arrived? *Blood isn't always thicker than water.* Gray knew that better than anybody.

How could he walk away, knowing what Lauren was getting into? Gray cared for Lauren in ways he had never thought himself capable, and he knew she cared for him. There had to be a third angle here, something he was missing.

"But I don't want you to go," Sarah mumbled, her head hung in disappointment. "You promised to take me to the rodeo and to teach me to ride all by myself."

Her words stole his breath. Gray crouched down to her level. How could he explain the games adults play and make her understand? He couldn't. "I'll be back, Sarah, you have my word."

She looked at him, tears shining in her sad eyes. "You promise you won't forget about me?"

Gray felt the sting of his own tears. He forced a smile for his daughter. "Sarah—"

"You don't have to worry, sweetie, Gray will never forget you."

Gray's head went up at the sound of Lauren's weary voice. What was she doing out of bed? He stood, uncertain of what she intended. Was she here to see that he cleared out? Whatever her reason, he yearned to touch her.

Sarah rushed over to hug Lauren's legs. "You feel better now, Mommy?"

Lauren patted her on the head. "Lots better now." She lifted her gaze to Gray's. "I need to talk to you."

Gray couldn't imagine what she would have to say to him now, but he would listen. Pride would not prevent him from following his heart as it had so many times in the past. "Sarah, why don't you take that bag out to my truck." He gestured to the small saddlebag.

"Wait, sweetie," Lauren said as she all but crumpled into the nearest chair. "Come over here and sit in Mommy's lap."

Sarah looked from Gray to Lauren, then obeyed her mother. Gray stood stock-still, waiting for the other shoe to drop. He couldn't read Lauren's feelings. But he could feel her trepidation or maybe resignation.

Lauren smiled at her daughter and gave her an affectionate hug. "Sarah, you don't ever have to worry about Gray forgetting about you, because you're too special to him."

Sarah's eyes lit up. "I am?"

Lauren nodded. "That's right. You know how Elly and Missy have a mommy and a daddy?"

Sarah nodded slowly. "But I don't."

"Yes, you do," Lauren said, her voice quavered.

Gray's heart surged into his throat. What was she doing?

"I do?" Sarah's eyes widened.

"Gray is your father, and he loves you very much." Sarah peeked shyly at him, then turned back to Lauren, her face expectant. "He would have come to see you a long time ago but he didn't know you had been born. He came as soon as he found out."

"Nobody tolded him about me?"

Lauren shook her head slowly, unshed tears brimming in her troubled eyes.

Sarah frowned up at Gray. His gut twisted with anxiety. Was she disappointed? Would she still want to be with him now that she knew the truth? How could he expect a child to understand her father not coming to see her in all these years?

"How comed you didn't tell me?"

"I wanted to, Sarah, but—"

"I asked him not to," Lauren interrupted. She swiped at her cheek. "I was afraid you would love him so much that—" her voice cracked "—you wouldn't need me anymore."

"You're silly, Mommy," Sarah said, making a funny face. She hugged Lauren. "I love you bunches and bunches." She bounced out of Lauren's lap then. She set her little hands on her hips and peered up at Gray. "If you're my daddy you have to stay." Before he could respond, the child made a mad dash for the door. "I'm gonna go tell Aunt Rosemary that I got a daddy, too."

Gray released the breath he'd been holding. When he'd composed himself, he turned to Lauren. She stood now, only a few feet away, twisting her hands nervously in front of her.

"I'm glad you're feeling better." He wanted to reach out to her, to touch her and make her admit what he knew she felt. He wanted more than he had ever wanted anything in the world to believe in her...in them.

"I was wrong," Lauren explained. She took a deep breath and struggled for calm. "I was afraid that you would take Sarah away from me and I'd never see her again. When Don told me that I would have a better chance of winning at least some rights to her by presenting the picture-perfect family setting, I believed him. I was desperate not to lose her." Her lips trembled. "But I was wrong. I had no idea what Buck was capable of. I'm certain he somehow influenced the way the test turned out. But he's not going to get away with it.''

Gray studied the determination in her eyes, in the set of her mouth and shoulders. She was serious. ''You're going to stand up against Buck, throw away all he can offer you, for me?'' He heard the disbelief in his voice.

''Yes.''

Gray closed his eyes and steadied himself. In his entire life no one had ever done that for him. After a moment he leveled his gaze back on Lauren's. ''Why would you do that?''

''Because you're Sarah's father.'' She straightened, squaring her shoulders. ''Because you're a good man and you deserve better than this.''

''I can fight my own battles, Lauren,'' he countered. Gray didn't want her facing Buck, especially not alone.

''This isn't just your battle, it's *our* battle. Buck used me to hurt you. I don't understand why yet, but I won't let him use me again.''

''Buck has a long-standing grudge against me,'' Gray told her with resignation. ''I don't think anything is going to change that.''

''Because you're his half brother?''

''You figured that out, did you?'' he asked, a bit surprised.

She nodded. ''I want you to stay here, Gray, with us. You may never trust me again or feel about me the way I feel about you, but I don't want you to go. Sarah loves you.''

''The people in this town don't want me here, remember?''

''They'll get over it.''

''And exactly how is it that you feel about me?'' He had to hear her say the words out loud.

''I'm in love with you, Gray Longwalker, and I'm willing to fight the whole town if necessary to keep you.''

Before Gray could respond, Lauren left, leaving him to make up his own mind about the future.

Their future.

LAUREN WAITED IMPATIENTLY in the parlor of Buck's ostentatious Spanish-style mansion. The place was as quiet and stifling as a mausoleum. This was no place to raise a child. How could she ever have considered bringing Sarah here? Lauren shivered and thanked God once more that she had seen through Buck and come to her senses. She shifted and suppressed the need to tap her foot. Though she felt tremendously better now, she had lost a full day already with the debilitating episode of headaches. She didn't want to lose any more time.

''Sorry to keep you waiting, sugar,'' Buck boomed as he swaggered through the door. ''I was on a business call to Houston.'' He winked. ''You know how it is.''

Lauren essayed a smile and braced herself for the obligatory kiss. Her stomach roiled at his touch.

''Have a seat, sugar, and I'll pour you a drink. You look as if you could use one.'' He busied himself at the antique sideboard that served as a bar. ''That Rosemary wouldn't let me see you or talk to you while you were feeling poorly.'' He glanced over his shoulder at Lauren. "I'm a little upset with that woman."

Lauren moistened her lips and drew in a bolstering breath. She couldn't just keep standing here putting it off. "I don't want a drink, Buck. I need to talk to you."

"All right." Buck left the drinks on the bar and crossed the thickly carpeted floor to stand beside her. "What seems to be the problem?"

"I made a mistake," she told him flatly. "I can't marry you."

Buck lifted one skeptical brow. "A little late for second thoughts, don't you think? After all, we have a contract."

Lauren's temper flared at his audacity. "You tricked me." She lifted her chin in challenge and added, "And you tricked Gray. I don't know how you got the results of that test rigged, but I'm sure Gray's attorney will get to the bottom of it. You'd better hope it isn't against too many laws to do what you've done."

"Now, sugar," Buck's gaze turned hard. "I don't think you have much choice in the matter. A deal is a deal. The whole town is geared up for this wedding, and I, for one, don't plan to let them down. Longwalker and his attorney can't prove a thing. I have friends at LabTech, and friends take care of friends."

Lauren held her ground. "Is that a confession, Buck? I may not be as wealthy as you, but I think my word against yours might be an even match."

Buck stepped intimidatingly nearer. "I don't think you quite grasp the magnitude of the situation, sugar."

"I will not marry you, Buck." Lauren didn't flinch.

She would make this right. This was a free country, he couldn't make her marry him.

"We have a contract," he said furiously.

"So sue me," Lauren retorted. "I don't know what you hoped to gain by doing this, but I'm certain that you didn't go to all this trouble just to have me as your wife."

"I told you this crazy scheme wasn't gonna work."

Startled, Lauren glanced at the door to find Willy staring wild-eyed at her.

"Shut up, Willy," Buck commanded.

"I won't shut up," he shot back as he stalked across the room. "You went about this all wrong, big brother. Start thinking with your head instead of your—"

"I said shut up, Willy!" The threat in Buck's voice made Lauren jump. He looked ready to kill his younger brother.

"Just tell her what you want and what you'll do if you don't get it," Willy ground out. "That tactic worked just fine with that tramp Sharon."

Fear crept into Lauren's chest. "What about Sharon?"

Willy smirked. "She was easy. I just let her know that if she ever told Longwalker about that little girl of his that I'd see that she was sorry. Children come up missing all the time."

Outright panic slammed into Lauren then. "Why would you do such a thing? My God, Willy, do you know how that sounds?" The sneer on his face told her that he knew exactly how it sounded.

"Let me handle this," Buck snapped.

"You've screwed it up bad enough. It's my turn now." Willy turned his attention to Lauren, and she trembled inside. "That crazy old man of ours went and changed his will a few years back—"

"That's enough, Willy." Buck snagged him by one arm. "Don't say another word!"

Willy jerked out of Buck's hold and glowered at him. "The old man's conscience got to him, and he left one third of everything to that kid of Long-walker's. The fool thought that would make up for the way he'd treated Longwalker and his mother." Fear-lessly Willy held his brother's gaze, daring him to try and stop his tirade. "In three more months, when the will comes out of probate, we'll have to turn over one third of everything to that kid. Unless, of course," Willy turned his haughty gaze to Lauren then, "you marry Buck and then everything will stay in the fam-ily."

Lauren couldn't respond at first. Her shock was so complete that she could only gape at the two men. "This whole thing has been about your father's es-tate?" Lauren heard the stunned disbelief in her own voice.

"Don't listen to him, Lauren," Buck put in quickly. "This is between you and me. My father's will has nothing to do with it. I'll admit that keeping things in the family is the reason I started this, but I have come to care for you."

Lauren shook her head. "I won't marry you, Buck." She backed away a step. "Tell your attorney to check with Don about what we can do to resolve this. I don't want anything to do with Buckmaster money, and I'll do whatever possible to rid Sarah of any connection to this. Sarah is a Longwalker, not a Buckmaster."

Before either of them could say anything else, Lauren dropped the engagement ring Buck had given her onto the nearest table, turned and hurried away. She had to tell Gray the truth about why Sharon had kept Sarah from him. She had to find out if there was any hope for the two of them.

For Sarah's sake.

LAUREN RUSHED into her empty house. Gray's truck was gone. As was Rosemary's car. Where was everybody? Surely nothing had happened. She shivered at the possibility. She hurried to the kitchen to check the message board. Rosemary always left her a note if she had to leave for some reason. The telephone rang just as Lauren picked up the note. Rosemary had taken Sarah to town to run a few errands. At least she knew where Sarah was. But what about Gray? Lauren pulled the receiver from its base before it could ring the fourth time. "Hello."

"Lauren, this is Bill."

Dr. Prescott? Lauren frowned. Why would he be calling? It wasn't time for her to see him again. The medicine, she realized then. He would have the test results. "You have my new prescription ready?"

"Not exactly," he said hesitantly.

An uneasy feeling stole over Lauren. "What's wrong?"

"Lauren, because of the possible side effects of this medication, the lab checked for the presence of HCG."

Lauren's frown deepened. Was there something else wrong with her?

"I don't know any other way to say this," he told

her. "Lauren, you're pregnant. When did you have your last cycle?"

Pregnant. Shock, fear and finally wonder swept over her. She was pregnant. *Gray.* She was pregnant with Gray's baby. A feeling of complete happiness blossomed in her chest. Sarah would have a brother or sister.

Sadness quickly overshadowed the happiness. What if Gray didn't want a future with her after what she'd done?

Dr. Prescott's voice dragged Lauren back to the conversation. "You'll need to discontinue your current medication, as well. I'll prepare you a prescription for an appropriate alternative." He paused. "Lauren, you'll need a more complete examination. When can you come into the office?" Concern filled his voice.

"In a few days, Bill." Impatient to be on her way, she said, "I have to go now. Call that prescription in to the pharmacy for me, and I'll pick it up. I'll be sure to call you early next week for an appointment." Goodbyes said, Lauren hung up and hurried out the door. She had to find Gray, and somehow she had to convince him to trust her again. But where could he be? He didn't have any friends in town...Mrs. Jennings. Gray had said she took him in after his mother died. Maybe she would know where he was.

Sarah wasn't the only one depending upon them now.

LAUREN KNOCKED ONCE MORE on Mrs. Jennings' screen door. Impatience and anticipation buzzed inside her. She was going to have Gray's baby! Tears of joy welled in her eyes and she had to struggle to keep from hyperventilating. Sarah would be so thrilled. She prayed Gray would be as well.

"Yes?"

The sound of the elderly woman's voice jerked Lauren back to the here and now. "Hello, Mrs. Jennings, I'm Lauren Whitmore."

The screen door opened with a creak. "I can see that." The elderly woman scrutinized Lauren from head to toe then met her gaze. "What can I do for you, Miss Whitmore?"

Lauren refused to allow the woman's wariness to dampen her sprits. "I'm looking for Gray Longwalker. I thought that maybe you had seen him today. He mentioned that you had been good to him in the past, so I figured he might come by to see you."

One gray brow winged upward. "Is he leaving town again?"

"Not if I have anything to do with it," Lauren replied bluntly. But the choice was his. She could only hope that he would be willing to give her another chance.

"I hope he isn't leaving. This is his home. And that little girl you're raising is his daughter," Mrs. Jennings said firmly. She stepped onto the porch and allowed the door to close behind her. "He's a good man. Considering the odds that have been stacked against him his entire life, he's done exceptionally well in my book."

Lauren smiled. "I agree."

Mrs. Jennings eyed her somewhat skeptically. "And just what do you intend to do if you find him?"

"Well." Lauren drew in a deep breath for courage.

"If he doesn't ask me to marry him, I'm going to ask him."

Amusement flickered in the elderly woman's eyes. "In that case, you might find him at Jeremiah Manning's place. Gray has been working with one of Manning's horses."

Lauren hugged the woman. "Thank you!" She released a startled Mrs. Jennings and bounced off the porch. She had to find Gray. She had to know if he could forgive...if he could love her the way she loved him. She needed him. Sarah and the baby needed him. But mostly, she loved him.

LAUREN PARKED near Gray's truck. Mrs. Jennings had been right. Lauren studied the scene before her as she emerged from her car. Mr. Manning and a half dozen of his hired hands were standing around or hanging on to the corral fence near the barn. Lauren slowly walked in that direction. For so many cowpokes to be banded in one place, the silence was deafening. She could have heard a pin drop.

When she reached the corral, she understood. Gray was attempting to mount a beautiful black stallion. The horse sidled away whenever he attempted to climb into the saddle. Lauren leaned against the fence and watched. Gray moved closer to the horse's head. He spoke softly to the animal and stroked his neck. Long minutes of this whispered communication went on before Gray again attempted to mount the horse. The horse hedged, then stilled.

Lauren held her breath as Gray placed one booted foot into a stirrup and slung his long leg over the animal. The horse shifted nervously from side to side with the unexpected weight. Gray leaned down and spoke to him in those quiet tones once more. While the crowd watched, man and horse became one. The powerful strides of the stallion moved them around the corral; Gray's body moved in concert with the animal's. It was a sight to be behold.

"I'll be damned," Mr. Manning muttered. "He did it."

Pride swelled in Lauren's chest. Gray trotted the horse for a few minutes more before he dismounted. He gestured for one of Manning's men to take over. Gray soothed the horse as the other man mounted. A wave of murmurs swept over the crowd hanging on the fence.

"That's one fine job you did, Longwalker," Manning said.

"Shadow's a fine horse." Gray removed his hat and tunneled the fingers of one hand through his hair before settling it back on his head. "He'll bring you a fair price."

"Thanks to you," Manning acknowledged. "In fact, I've decided to keep him."

Gray's gaze captured Lauren's, and he moved to stand beside her. "I'm glad to hear it," he said to Manning.

She took a deep breath, and a smile tilted her lips. She was going to have his baby. The realization warmed her to the core of her being. She pressed her palm to her flat abdomen and silently thanked God for this wondrous gift. She couldn't wait to tell Sarah, but she had to tell Gray first, and she wouldn't tell him until they had resolved the issues standing between them. Lauren had to know if he loved her.

Gray inclined his head and studied her face as if searching for the answer to his question even before he asked.

Lauren looked into his handsome face and considered that their child would be dark like him, like Sarah, and probably just as beautiful. "That was pretty amazing, Longwalker." She smiled again. God, how she loved this man.

"You spoke to Buck?"

She nodded. "He admitted that he'd influenced the test results."

Gray let go a heavy breath. "I suspected as much."

"And Sharon," Lauren blurted, remembering. She had so much to share with him, she didn't know where to begin. "Willy threatened to harm Sarah if Sharon ever told you about the child."

Fury darkened his silvery gaze. "Both of them will answer to me for that, and for hurting you."

"It was because of his father's will," she explained. "Mr. Buckmaster had apparently developed a conscience a few years back. He wanted to make up for what he'd done to you and your mother, so he left Sarah one-third of everything." Lauren moistened her lips and swallowed hard. "That's why Buck wanted to marry me, so he would retain control of Sarah's portion of the estate. I told him we didn't want any part of Buckmaster money." It occurred to her then that she might have been hasty in that decision. Gray might want what was rightfully his.

"Good," he said, to her relief.

Lauren stared at the dusty ground at her feet. "I'm sorry, Gray. I made a terrible mistake." She lifted her gaze back to his. "Can you ever forgive me?"

Understanding replaced the fury in his gaze. "How can I blame you for something I drove you to do? I tried to take Sarah from you. I left you no other choice. You don't need my forgiveness, Lauren. You did what any mother who loved her child would do. I pushed you into Buck's trap."

Lauren took his hands in hers and drew in a steadying breath. "I love you, Gray. I love you for who you are and what you are—a proud, wonderful man. I don't ever want to be with anyone else." The strength of her emotions made Lauren tremble now. She loved him so much, would he trust her enough to believe in that love?

A heart-stunning smile slid across Gray's lips. "I love you, Lauren, and my offer still stands." He pulled off his hat and stepped closer to her. "Marry me," he murmured, his mouth close enough to kiss.

The sound of flying gravel and tires skidding to a stop jerked both their gazes in that direction. Buck and four of his men emerged from the vehicles now parked haphazardly in Manning's drive.

"Go inside the house, Lauren," Gray said in a low voice. "Have Mrs. Manning call the sheriff."

"What does he want?" Fear pounded in Lauren's chest. Hadn't Buck done enough already? Why didn't he just leave them alone?

"Go, Lauren."

Before her body could assimilate the command to run, Buck and his men spread out in a line a few feet away.

"I want you out of my town, Longwalker," Buck commanded bitterly. "And you can take that *woman* and the kid with you."

Gray stepped toward him. Lauren's breath became trapped in her lungs. How could Gray take on all of them alone?

"It's a free country, *brother*," Gray returned easily. "But if you think you're man enough, you can try and make me go."

Fury tightened Buck's features. He didn't take a step forward, but he held his ground. "People in this town don't want your kind here. If you want a piece of me before me and my boys run you out of town, then come get me." Buck wiggled his fingers in invitation.

"This is my property, and Longwalker ain't gonna leave until he's danged well ready." Manning stepped forward, aligning himself with Gray.

"Stay out of this, old man," Gray warned, obviously concerned for the older man's well-being in spite of the odds against him.

"I'd listen to him if I were you," Buck added haughtily.

"I live in this town, too," Manning went on, "and I'd a whole lot rather have men like Longwalker around, than snakes in the grass like you. If anybody's gittin' off my property, it best be you."

Buck aimed his fury at Manning now. "And how do you plan to make me, you old fool?" he growled.

All six of Manning's men moved up behind him and Gray then. Emotion welled in Lauren's chest at the show of support.

Manning chuckled at Buck's look of utter surprise. "Oh, I s'pect it'll be easy enough."

"You haven't heard the last from me, Longwalker," Buck threatened as he and his men backed away.

"I'd be disappointed if I had," Gray assured him.

Buck and his men roared away leaving a thick cloud of dust in their wake.

Lauren's feet finally accepted the command to move. She hurried to Gray's side.

Gray and Manning eyed each other warily for several long seconds before Gray spoke. "Thanks for backing me up." Gray extended his hand.

Manning's hand closed around the offered one and gave it a good shake. "T'weren't nothing. That boy's been needing to be put in his place for a long while now." Manning grinned sheepishly. "Just glad I lived long enough to see the truth and to be the one to do it." He slapped Gray on the back then. "There's a fellow over in Bear Creek got a slew of wild horses needin' the right kind of attention. You interested?"

Gray chuckled. "I am."

Manning nodded, then turned to bark orders at his loitering men.

Lauren slid her hand into Gray's. "Before I say yes to your proposal," she qualified, drawing his full attention back to her, "there's something you need to know."

Gray lifted a speculative eyebrow. "I think we've had enough excitement for one day, are you sure it can't wait?" He tightened his fingers around hers and pulled her closer. "I was hoping to take my future wife home and make love to her."

Lauren placed his free hand on her abdomen. "I just wanted you to know that we're having a baby."

Surprise, then awe filled his beautiful eyes. "You're sure?"

Lauren nodded. "Dr. Prescott called just before I came over here."

Gray hauled her up against him. "Why didn't you say something before?"

Clutching his shoulders for balance, Lauren smiled up at him. "You were a little busy." She tiptoed and tilted her chin upward to align their lips. His warm breath whispered across her mouth, making her lips quiver. "But now I expect your undivided attention."

"Is this what you really want, Lauren?" he murmured, uncertainty in his soft voice.

"More than anything." She breathed the words, yearning for his mouth to cover hers. "Now kiss me, Longwalker."

Desire barbed low in her belly at the first touch of their lips—his firm, hers much softer. She pushed her arms around his neck and held on tightly. His kiss was long and deep, branding her heart and soul as his own, as a Longwalker.

* * * * *

Don't miss the next
COLBY AGENCY *story,*
PROTECTIVE CUSTODY
by Debra Webb.

*A Harlequin Intrigue coming
in April 2001.*

*Harlequin Intrigue
Your source for outstanding
romantic suspense.*

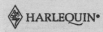
HARLEQUIN®

AMERICAN *Romance*

This small Wisconsin town has some big secrets...and the newest scandal is about to hit!

RETURN TO TYLER

SECRET BABY SPENCER
by Jule McBride
11/00 AR #849

PRESCRIPTION FOR SEDUCTION
by Darlene Scalera
2/01 AR #861

PATCHWORK FAMILY
by Judy Christenberry
12/00 AR #853

BRIDE OF DREAMS
by Linda Randall Wisdom
3/01 AR #865

And in January 2001, be sure to look for this special 3-in-1 collection from Harlequin Books!

TYLER BRIDES
by Kristine Rolofson
Heather MacAllister
Jacqueline Diamond

Warm as a cherished family quilt and bright as a rainbow, these stories weave together the fabric of a community.

Available at your favorite retail outlet.

HARLEQUIN®
Makes any time special™

Visit us at www.eHarlequin.com

HARRTT

HARLEQUIN®

AMERICAN *Romance*

presents

2001 Ways to Wed

Meeting the perfect groom isn't easy.
Sometimes a woman needs a little help.

Join three friends as they begin their husband
hunt following the advice of *2001 Ways to Wed*,
a book guaranteed to provide satisfaction!

Find out who marches down the aisle first—

RENT A MILLIONAIRE GROOM
Judy Christenberry
March 2001

TAME AN OLDER MAN
Kara Lennox
April 2001

KISS A HANDSOME STRANGER
Jacqueline Diamond
May 2001

Available at your favorite retail outlet.

HARLEQUIN®
Makes any time special ™

Visit us at www.eHarlequin.com.   HAR2001WTW

From bestselling
Harlequin American Romance author

CATHY GILLEN THACKER

comes

TEXAS VOWS

A McCABE FAMILY SAGA

Sam McCabe had vowed to always
do right by his five boys—but after
the loss of his wife, he needed the small-town security
of his hometown, Laramie, Texas, to live up to that
commitment. Except, coming home would bring him
back to a woman he'd sworn to stay away from.
It will be one vow that Sam can't keep....

On sale March 2001

Available at your favorite retail outlet.

HARLEQUIN®
Makes any time special ™

Visit us at www.eHarlequin.com

PHTV

HARLEQUIN®

AMERICAN *Romance*

&

HARLEQUIN®

INTRIGUE

Present

IDENTITY *Swap*

**Two different women,
one near-fatal accident.
Their lives become hopelessly entangled—
their fates forever entwined...**

Don't miss this exciting cross-line duo by

CHARLOTTE DOUGLAS

MONTANA MAIL-ORDER WIFE
Harlequin American Romance (#868)
March 2001

STRANGER IN HIS ARMS
Harlequin Intrigue (#611)
April 2001

Available at your favorite retail outlet.

HARLEQUIN®

Makes any time special ®

Visit us at www.eHarlequin.com   HARIIDENT

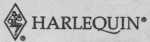 **HARLEQUIN®**

makes any time special—online...

eHARLEQUIN.com

your romantic escapes

—Indulgences—

♥ Monthly guides to indulging yourself,
such as:
★ Tub Time: A guide for bathing beauties
★ Magic Massages: A treat for tired feet

—Horoscopes—

♥ Find your daily Passionscope, weekly
Lovescopes and Erotiscopes

♥ Try our compatibility game

—Reel Love—

♥ Read all the latest romantic
movie reviews

—Royal Romance—

♥ Get the latest scoop on your favorite
royal romances

—Romantic Travel—

♥ For the most romantic destinations, hotels
and travel activities

HINTE1

#1 *New York Times* bestselling author

NORA ROBERTS

brings you more of the loyal and loving,
tempestuous and tantalizing Stanislaski family.

Coming in February 2001

The Stanislaski Sisters
Natasha and Rachel

Though raised in the Old World traditions of their
family, fiery Natasha Stanislaski and cool, classy
Rachel Stanislaski are ready for a *new* world of love....

*And also available in February 2001 from
Silhouette Special Edition, the newest book in the
heartwarming Stanislaski saga*

CONSIDERING KATE

Natasha and Spencer Kimball's daughter Kate turns her
back on old dreams and returns to her hometown, where
she finds the *man* of her dreams.

Available at your favorite retail outlet.

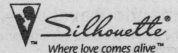

Where love comes alive™

Visit Silhouette at www.eHarlequin.com   PSSTANSIS

CHAPTER FIVE

AT LEAST SHE had a tree. That was the glittery lining to this strange little afternoon. It hadn't been entirely unpleasant, spending time with Ryan. It hadn't been entirely unpleasant being subjected to the small moments of unintentional flirtation. But it would've been better if they were intentional. Or if they were moments she could respond to.

Had she been on a date, complete with a walk in the snow, hot cider and a beautiful Christmas tree, it would have been a lovely afternoon. One full of banter and naughty jokes that made her feel warm and excited. That heated her from the inside out.

As it was, it had just been awkward, with a side of awkward, rolled in awkward and flash fried in *oh dear God why*.

At least the drive back into town was uneventful. They stopped for gas, chatted with the station attendant, and then she talked him into making a stop at the store for apple juice because her earlier thoughts about cider had made her crave some.

By the time they pulled into her driveway, she had almost forgotten his words up in the mountains. Almost.

Every so often they replayed in her mind. Deep,

rough, sexy. *Next thing you know you'll be sleeping in my bed.*

He had no idea that was one of her most cherished fantasies. Still. Yes, now that she was being honest with herself, she could admit that it *still* was.

That's probably why you've never slept in anyone else's bed.

She winced at her own line of thinking. She did not need to go thinking about sex again in his presence. Particularly her lack of experience. Her stomach sank when he turned off the engine, and she realized she needed his help getting more than one thing into the house.

"Can you help me with the tree?" she asked.

"Of course. I'm not going to leave you to struggle with a giant pine."

Giant pine. There was another one. She was getting kind of prurient. All she needed to do was not say anything about wood. "Thank you," she said, the words stiff, cautious.

"I assume you need help getting those bins into, unless you wrangled them in yesterday."

"No, no wrangling was done. They're still sitting in the back of my car."

"Okay, I guess I can put my muscles to use for you. No one else is using them."

She closed her eyes and tried very hard not to think about how many uses she could find for his muscles. "Yeah, we…we established that. And I'm happy to. Make use of them. To carry heavy things…not… Right."

"You can go ahead inside the house, get the tree stand set up. I'm going to have to cut off some of the bottom for the stand up in your living room, I'm almost sure of it."

And she was going into the house. She was not going to stand outside and watch him, engaging in Ryan-based lumberjack fantasies that she had no business having.

Anyway, she'd already done that earlier when he'd chopped the tree down in the first place.

"Okay." She got out of the truck, holding her grocery bag with the juice in it. "I'll go put the cider on."

"You have booze for that?"

"I'm not a Philistine, Ryan. It isn't the holidays if you can't get pleasantly sauced around the tree. Or, in my family, people just got drunk and skipped the tree."

"Sounds like my kind of Christmas," he said.

She swallowed, trying to suppress the unpleasant memory. It was her own fault for bringing it up. "Yeah, not really. Trust me."

"Sorry," he said.

"No, don't be. I made the joke. But hell, we all have baggage. No need to dwell on it."

"Why is it that airlines never lose emotional baggage?"

"*That* is a good question. I'll go...do the cider."

She walked inside, kicking her boots on the edge of the doorframe to knock off most of the mud. She left it cracked so that Ryan could push his way in easily when he was ready. She looked around her living room, imagining how it would be when it was full of friends and surrogate family, decorated for the holidays and smelling like cinnamon and cranberries.

Her house was another thing Margie and Dan had helped her with. She wondered if Ryan even knew that. They'd given her the down payment on her beautiful craftsman style home. It was modest, but it was the first thing she ever owned. She was almost certainly the first person in her family to own a house.

What she owed them was endless.

She set to work, putting a blue and white speckled pot on the stove and dumping the jug of cider in, then adding a few cinnamon sticks and some nutmeg. She turned the burner on high and covered it with a dented lid.

A few moments later, Ryan appeared with the tree. "You can set it over there, where the stand is," she told him. She'd moved it into place last night.

He grunted, and she was powerless to do anything but stare as he carried the tree through the living area, his footsteps heavy on the wooden floor. She cursed winter yet again, because it necessitated him wearing all those layers, and covered up what she was certain was a pretty darn good show.

Get a grip. You're supposed to be dealing. Not pining like the idiot you've been for all these years. When you leaned in toward him yesterday, he jumped back like you growled at him. He does not want you.

Part of the problem was that she'd never moved on. It was easy to convince herself that what she felt for Ryan all those years ago was a crush, but the proof was in her actions. She'd never gone on more than two

dates with anyone. She never let anyone get past her
front door, never let them get into her heart or her body.

It was easy enough to dismiss all that. She had trust
issues. A dad who had never bothered to be faithful to
her mom, a mom who had abandoned her because of a
mistake she'd made.

She happily blamed her lack of love life on all those
things. The Ryan factor was a lot less comfortable.

She gritted her teeth and headed back over to the
stove to needlessly stir the cider and try to get a handle on herself.

By the time she looked up again, Ryan was walking out the door, probably headed out to grab the bins.
Then he would bring them in, then leave. She could
decorate her home in peace and quiet and not think
about all of the old feelings that were stirred up inside her.

He appeared a few moments later with two bins,
one stacked on top of the other, dropped them just inside the doorway and headed back outside for the third.
When he came back, he surprised her by closing the
front door and pulling the lid off of the first box. "Do
you need help with any of this?"

"Well, I'll need help with the outdoor things, but it's
too dark to do that now."

"What about the stuff going inside? Need any help
with the garlands, or anything?"

"Why are you being nice to me?"

"Because I've been distinctly not nice. And I'm
sorry. Holidays have never been a big deal for me.

And I was insensitive. So let's just get back to the way things were."

She had an awful feeling that this had nothing to do with his grumpiness, and everything to do with the strange sexual tension that had wound itself around all of their actions for the past couple of days. He wanted to get rid of it. He probably figured he had two options: go back to his boat and hide from it, and do battle with the next time they saw each other, which was a bit more frequently right at the moment, or try to make things normal again.

Obviously he had taken option two.

Her disappointment was a bitter pill. It shouldn't be. She should be thrilled. She'd just been trying to talk herself into not acting like a sex-starved idiot.

But you are *a sex-starved idiot.*

Okay, she had a point with that one.

But no more. Her New Year's resolution would be to put an end to all of that. She would get a kiss, from someone she didn't know maybe. A handsome stranger. Too bad there were nothing but handsome acquaintances in Copper Ridge. Such were the hazards of life in a small town.

Maybe she would celebrate the holiday in Tolowa. Or in Portland. She could get a fancy dress, and drink fancy drinks, and in general be fancy. And make out with someone.

"You're frowning awfully deeply for somebody who's just stirring juice."

She blinked and returned her focus to Ryan, who

was standing there looking at her like he was afraid she was going to bite his hand.

"I was just thinking," she said.

"About Christmas decorations?"

"Coordinating events is my business, I take it very seriously. I have a whole idea in my head." That much was true, though thinking about party decorations didn't make her frown. It made her happy.

"Okay. So you say what you need, and I'll do it. I'm your slave for the rest of the evening."

She swallowed hard, biting the inside of her cheek. She did not need that mental image. "Thanks. Well, some of the Christmas lights and garlands are wound in pretty heavy bundles. If you could help get that sorted, that would be helpful."

"Okay. In return do I get some dinner?"

She treated him to a mock scowl. "I should've known you had ulterior motives."

"Me? My motives are pure. And hungry."

"I have some cheese and crackers. I'll get those out and then I can put some pot pies in the oven."

"I won't say no to that."

She readied the plate of cheese and crackers, then fiddled about in the kitchen so that she had a little bit of distance from Ryan. The pies went into the oven before she arranged some vegetables and dip on a platter. If there was one thing she always had a lot of, it was various appetizers and munchies. The perks of working parties. Especially weddings. The happy couple left, and after she saw to the work of preserving what was left of their wedding cake for them, she typically ended up with the other food from the reception, since it would go bad before they got back from their honeymoon.

Of course, it was potentially bad for one's diet to have a steady stream of crabcakes, puff pastries and bacon wrapped everything. She tried to eat a lot of salad to counterbalance it.

She walked out into the living room with the vegetables and the cheese and crackers, then sat both plates on the couch. Ryan had already unpacked all of the bins. The tree ready to decorate, garlands and strands of lights unrolled and laid out across the floor.

"Christmas command central," he said, gesturing to the display in front of her.

"It looks like a reindeer threw up in here."

"I know. It seems like the kind of thing you would like."

"I don't like it." She smiled when he frowned. "I love it."

"Holidays are a big thing to you, aren't they?"

She lifted a shoulder. "In my line of work? Of course the holidays are a big deal to me. Plus…" She hesitated. "We didn't celebrate anything when I was a kid. My parents just…didn't see the point. Getting to plan parties like this, to share in all of these special moments of people… It's kind of like making up for every party I didn't have."

Ryan frowned and her heart contracted, embarrassment over the fact that she just admitted that making her cheeks sting with heat. "Did you ever have a birthday party? Before Dan and Margie?"

His words brought the night of her eighteenth birthday to mind. Her parents had agreed to come and take her out, and then they hadn't showed. She'd been standing there on Dan and Margie's lawn in a dress, not wanting to go back in and admit that her parents had flaked out on her.

And then Ryan had come up the walkway, looking every inch like the only present she would ever really want. He'd touched her then. Hugged her. She'd wanted to stay in his arms forever, but it had only lasted a moment.

Just one more disappointment.

She bent down, picking up one of the green garlands. "Doesn't matter. I have big parties now. All the parties I want. I plan the best ones."

"Holly…"

She looked up and froze, immobilized by the look in his eyes. Sympathy. Sympathy from Ryan Masters. A man who would quite possibly shout *bah humbug* at a Dickensian street urchin. And he was standing there feeling sorry for her.

Just like he had back then. She wanted so much more than just his *sorry.*

"Don't give me that look," she said, frowning and gathering one of the garlands into her arms. "You're thirty-four, single, and live on a boat." She swept over to her mantel and climbed up onto the raised brick hearth of the fireplace to place the garland over the bare, polished wood.

"You want me to apologize for feeling something?"

"I don't need pity. My childhood sucked. A lot of

people had it worse. I was fortunate enough to end up with the best foster parents in the entire world. Foster parents who still care about me, who still treat me like one of their children. How many people can say that? And now I'm a grown-up who deals in fancy foods and decorations for a living." She snorted. "Pity yourself, boat man."

He ignored the dig. "We have quite a few things in common," he said.

"Do we?"

"Besides the obvious foster kid situation, neither of us wants sympathy. Neither of us has a whole lot of attachments, either. Don't act like you're so different from me."

"I don't think our situations are exactly comparable," she said, climbing down from the fireplace and making her way over to one of the bins that was filled with ornaments. "I'm a stable, happy business and home owner. You, on the other hand, are alarming."

His dark eyebrows shot up. "I'm alarming?"

"A little bit."

"How so?"

"You spend a lot of time alone. With fish."

"I'm a fisherman."

"So the fish don't even like you. Because you kill them."

He treated her to an unamused look. "I'm not exactly worried about the finer feelings of fish."

"You can't afford to be."

"No, I can't. But I worry a little bit about your finer feelings."

Her stomach clamped down hard, and she had the inescapable feeling of being caught at something. "Oh?"

"You're so concerned about my constant grumpiness. I worry a little bit about your constant cheerfulness."

"Oh. Ha! As if being a...a...jackass all the time is more emotionally healthy than being an optimist?"

"No, being honest is healthier. You're just pushing it all down."

"Why would you say that?" she asked. "I can't imagine that you want to sit down and talk about my feelings. We had a crappy start, we both did. But why wallow in it? And why talk about it."

"I didn't say we had to talk about our pasts. I'm just pointing out you shouldn't get real smug up on your high horse there. You're emotionally healthier than me? Bullshit. You're holding so much in that one of these days you're going to explode."

Holly wanted to punch him in the face. For being so right. For being part of the problem. But even while she was feeling so angry she was afraid she might explode, she was watching his mouth. Imagining, yet again, what it would be like to be kissed by him. What it would be like to have those large, masculine hands touching her. What he might have looked like carrying all those heavy boxes in without all the layers of clothes on. What he might look like without all those layers of clothes. Without any clothes at all.

It was sick. Sick and perverse. He was right. She was going to explode.

"Okay," she said, swallowing hard. "Maybe you're right. Maybe I am holding things in. Maybe I've been holding some things in for too long. Hiding them too well." She regretted saying that, the moment the words left her mouth, because if he asked for an explanation, she would have to give it. He knew her. He knew this wasn't about a serious relationship. Knew that it wasn't about work. It wouldn't take long for him to figure out what it was about.

"Is that so?"

She gritted her teeth. "Yes. I know what it's like to feel something that you can't act on. To feel something huge, something there isn't any room for, not inside of you, not in your life. And you push it down because it... It would just ruin things."

"That's not something that can last," he said, taking a step toward her.

"Obviously," she said, moving nearer to him.

His eyes were sharp, hot on hers. "What are you holding in?"

This was very bad. Very, very bad. He was talking about feelings, and she was making it about sex. She felt like some kind of gender role had been flipped. Unless he was talking about sex now too. But she doubted that. Because he seemed opposed to the idea of introducing a physical relationship into...their friendship? Their strange, pseudo-familial relationship? Whatever it was they had.

There were reasons she'd never made a move on him. Yesterday being an exception.

The Traverses meant everything to her. Everything.

If things went south with Ryan…it would complicate everything. Compromise things with the only family she'd ever known.

But you don't want a relationship. You aren't that stupid anymore. And he probably doesn't want one either.

She thought about her distant New Year's resolution. To get a kiss again. To move on. Suddenly, she had a very bad, very self-indulgent idea, that felt like it bordered on genius. Because it meant she could have everything she wanted without any repercussions.

A holiday fling. With the one man she'd always wanted. A man who didn't want a serious relationship. She would go into it with her eyes open. Go into it for the physical only, no unrealistic expectations.

She would ring out the old year with Ryan, and ring in the New Year ready to move on.

"I like One Direction." She had no idea why, but those were the words that escaped. Probably something in her brain trying to save her at the last minute. Giving her an out.

The left side of his mouth lifted. "Do you?"

She nodded. "Deep, dark secret."

"Somehow, I don't think that's what you were talking about."

"And now you're an expert on secrets?"

"Just on yours. Or, more to the point, I can tell when you're lying."

"You can?" She really hoped that wasn't true.

"Or, in this case holding something back. Maybe you do like One Direction. I'm not even sure who that is."

She swallowed hard, her hands shaking, her stomach tightening. "Okay, yes, I am holding something back. Bacon is only okay. It doesn't need to be put on everything. Wow, I feel better now."

He took another step toward her. "You be careful with heresy like that."

"Come on, bacon chocolate chip cookies. It's gone too far." Her face was hot, her heart beating so fast she could hardly breathe.

She didn't know what was happening. Sometime in the past few minutes things had changed. He had changed. He could see inside of her, she was sure of it. There was a heat in his eyes that spoke of only one thing. The kind of heat she'd never seen in Ryan's eyes before.

It scared her. And she wanted it.

"Holly, what are you hiding from me?" His dark eyes were intense, level with hers. The air felt thick between them again, like it had yesterday in the attic at his parents' house. "You're the one who brought it up, so I can only assume there's something you actually want to say. But don't want to say."

"That doesn't make sense."

"So, I'm wrong?"

"No," she said, her tone wooden. "But if I say it, I can't unsay it. And you might run away. And never speak to me again. And embarrass me in front of the Traverses."

He paused. "You don't really think I would do that."

"Okay, not anything except for the leaving. I do think you might leave."

He said nothing for a moment, swallowing hard, his Adam's apple bobbing up and down. "If I were you, I would clarify. And quickly. Because you're leaving me a lot of space to make assumptions, and you may not like the conclusions I'm drawing."

"Are they interesting conclusions? Because I might want to hear them before I admit to anything."

"Holly…"

She licked her lips, hesitating a moment before closing the distance between them and wrapping her arms around his neck. He didn't move away, not this time. And she acted before waiting for a response. Then she closed the distance between them, and pressed her lips against his.

CHAPTER SIX

SHE TILTED HER HEAD as their lips met, the shock of heat and arousal that rioted through her intense, unexpected. Yes, she'd known that touching him like this would be amazing, but she hadn't realized it would be so…all over.

Kissing—in her experience—involved her mouth and very little else. Possibly roaming hands, but she'd never let it continue on very long. So, not even usually that.

One brush of Ryan's lips against hers and she felt the impact everywhere.

It took her a moment to realize that he was frozen beneath her. She had to cut through the heat, the fire and flame, to get any sort of sense of his reaction. But now that she had it, she felt slightly horrified. She raised her head, breaking the contact between their mouths. "I'm sorry," she said.

The moment the words left her mouth, Ryan's hand shot up, his fingers digging deep into her hair, holding her tight. "Don't apologize for that," he said, his voice almost a growl, a look in his eyes she'd never seen there before.

"Well, you didn't… You didn't kiss me back."

"I need to make sure you know what you're asking for," he said.

"You need to make sure I know what I'm asking for?" she parroted.

"I don't want to kiss."

"Oh?"

"I haven't had sex for more than a year. And you're the last person that I should ever touch. What I need... It's physical. Only physical. And it's not just a kiss."

"Good. That's all I want too. I... I've wanted you for a long time. But you're part of...you're part of the most important people in my life. You don't lift out of the picture. And I don't want you to lift out. It always seemed like something way too important to screw up for a few orgasms."

"Being horny means never having to explain why."

She laughed, a short, distressed laugh. "Wow, that's profound."

Suddenly, his arms were around her, and he was pulling her up against his body, letting her feel the evidence of just how aroused he was. She was shaking now, from the inside out, all of the words in her head suddenly jumbled and tilted on end.

"I'm not even sure what I said. There's no blood left in my brain."

"Nothing changes," she said, while she could still figure out a way to form sentences.

"I'm good with that."

"I mean it. Nothing changes. After this we go back to how it was. I know that you don't want to marry me.

I certainly don't want to marry you and go live on your boat, and deal —"

Her words were cut off by the hot press of his mouth against hers, his tongue sliding against the seam of her lips, forcing them apart. She had no idea how they'd gone from never having touched romantically to making out in her living room in five seconds flat, but they most certainly had.

There were very few things that lived up to their promise. Very few things that possessed even a shade in reality of what they had promised in fantasy. Ryan's kiss was one of them. In reality, his kiss superseded the fantasy. Everything his lips had promised to be, they were more. His hands were strong and hot on her back, sliding down her waist and to her hips, gripping her tight as he angled his head and took the kiss deeper, harder.

She couldn't believe it was happening. Finally. It felt like the last piece had fallen into place. The last part of human contact she'd been missing. Margie and Dan had given her love like parents, love she'd been missing all of her life. Elizabeth had been like a sister. When it came to romantic relationships…there had been nothing. Not anything real.

Ryan was the one she'd wanted. His touch. His kiss. It was happening now. And it was everything.

He groaned, walked her back and pressed her against the wall, his body hard and hot in front of her, the surface of the wall unyielding and cool behind her. She clung to him, her fingers fisted into the fabric of his shirt as she learned the surface of his lips and became accustomed to the slick friction of his tongue against hers. As the ache between her thighs deepened, intensified, became a ravenous, hollow hunger that needed only him to be satisfied. She rocked against the hardened length of his arousal, his height making it impossible for her to feel him precisely where she needed him most.

"Ryan," she said, tearing her mouth away from his, "Ryan... I need..."

"I know."

And he seemed to, because he slid his hands down from her hips to grip her thighs, tugging them apart and forcing her to wrap her legs around his waist. Opening the center of her need to him, grinding the hard ridge of his cock against her as he held her firmly against the wall.

"Oh!" She'd officially gone past the point of all previous experience. But then, she felt as though she'd done that the moment their lips had touched. Kissing Ryan was an entirely separate activity from what she'd experienced in the past.

He slipped his hands away from her thighs, using the strength of his body and the wall to hold her in place. He cupped her face, tilted her chin up and deepened the kiss, tasting her, savoring her as though she were a delicacy, and he a starving man.

She knew what that was like. It had been more than a year since he'd had sex, but she was a twenty-seven-year-old virgin. She was pretty sure she won.

She was suddenly struck with a jolt, not of nerves, but of extreme excitement. She was finally touching him in the way that she wanted to. Finally kissing him like she'd always fantasized about. No, it wouldn't end well. But she had accepted that, and she was just free to enjoy now. Everything she could have. Everything he would give her.

Scratch that. Everything she could *take*. She wasn't passive in this. She *refused* to be. This was her fantasy come to life. She doubted it was the same for him. For him, this was just a drink of water after a long dry spell. For her, this was the oasis she had always desired after years in a desert. For her this was the fulfillment of a specific fantasy, not a generic need.

Those thoughts spurred her on, made her bold. Virginal nerves had no place in this. Later, later she could sit and have a postmortem. Be horrified by her behavior, maybe. But now, *now* she was just going to have what she wanted.

She moved her hands down his chest, feeling his muscles through the thin cotton of his shirt. Yes, they were as hard as she'd imagined. Everything about him was all that she'd dreamed of, everything and more. She moved her hands down lower still, pressing her fingertips up beneath the edge of his T-shirt, her hands making contact with his hot skin. He had just the right amount of hair on his well-defined stomach, enough to remind her that he was a man, and she was a woman. She moved her hands higher, to the hard wall of his chest muscles. Oh yes, he was very much a man.

"Off." That was the best she could do. The most she could say.

He said nothing in return, releasing his hold on her

to take a moment to take off his jacket, and wrenched his shirt over his head. She whimpered, surveying the perfectly defined lines on his chest and stomach, the V that disappeared down beneath the waistband of his jeans, an arrow pointing to the part of him she most craved.

She didn't know who she was right now, this wild, hungry creature who craved Ryan at the expense of everything else. Damn her pride, damn common sense.

Okay, that was a lie. She knew exactly who she was. She recognized this woman. This was the woman she was in her fantasies. The woman she was late at night when she allowed dark, heady thoughts of him to enter her mind. This was the woman she'd always wanted to be.

That thought made a smile curve her lips.

"You like what you see?" he asked.

"That's an understatement."

"I think this calls for a trade," he said. "Remember, it's been more than a year for me."

"It's been quite a while for me too," she said, ignoring the fact that the statement fudged the truth a bit. "So I'm going to need some time to enjoy the scenery myself."

"Enjoy it topless."

He didn't give her a chance to respond. He reached forward, tugging her sweater up over her head, taking her beanie off with it, leaving her standing there in her plain, white bra. She wished suddenly that she had underwear more befitting of the vamp she felt like she was in this moment.

This was definitely virgin underwear. But she would try not to let that deter her.

The underwear wasn't going to stay on for long anyway.

A crease formed between his brows, his lips turning down. That couldn't be good.

"No woman wants a man to frown at her breasts, Ryan."

"That's not what I'm frowning at," he said.

"That's only slightly reassuring."

"I'm pretty sure every member of the Travers family will kill me if they ever find out about this."

"I'm not going to give Elizabeth the gory details." That seemed strange in a way. Elizabeth had most certainly told Holly when she'd lost her virginity. But Holly was an expert at deflecting questions about her love life, about crushes she might or might not have. Because she didn't want to admit to her friend that she'd never actually had sex. She'd always managed to keep her feelings for Ryan under wraps. She'd also managed to never exactly admit she'd never had sex before. This would just be an extension of all of those secrets, all of those little lies.

Again, worth it.

"You've always been…"

"If you say *like a sister to* me I'm putting my sweater back on."

"No. Not that. But, a lot younger."

"Four years. That isn't so much."

"It was when we met."

"That has nothing to do with now. Nothing to do

with where we're at. We are both adults. And we are both almost naked. So, really we should just get all the way naked and get on with things."

He chuckled, reaching out and brushing her hair out of her eyes. "You definitely seem to know what you want."

"Definitely." She looked down at the very clear bulge pushing against the denim. "Pants off."

There. Regardless of the sexual status of her underwear, she was doing a pretty good job of holding her ground.

What she'd said earlier about her job making up for all of those missed parties? It had been a lie. This, right now, was every atonement for every missed party. For everything she'd ever wanted that she hadn't gotten. For every night she'd gone to bed hungry, every day she'd gone without a hug, without so much as a sideways glance.

She would take this as atonement for all of that.

Which was potentially a lot of pressure to put on Ryan's body, but if he didn't know, he wouldn't mind.

He put his hands on his belt buckle, worked the end slowly through, undid the snap, then the zipper. She couldn't look away, didn't want to. She was pretty sure Santa and all his reindeer could stampede through the living room and her eyes would still be glued to what Ryan would reveal next.

He pushed the pants down his lean hips, taking his underwear with them, leaving himself completely naked in front of her.

She sucked in a sharp breath and nearly choked on

it. She'd never seen a naked man in person. Naked, and erect. Very, very erect.

She swallowed, trying to force her heart back down into its proper place. She looked back up at his face, and saw him studying her with an odd expression.

"You're staring," he said.

"Because I like what I see."

"Okay, I wasn't sure. You looked slightly terrified. I wasn't sure if maybe something had mutated from all the disuse."

"A *year*? Seriously, don't be dramatic. Nothing mutated. As near as I can tell." She bit her lip. "Of course, I might need to examine everything a little bit closer."

"I think we can stop bantering now," he growled, pressing her back up against the wall again, kissing her deep and hard. She wrapped her arms around his neck, losing herself in this, in him, in the rough feeling of his hands on her body, of the heat of him pressed so tightly against her.

Somehow, he managed to get her jeans and panties off, never breaking their kiss. He cupped her cheek, tracing a line along her jaw, down her neck, pausing for a moment, cupping her breast and squeezing it tight. Brushing his thumb over her nipple, he pinched it lightly between his thumb and forefinger before allowing his fingertips to glide over her stomach, down between her thighs. He stroked her there, where she was wet and ready for him. She gasped, letting her head fall back, giving herself over completely to the sensation.

"I don't know if I can take this as slow as I should."

That was fine with her. She'd wanted him for the last fourteen years. In her opinion, slow was overrated.

"Kiss me," she said, barely recognizing the rough, husky voice as her own.

He obeyed, his fingers moving over her clit as he slid his tongue over hers. Then he cursed, pulling away from her sharply. "I don't have a condom."

"Oh no," she said. "I don't have—" Suddenly, she remembered the basket sitting in her hall closet. The basket decorated with fluorescent pink and purple ribbon, filled with favors from the bachelorette party she'd helped plan a couple of months ago. "Hold that thought."

She extricated herself from his hold to scamper down the hallway, completely naked, well aware that his eyes were on her backside. And that it probably jiggled a little bit with every step she took.

Darn bacon-wrapped everything. Bacon really was overrated.

She opened up the closet, and rummaged past a bin filled with ribbon, a few rolls of wrapping paper, until she found the basket. Inside of it were little party favors. And within those party favors, she knew she would find the required protection.

She pulled out one of the pink, iridescent bags, her face heating as she saw the phallic shaped whistle attached to the outside.

"What is *that*?"

She looked up, and over at Ryan. She'd been hoping to pull the condom out of the bag without him having to see it, or any of its other contents.

"A party favor. From a party I coordinated." She pressed her lips to the end of the penis whistle, and blew. "Festive."

He laughed, and at the same time, his cock twitched. "I'm not sure how you can make me laugh, and make me want to ravish you at the same time."

She blinked. "A hidden talent?"

"Very hidden. But then, in fairness, I wasn't looking for this kind of thing with you."

She stood there, holding the bag filled with obscene party favors, completely naked, not sure if she wanted to hear what he had to say next. It was so ridiculous, she kind of wanted to laugh too. Unless he was going to say something that hurt her feelings. "I'm not sure how to take that."

"You had to be off-limits. You were too young. Then you were just a lot sweeter than me. You were always beautiful, Holly. And even though you give me a hard time about it, you let me be grumpy. You listen. And you never tell me to just smile through anything. You're damn pretty, but that means a lot more than pretty ever could."

Her heart felt swollen, and that was bad, considering she was trying really hard to keep her heart uninvolved. She didn't say anything; instead she opened the bag, grimacing when she encountered an anatomically correct action figure, a tube of red lipstick also shaped like the male member, what looked like a pair of hard candy panties, folded up in a plastic bag, and finally, on the bottom, a fun size packet of condoms.

She fished out the protection, dropping the rest onto the floor. "See?"

He took the little packet from her hand and tore it open to reveal four individual condoms inside. "They're purple," he said.

She released a heavy breath. "Of course they are."

"I'm fine if you're fine. I don't really care what color it is. It's not what's on the outside that counts, after all. It's being inside you."

"We don't really have an alternative. Except not doing this. And that isn't acceptable."

He smiled, tearing one of the packets open and discarding the rest. And she forgot how ridiculous the situation was. Forgot that they had a living room cluttered with Christmas decorations, forgot that the condom he was currently rolling onto his thick length was purple, and had come out of the bag with a penis whistle.

Nothing else mattered but this moment. But this man and how much she wanted him.

He closed the distance between them, kissing her deeply, devouring her. She wrapped her arms around his neck and pulled, bringing them both down to the floor with him on top of her between her thighs. The floor was cold, and she didn't care. It was hard, but it didn't matter. All that mattered was this, with him. She didn't have time to try and make it to the bed. She didn't have time for anything but this. And she needed this. Needed it more than she needed her next breath.

"Please, Ryan."

He shifted, the blunt head of his arousal pressing against the entrance to her body. And that was when the nerves hit. She gritted her teeth, screwing her eyes shut tight as he thrust deep inside her. The pain was sharp but brief, fading quickly into something that felt foreign, and not entirely pleasant.

She clung to him, holding onto his shoulders, getting used to the sensation of him being inside her.

"Are you okay?" he asked, his voice strained. If he suspected that she'd never done this before at all, she couldn't tell.

"Yes," she said, not entirely certain she wasn't lying.

She felt full, emotional. Her heart raw and tender. And that was more intense than any pain or pleasure.

Then he moved, sliding his hands down the line of her spine and cupping her butt, lifting her hips to push himself more deeply inside. When he did that, it brought his pelvis up against the bundle of nerves at the apex of her thighs, sent a lightning bolt of pleasure through her so sharp, so focused that it stole every thought, channeled all of the sensation that was building up in her chest to pop and crackle through her veins, absorbing her entire being in the pleasure he created with his movements.

He established a steady rhythm, pumping into her hard and perfect, driving them both closer to the peak she knew was up there somewhere, even if she'd never reached it with anyone else before.

He lowered his head, kissing her neck, his breath coming in harsh gasps as his movements quickened. He tightened his grip on her hips, drawing her up against him each time he thrust home. "Come on, baby," he said, his words broken, jagged like glass. "I can't last."

It was that admission, that hard, rough admission, that broke her. That pushed her to a height she'd never known existed and sent her over the edge. Her heart was beating so hard she thought it would burst through her chest, her internal muscles tightening around him as pleasure exploded in her midsection, flooding through her, overtaking her completely.

She was floating on a white, endless snowdrift. And when it set her back down it was on the hard floor of her hallway. But it was still perfect, because she was with Ryan. And as long as she didn't think about the future, that was enough.

CHAPTER SEVEN

HE'D ALWAYS KNOWN that kissing Holly Fulton wouldn't lead anywhere good. He'd been right. He should have listened to that instinct.

Granted, his instinct had not informed him that kissing her would end with him wearing a purple condom and taking her virginity, but he'd known it would be a bad idea.

His knees hurt. He realized that was because he was still braced on the hard floor of her hallway, still inside her and reeling from the explosive climax they'd just shared. As a reintroduction into sex went, it had been mind-blowing. As far as decent human behavior went, it was a new low.

He moved away from her, rubbing his hands over his face. "Just a second," he said, pushing into a standing position and walking down the hall, calling on all of his self-control to keep from looking back at her naked body as he made his way to the bathroom. He took care of the condom, then went to stand in front of the sink, running water over his face as he looked at his reflection in the mirror. Bad idea. He was singularly unimpressed with the guy he saw standing there, looking a lot more satisfied and smug than he had a right to.

Had she really been a virgin? Or was he just hallucinating? She'd said it had been a while. Maybe that's
why it felt different. Maybe it was him. Maybe he was
imagining all of it. Maybe he was hallucinating all of
this and he'd never kissed her back when she'd leaned
in. Had never touched her or told her to take her clothes
off.

Maybe he was still standing there waiting to make
a move. Damage not done.

He looked back up and saw his all-too-real reflection. If he'd felt any humor around the situation, he
might have laughed. Since they had just been discussing emotional honesty and all manner of other bullshit.
And here he was taking solace in very clear denial.

He turned and started to walk out of the room, then
stopped. He was still naked, and even though they'd
just had sex, it felt wrong. She was still Holly. And
he was still Ryan. He wasn't sure walking out of the
bathroom wearing nothing but his skin was entirely
appropriate.

He reached out and grabbed hold of the fluffy pink
towel that was hanging on the towel rack. Purple condom, pink towel. Clearly, the universe was intent on
him paying his penance for the pleasure he just received. He wrapped it tightly around his waist, then
walked out into the hall, where Holly was standing,
still naked. She was looking at him with large, dewy
eyes. Shame crawled over his skin like an army of ants.

He was wrong. Maybe he'd always been wrong. It
was easy to forget when he was alone. Easy to forget when he was out on the ocean, down in his boat.

When he had the reassurance of Margie and Dan that he wasn't broken in any way.

But sometimes the feeling was impossible to shake. That there were certain things that were inescapable. That the darkness, the destruction, was all in him.

Now was one of those times.

"Holly," he said, his voice rough, even to his own ears. "Why the hell didn't you tell me you were a virgin?"

That was not what he'd intended to lead with. Too late to turn back now. Variations on the theme.

Holly looked like she wanted to fold in on herself, standing there completely naked and exposed. In that moment, he hated himself. "Well, we've never talked about those sorts of things," she said.

He sighed heavily, looking past her and at a spot on the wall. "Evidence that we really shouldn't have done what we did."

"I knew what I wanted."

"Did you? Did I hurt you? Do you need…I'm sorry."

"I'm fine. Don't apologize for having sex with me."

She sucked in a sharp breath through her nose, and released it slowly before turning on the ball of her foot and stalking into the living room. He was only human, so he watched the gentle sway of her hips, the slight bounce in her ass. He liked it. Liked it a lot. The softness of her skin, of her figure. The two little dimples low on her back, the full flare of her hips… Yeah, no question it was nice.

Like it a little less, you perv.

He rubbed his hands over his eyes and followed her

back into the living room. It looked like a war had been waged in there with Christmas decorations, everything left strewn across the floor like very cheerful debris. And amongst the decorations were their clothes.

Holly threw his at him, and he caught them, applying all of the focus he could muster to getting dressed, and not watching her. He didn't have the right to look at her.

He was buckling his belt when Holly spoke again. "I kind of liked the towel."

"Pink isn't really my color," he said.

"I disagree. I think we discovered a whole portion of the color wheel that suits you more than you might have thought."

"Holly," he said, his tone serious.

"Is this where you speak gravely of your regret over stealing my virtue? Or are you going to twirl your mustache and cackle over your conquest?"

He shoved his hands in his pockets. "You deserve better than that. Better than the floor in the hallway. A hell of a lot better than me."

"From where I'm standing it was pretty good." Color flooded her face. "What I mean is that I fantasized about that for a long time. You. Us. I needed that."

He felt like he'd been punched in the chest. He didn't deserve to be the object of Holly Fulton's fantasies, that much was true.

But now here he was, standing in front of the one woman he should have never touched, the woman he should have left a vague, misty fantasy. There was nothing misty or vague about it now. It was all harsh light, hard floors and naked skin.

"So that's what this is? Fantasy fulfillment? I shouldn't be *that* important to you," he said. "And why was there no one else? That's what concerns me."

She laughed. Not something small or polite. But she honestly doubled over laughing, as though he'd just said the funniest thing in creation. "Are you implying that… I was waiting for you?"

Heat stung his cheeks as he realized that was exactly what he'd been thinking. What he'd been worried about. "No."

"Yes, you were. That's what you were worried about. Ryan, you're very handsome. Don't get me wrong. But I had a crush on you when I was like…sixteen. It's not like I've been sitting around pining for you."

"Then why? I feel like I have a right to know since I'm the lucky man who broke the drought."

She bit her lip and looked down, her cheeks turning a deeper shade of red. "I just… Relationships are hard for me. And there's the Travers connection. It's complicated. It's the same with friendships. I have Elizabeth. Through her I have a couple of other friends, but none of them mean as much to me as she does. I've known you for a long time. I trust you. Not for like, love, or marriage or anything like that, but I know you. I know that you won't just look at me with blank eyes one day like you don't even know who I am."

"Holly…your parents… Whatever happened with them, they weren't normal. It has nothing to do with you."

"I know," she said, her voice a whisper, "I know. But it doesn't take away the anxiety. The fear of caring for someone who will never care for you in the same way. I loved them. Part of me still does even though I haven't seen them in years. For a long time I wished it would change. So much. My mom had me hoping I would fix her marriage. And I didn't. Instead, I made everything harder. So they just...stopped taking care of me." She blinked rapidly. "I couldn't bear loving a man and having him look at me one day and say the same things. I'll... I'll get over that. I'm getting over that. But it's held me back for a long time. Knowing you, trusting you, makes it safe."

His heart felt warm, thundering heavily in his chest. There was something both deeply gratifying and slightly unsettling about her words. He liked the idea of being safe for her. But part of him rejected it. Because if a man was going to be someone's fantasy, finding out he was a fantasy of *safety* wasn't the biggest ego boost."Before I go saying anything else, you have to tell me something."

"Okay, what?"

"Are we going to do this again?"

Heat flooded his body, his cock getting hard just from the thought of it. "It wouldn't be the best idea."

"Who cares if it's the best idea?" She planted her hands on her hips. "Are we going to do it again, or not?"

"You were a virgin."

"Can we stop fixating on that? It's not that big of a deal."

His chest felt tight. "It's a big deal to me."

"Fine. It's a big deal to *you*. But it's too late to do anything about it, the damage is done. Here's my proposition: we finish out the year with a bang, no pun intended, and once the new year rolls in, we stop. Clean slate, no damage done."

"There's never a guarantee of no damage." He hated himself for saying it, hated himself for trying to make her change her mind. Because he wanted this. Needed this. She was going through some stuff, but he'd been through his share too. He could damn well use a little bit of physical relief.

But this was Holly. She was more than physical relief. She was important to him. That meant he had to be honest.

"Okay," she said. "But I want you." She met his eyes, the statement simple, direct, and more temptation than he could handle. He'd tried to be the good guy years ago. Hadn't followed his instinct to kiss her on her eighteenth birthday as he'd known he would only add to her pain. Except now he apparently had less restraint than he'd had almost a decade ago.

He took a step toward her, reaching out and taking hold of her chin between his thumb and forefinger. Before he could think better of it, he leaned in, pressing his lips to hers. Kissing her like he'd wanted to do all those years ago. Soft at first, gentle, a slow, measured tasting that gave respect to her inexperience. Then deeper still, a tribute to his hunger.

"I take it that means we'll do it again?" she asked when they parted.

"Definitely," he said. His good intentions had lost the war. "But first, we'd better finish decorating the living room."

He didn't actually want to decorate. He wanted to take her straight to bed. Wanted to go ahead and revel in this very bad, selfish decision he'd made. Now that he was committed to it, he was all in. But she'd been a virgin, and the last thing he wanted to do was cause her any pain. Any more than he already had.

Just then, the oven timer went off. "Oh yeah," Holly said, sounding dazed. "I forgot about the pot pie."

"Right about now pot pie seems anticlimactic."

She laughed. "Definitely not the sexiest of foods. Hearty, certainly comforting, but not sexy."

"Do you have champagne and chocolate-covered strawberries?"

She lifted a shoulder. "Fresh out."

"I guess we'll have to make do with the pot pie and cider."

She smiled at him, this kind of glowing, dreamy smile he'd never gotten from anyone before. A smile he was certain he didn't deserve. "You know, I can't think of anything better."

CHAPTER EIGHT

HOLLY HAD NEVER had so much fun planning a party in her life. And planning parties was her passion. She loved weddings and the fact that they were a celebration of two people coming together for the rest of their lives. She loved holiday parties, full of family and friends gathering to enjoy not just the season, but each other's company. Bachelorette parties that were all about female friendship, and the celebration of new stages of life.

But putting together the Christmas party to honor Dan and Margie was definitely the best. Of course, her enjoyment could have had more to do with the fact that she was burning up the sheets with Ryan every night.

If she'd known how good sex could be, she probably wouldn't have waited.

Okay, that wasn't true. Because Ryan was what made it so good. And if it wasn't with Ryan, she doubted it would be even half as amazing.

Damn, she had it bad.

He'd made it a priority to get some standard protection at the grocery store the day after their first time, and he'd been sleeping at her house instead of on his boat. It probably shouldn't flatter her since a full-size bed was going to be better than one of those bunks any day. But she chose to let it flatter her.

She also chose not to worry about the future. About the fact that in a week all of this was supposed to be over. That all she would have to look forward to after Christmas were nights in an empty bed, nights without Ryan.

It wouldn't work. Not for either of them. She couldn't need him. She couldn't afford to need him. But that was a problem for later. Now, this week, they were together.

They were meeting up today after he got through with work, and she was planning on cooking him dinner. She didn't have to cook all that often thanks to the steady stream of leftovers she took in from the various events, but she wanted to make something for him. Something special, which was why she was currently at the mercantile in Old Town that sold specialty foods.

She already had a few nice, flavored olive oils in her basket, some pasta that had been imported from Italy, and a tub of fresh, organic pesto made by some local women. She paused in front of a display that had a few types of bread all fresh from the oven.

A flash of movement outside caught her eye and she looked up in time to see a woman with bright red hair walking down the sidewalk. Her heart jolted.

The woman was definitely familiar. More than familiar. Before she'd made a conscious decision to do so, Holly found herself setting her shopping basket down on the red tile floor and walking out the door of the store, letting the door shut behind her. The woman was already passing by the cranberry-colored knickknack shop the next building up. Holly should let her go, she knew that. But she couldn't.

God help her, she couldn't.

"Mom?"

The woman paused for a second, and turned partly, her face white as snow, her eyes hollow. There was nothing there to read, no flash of recognition, no happiness. Holly found herself staring, drinking in her mother's face with a surprising amount of hunger. She hadn't known how much she'd missed her. Hadn't realized she'd missed her at all. Not after all the pain she'd put her through.

Not after the horrible parting words. Not after her mother had called Child Services herself to say she couldn't take care of her daughter anymore. Because Holly had betrayed her. Old guilt, crippling sadness and longing filled her chest until she could barely breathe. She wanted to yell. She wanted to apologize. She couldn't do any of it, so she just stood and stared.

The other woman looked older, thinner. Holly looked at her left hand and saw that she didn't have a ring on. Were her parents even married anymore? They'd moved years ago, and she hadn't heard from them since. Running into her mother now was unexpected. Painful. And she should turn away. She shouldn't have come out here. She shouldn't be standing here like an idiot.

She shouldn't say anything. But she couldn't hold it in.

"Mom," Holly said again, taking a step toward her.

The other woman shook her head and turned away,

walking briskly across the street as though Holly hadn't spoken at all. Holly could do nothing but stand there, staring after her, unable to believe what had just happened. She had seen her mother. Her mother hadn't spoken to her at all.

All she could do was stand there, torn to shreds on the main street of Copper Ridge.

She felt like she'd been hollowed out, angry, stinging tears forming at the backs of her eyes, an intense pain resting at the base of her throat.

"Holly?"

She turned around and saw Ryan standing there, his hands clenched into fists at his sides.

"I…"

He took a step toward her, closed the distance between them and pulled her into his arms, his hold so tight she could barely breathe. And she was grateful for it. For the comfort she found there, for his strength. For the fierceness in his hold, because there was nothing tentative about it. Nothing temporary. It was real, sure, firm, overtaking everything. He held her so hard it almost hurt, canceling out the ache that had wound its way through her chest, wrapped itself around her heart.

"She's wrong," he said, finally speaking after holding her in absolute silence for a while. "Not you. Never you."

"How?" It was the only word she could speak, the only word she could think of.

If her parents didn't love her, surely something was wrong with her. If she'd managed to make her mother send her away then surely she must be a monster. She realized then the real reason she'd never gone after a relationship before, with Ryan *or* anyone else. She didn't know who she could trust. Elizabeth was a wonderful friend, and had been for years. Dan and Margie cared for her; they had from the moment she'd been brought into their home. But…new people. How could she ever trust them? If her own parents could just stop caring one day…anyone else could, too.

Ryan made her feel like that wasn't true. Like it couldn't be true. She knew he didn't love her, not like that. But he held her like she mattered. It felt true. It felt right. And so did the words he was speaking. Reassuring, fierce words that spoke of his protectiveness.

She could feel how much she mattered in each and every one of them. And if she mattered that much to him, a man who didn't even want a relationship with her beyond next week, then surely she should matter to her parents. Surely she deserved more than a blank look on a public street.

She wrapped her arms around his waist and rested her head against his chest. "I was going to make you dinner," she said. "I left the basket in the store."

"I have a better idea. I'm going to take you out."

CHAPTER NINE

AFTER THE ENCOUNTER with Holly's mother on the street last night Ryan had taken her to the nicest restaurant in town. He hadn't cared who'd seen them, if people would draw conclusions. He sort of hoped her parents would see them. Anyone who had ever ignored her. Hoped that they would see her out with someone who knew she was worthy of attention. Most people would look at them and assume nothing much. After all, they'd been surrogate family for years. But there might be a few who wondered if things were romantic between them.

That didn't bother him, either.

He'd just wanted people to see her being treated as she should be. With respect. Reverence.

Everyone who'd ever wronged her should know how wrong they were just by looking at her. Maybe they did. Maybe that was why her mother couldn't bear to speak a word to her. He didn't know.

All he knew was that when he'd witnessed that, the pain he felt had been a clear echo of her own. And not just pain. Anger. Rage. He'd always known they were terrible, that they'd neglected her, but he'd had no idea just how bad it was.

He wanted to do more, wanted to give her something, but he didn't know what. He wasn't exactly known for making situations better.

But after a stroke of genius, he'd come back to shore early today to get some supplies. He'd let himself into Holly's house before she'd gotten home. All of the Christmas decorations were up, the outside of the house lined with white lights, the inside decked out from head to toe. He'd noticed that she liked to keep a pan of cinnamon sticks boiling on the stove with a few drops of vanilla to make the air smell good. Something Margie always did.

He put some in for her, so that everything would smell nice when she arrived. And then he'd taken out the bag of decorations he'd bought at the store on his way home. He knew that she probably had birthday party decorations. More than any other person, he imagined. But that wasn't good enough. He'd wanted to choose them.

The memory of her eighteenth birthday, of how desolate she'd been, was stronger in his mind today than ever. He'd been thinking about that night a lot lately, because it was the moment when he'd almost kissed her. But now he was thinking about it because it was the first moment he'd really understood just how badly her parents failed her every day. That realization had been reinforced tenfold yesterday.

And today he wanted to do something to fix it. To begin to restore those years that had been eaten away by neglect.

He pulled the *happy birthday* banner he'd selected

out of the bag. Pink and purple, for obvious reasons. He was sure that it was kind of cheesy, but he'd chosen it. For her. He set to work, blowing up balloons and hanging up the banner over one of the Christmas garlands. It was a mashup of holidays. Which gave him another idea. He walked to the hallway and opened the closet, looking at the vast array of labeled bins filled with decorations.

He took a sampling of each. Valentine's, bachelorette, St. Patrick's Day, Hanukkah, and put them in with all of the other decorations. It would be every party that she'd missed.

He stood back, surveying his work. It was...weird. The colors most definitely clashed. But he kind of liked it.

He realized suddenly that he was standing there smiling at the most cheerful sight he could have ever conceived of. It was a little bit out of character. But sometimes Holly made him feel out of character. Or like a new character entirely. It wasn't just the sex, though that was great. It was something else. Something he couldn't quite put his finger on. Something he kind of didn't want to.

He walked back to a side table and took the candles out of the bag to place them onto the cake he'd bought, the one that said her name. That was when the front door opened to reveal a very shocked-looking Holly, who was taking in her surroundings with wide eyes and an open mouth.

"What is this?" she asked.

His throat felt tight suddenly, and he couldn't rightly

say why. "Happy birthday. And Hanukkah, and St. Patrick's Day, and Valentine's Day. Christmas too."

"It's not..." She looked all around. "It's not my birthday."

"I know. But I think you deserve some extras." He nodded. "I know you do. You remember... Your eighteenth birthday."

She smiled weakly. "I try not to."

"I don't blame you." He walked from the kitchen over to where she was standing. "I almost kissed you then." He took hold of her hand, drawing her close to him. "You were so pretty. And sad. But only eighteen. So I didn't. I've always remembered. I should have done this then. I should have gotten you a cake then, and made you a party. Made sure you had something. I should have told you then how wrong your parents were." He let go of her hand, bracketing her cheeks with his hands, looking deeply into her eyes. "And I should have kissed you."

He did so then, kissed her with everything he had, kissed her until he tasted salt on her lips. He opened his eyes, saw tears streaming down her cheeks. "Are you okay? Did I hurt you?"

She shook her head. "No. I just... I can't believe you did this for me."

"I know you said you get to throw all the parties you never had, but I couldn't help but think it wasn't fair no one was throwing parties for you for so many years before Margie and Dan." He swallowed hard, trying to lessen the knot of emotion that was building in his chest. He wasn't quite sure what was wrong with him. Why he was feeling such deep regret. He'd had a similar upbringing, and this stuff—parties and other moments of fun—wasn't something that had ever mattered to him. But they mattered to her. And that made him feel it. There was something about her that made him feel connected to things in a way he wasn't usually. Not just his own feelings, but hers.

He'd never wanted to do anything like this for another person. Had never wanted to fix things for someone. To matter to them.

He wanted to matter to her. To fix every broken thing inside of her. But how could he? How could he when everything in him was still fucked all to hell?

Her hands went to his chest, slid down his stomach, pushing beneath the fabric, her fingertips hot on his bare skin. And he figured he would worry about feelings later.

"Hey, I didn't light your candles yet," he said.

She stretched up on her toes and kissed him. "This is what I want for my birthday. That kiss you should have given me then."

"If you keep touching me like that it's going to be more than a kiss."

"I hope so," she said, pushing her hands up farther beneath his shirt, gathering up the material. He lifted his arms and she pushed the whole thing up over his head. He cast it onto the floor, wrapping his arms around her, holding her tight, sliding his tongue against hers.

"What about your cake?" he asked.

"You're better than cake," she said, her voice husky,

her lips soft against his. "You're better than any party. Even half a dozen parties in one."

"That's pretty high praise." He angled his head, grazing his teeth across her jaw, gratified when she let out a sharp, needy sound.

"For me? There isn't any higher praise."

"I know."

As he held her in his arms, as she ran her fingertips over his body after she divested him of his clothes, he couldn't fathom how such a warm, beautiful woman had come from a place of such coldness and neglect. She was too good for them.

Too good for *him*, a boy who'd been raised under the iron fists of a man who didn't believe in kindness. He didn't think he would ever hurt her, not like his father had done to him and his mother. But he didn't know how to love either. Not in the right way.

Holly had come out of such a terrible place still smiling. So much brighter, so much more genuine than him. He could never bear it if he stole her smile.

But tonight? Tonight he made her happy. They only had another week, so it didn't matter what happened after this. Now he could make her smile. For now, he made her happy. And so he would do it. The best he could, as long as he could.

He removed her clothes slowly, unwrapping her like she was the most precious gift. He sucked in a sharp breath, examining her every curve, her soft pale skin, her full, round breasts, the perfect pink nipples at the center. Her softly rounded stomach, and perfectly curved hips.

He would never get tired of looking at her. Of allowing himself this fantasy fulfillment of a dream he barely ever indulged in.

He'd always known she was too sweet for him. Had always known that his hands—rough, workman's hands—weren't fit to touch her. And yet here he was, skimming his hands over her every curve, over every inch of her beauty, claiming it like it was his, like he had a right, when he knew damn well he didn't.

He kissed her lips, pink and flushed, then down her neck, and down farther still, drawing one tightened bud into his mouth and sucking hard, relishing the sound of pure pleasure that escaped her as he did. He moved lower, forging a trail of kisses down to her belly button, then lower, gripping her hips hard, his fingertips digging into her skin.

"Ryan?"

He adored the question in her voice, the betrayal of her inexperience, of the fact that no other man had ever done what he was about to do. He shouldn't relish it, should feel nothing but guilt, and yet, he couldn't find any. Because there was nothing in him but pure fire, pure pleasure, and pure selfishness. He wanted to taste her, to know he was the only man to have ever done this.

More evidence that he was a bastard. But he didn't care.

He held onto her tightly, tugging her in toward his mouth, tasting her deeply, sliding his tongue through her damp folds until she cried out.

He wrapped one arm around her lower back, still

holding her hips with the other, pulling her down to the floor with him and laying her back gently before hooking her legs over his shoulders and burying his face between her thighs.

She was beautiful, she was perfect, the embodiment of every male fantasy. He was not worthy of the gift, but he would take it. He would take it hard, he would take it fast, and he would take it as many times as he could get it.

This was a party for her, but it was one for him, too. These whole two weeks were a party just for him. Until he had to go back to his life on the boat. Alone. Because he couldn't quite figure out how to make a life with other people work.

In that moment his heart ached for the things he couldn't have. For the things he couldn't be. For the first time in years he wished it could be different. That he could be everything a woman like her deserved. It was easy to be fine alone, living on a boat when there was no one around he wanted to share his life with. Share himself with.

If he ever did, it would be her.

That couldn't be. But they could have now.

He reached over and found his jeans, procuring a condom and rolling it on quickly. He braced himself over her, kissing her deeply before thrusting inside her body.

He was lost then, in her, in this. He could stay here forever, frozen in time, at every party for every holiday he could think of and find decorations for, celebrating the fact that right now he had her.

He lowered his head, kissing her neck as fire wound itself around his veins, stealing his control, pushing his heart into overdrive. His movements became erratic, uncontrolled. He could do nothing but simply give himself over to the experience. Pray that she found her release, because he was at the mercy of his.

She gripped his shoulders tight, her fingernails digging into his skin as she let her head fall back, the sound of her release perfection to his ears, her internal muscles clenching tight around his cock as she gave herself over to her pleasure. That was his permission to surrender to his own. Release roared through him like a beast, but it wasn't a relief. It tore at him, tormented him, dragged him down into hell and back, showing him a taste of bliss and eternity that could never fully be his before wrenching him back into the real world, spent and exhausted, and so far from satisfied. He would never get enough of this. Never get enough of her. But he would have to. Because at the end of next week, all of this would be over. And there wasn't a damn thing he could do about it.

MORE OFTEN THAN NOT they seemed to end up on the floor somewhere in her house, only making it to the bed later.

She smiled and snuggled deeper into his hold, trailing her fingertips over his chest. She enjoyed the physical pleasure she found with him, but it was more than that. It was these moments of intimacy. Of quiet. Where they held each other and said nothing. Where she felt overwhelmed by the comfort and familiarity of being in his arms, and the exhilarating, electrifying newness of it. Of knowing him this way. Of deepening an existing bond that was stronger than she imagined.

"The day I came to live with Margie and Dan was the day I got out of the hospital," he said, his voice rough.

Holly curled her fingers into fists, tightening her hold on him. "Ryan, you don't have to…"

"I'd been taken out of my parents' house before. But they would do the classes, and I would go back. But not after this one. The one favor my mother ever did for me was calling an ambulance after my dad beat me that last time. I'm sure once he got out of jail it didn't work out so well for her."

"Ryan…"

"I'm not telling you this so you'll feel bad. I just want you to know. I want you to understand, I guess." He cleared his throat. "I don't usually care if anyone understands. But I want you to."

"I do. I think I always have." She wouldn't tell him she knew he was only grumpy in order to keep people away so he didn't get hurt. Because he would deny that. But she did. "I know you," she said instead.

"Make me understand you, Holly Fulton. Tell me your story."

They'd known each other for a long time. Lived in the same house, spent holidays together. But they didn't talk about their lives before Margie and Dan. Not to anyone.

She wanted to talk to him.

Holly swallowed hard, her throat tightening up. As

though her body were trying to keep her from saying out loud things she had kept inside for the past fourteen years. "Child Protective Services had been out to my house before too," she said, each word coming slowly. "I'd been removed temporarily, and brought back. Like you said, parental classes, and things like that. But my parents never hit me. The school would call because I was stealing food in the cafeteria because I was hungry. They'd realized I wasn't eating at home again. My mom would always try for a while. My dad never really tried at all. I'm not sure if he noticed when I left. But that last day, it was my mom who called. She called them because she didn't think she could take care of me anymore. She didn't want to."

A tear slid down her cheek, and she didn't bother to wipe it away. She continued. "It was summer. I was home from school, and my mother was at work. My father came home with a woman. I didn't know her. I knew more or less what was going on, but I just did my best to ignore it. Later, the woman came out of the bedroom and saw me. I was really skinny, and I must have looked hungry and kind of dull. She asked if I wanted anything. I wasn't allowed to just take food out of the cupboard without permission. My mom would get mad. The woman, Josie, I still remember her name, she didn't think that was right. She got some bread and peanut butter and made me a sandwich. She sat me at the kitchen table, and she talked to me. She was worried I wasn't eating enough. Then my mother came home."

She squeezed her eyes shut tight, trying to keep

any more tears from falling. "She was so angry. She knew my father had affairs. She knew he was unfaithful. She…she felt like she'd tried, at least. Tried to love me and then I betrayed her too. Accepting something from another woman, I guess."

"Holly," he said, kissing her forehead. "You have to know that wasn't a betrayal on your part. You have to know that."

"I do know that. But it's why I was sent away. Reality didn't matter. She was already under stress and that was the last straw. The one she couldn't handle. If I had done something different—"

"You might never have gotten out. They were wrong, Holly. That's all there is to it. They were your parents. Parents are supposed to take care of their children. Parents aren't supposed to hit their children. Parents aren't supposed to try and use their children as a Band-Aid. Parents are supposed to feed their children. Hug them. They're not supposed to send them away. You didn't do anything wrong."

"Neither did you," she said.

He said nothing to that, only tightened his arms around her. "Thanks for talking me into this," he said. "The Christmas party, I mean. You didn't talk me into *this*." He clearly meant the two of them lying naked under the Christmas tree.

"Me too." But she meant more than just the Christmas party, and she was happy enough if he didn't realize that. If he didn't realize just how much this moment, and he, meant to her.

He was warm. He was holding her. She'd spent a

long time cold and alone. This might not be forever, but it was one of the most beautiful moments she'd ever experienced. No matter what happened later, she would always be glad they had the now.

CHAPTER TEN

THE COPPER RIDGE AIRPORT had only one terminal and one baggage carousel. It didn't take long to catch sight of Margie and Dan coming through the revolving doors that brought them from behind the single line security checkpoint and out into the general area.

Margie pulled him into a hug without hesitation, and Dan clapped him on the back. "Good to see you," the older man said. "How's the fishing?"

"Hard work," Ryan said. "But doing for a living what most people retire to do isn't the worst gig in the world."

"It's not the same as sitting out in the middle of a lake in a motorboat, but I'm glad you're happy," Dan said, smiling. "Anyway, it's not Hawaii."

"Yeah, well, it gives me something to look forward to for when I'm old," Ryan said. "It's nice to know there are still better things on the horizon. I don't want to peak too soon."

"Your work should never be the peak, son," Dan said, looking at his wife. "Hard work matters. But in the end it's not what you're left with."

Ryan looked at Margie and Dan, thought of their legacy. The Farm and Garden was certainly part of it.

Everyone in Copper Ridge shopped there for something or another. But that wasn't what Ryan loved them for. It wasn't what he would remember.

For some reason, the thought made his chest feel tight.

The conveyer belt on the baggage claim started up and Ryan made a move toward it. "What color are your bags? Let me get them."

"They're the really ugly ones with the flowers. You'll know which ones," Margie said. "So much easier to see."

Ryan smiled, not commenting on the fact that he had a feeling Margie liked the loud, colorful bags better and had used the 'easy to spot' excuse on Dan so he would agree to carry a bag with flowers around.

Of course, Dan would agree to it, anyway. He agreed to whatever Margie wanted, and seemed to enjoy doing it.

He stood, waiting for the bags to come around, and looked back at the older couple. They were standing together, Dan with his arm around his wife, an easy silence settling over them.

It was a strange moment, standing there, thinking about what his future might look like.

Ryan made it a practice not to look too many steps ahead. There was no point. His life had been kind of a hard slog. Spending days avoiding his father's fists, then coming to live with the Traverses and hoping that he wouldn't get moved again. Wouldn't get sent back. He'd worked tooth and nail to get into his boat and to get his business established. Planning for retirement was a privilege he hadn't gotten around to yet. But it wasn't only that.

He'd never imagined himself as an old man. More, he'd never imagined who might be standing alongside him, and who wouldn't be.

Looking back at Dan and Margie, he knew he didn't want to be standing alone. He wanted someone to retire to Hawaii with. Or not retire to Hawaii, necessarily, but someone to be with him. He couldn't look up to his father, never had. He'd put his head down and taken the blows, but he'd never imagined for a moment that he wanted to be like his old man. He'd never much imagined what he wanted to be. He prized hard work, because Dan had shown him it was the key. Dan was a man who worked hard, who ran a good, honest business, and had made a good living at it. But he was more than that. He was more than work. He was a husband, and a surrogate father to many kids who'd gone through the foster system in Copper Ridge.

It wasn't enough to just work hard. Because at the end of the day, at the end of his life, he didn't want to just be a man with a boat. He wanted to be the man standing there with a woman who still looked at him like he was something special.

He wanted to stand there with Holly. Because it was only with Holly that he could actually accomplish any of this. Holly made him feel like more. More than just a guy on a boat. More than just a kid whose father had used him for a punching bag. If she wasn't broken, neither was he. And he knew that she was in. He also knew she deserved the best. He might never be the best, but he could be more.

It took him a moment to realize that he'd let Dan and Margie's bags pass by on the conveyor belt.

"Do you have something on your mind, Ryan?" Margie asked, moving to his side.

"Just thinking about everything you two have given me. Thank you. You know, my dad never taught me a damn thing, and just standing there you made me realize something. That's pretty amazing."

Margie pulled him back into a hug, squeezing him tight. "We've helped a lot of kids, Ryan. And no matter the outcome, we would do it again," she said. "But it isn't enough to just get advice. You have to follow it. You're one of the few who has. At least parts of it."

He knew what she was talking about. Of course, Margie wanted him married with kids and all of that. He swallowed hard. He was starting to think maybe he wanted that, too.

For the first time he believed he really could have more. More with Holly.

He would just have to convince her.

He went after the suitcases and pulled them off the conveyer belt, holding one in each hand. "Let's go," he said. "We actually have a surprise for you."

IT WAS CHRISTMAS EVE, and Holly felt profoundly morose. Decidedly strange because she had loved the holidays from the moment she first met the Travers family.

It wasn't a mystery why this one wasn't welcome,

though. It was because the arrival of Christmas meant her time with Ryan was coming to a close.

So tonight, the big triumph, the party, didn't seem like her goal, it seemed like an end. An end she was not looking forward to.

She had to pack up the party that Ryan had thrown for her. It'd made her heart ache, but she couldn't throw a Christmas party with a giant happy birthday banner set up in the middle of one of her garlands.

Everything looked perfect, even though the subtle, beautiful decorations she now had in her living room looked pale in comparison to how Ryan had decorated for their private party. The tree, the centerpieces, the small village on the mantel. All of the guests would be arriving soon, and Ryan had gone to the airport to pick up Margie and Dan. Elizabeth would be back in town a little bit later. Everything was going according to plan, except Holly just wanted to crawl underneath the table with a cheese log and eat the entire thing herself.

She was in mourning. Like, suffered-a-death mourning. Like she'd lost the love of her life. Not just sex. But no, she couldn't love him. It wasn't possible, and it made no sense. More, loving him could come to nothing.

Because it could all get yanked away. And she would be left blindsided when it did.

She heard a knock on her front door and her stomach tightened. She wondered if it was Ryan. And the Traverses. She was excited to see them. Except she didn't feel so right now. Because their arrival was all wrapped up in the whole end-of-their-time-together thing. She smoothed her red satin skirt and walked to the front door, flinging it open, trying to force a smile when she saw her pretty, dark-haired friend Elizabeth standing there beaming at her.

"Merry Christmas!" Elizabeth handed her a gift and walked in, looking around at all of the decorations with a look of wonder on her face. "This is amazing! Really, you've outdone yourself. You made all of Mom's old decorations not look quite so 1983."

"You're early. And I like your mom's decorations," Holly said.

"I know you do."

"Where's Todd?"

Elizabeth rolled her eyes. "I don't know. Probably manscaping something."

"Did you not have a good time skiing?"

"Oh, I had a good time skiing. But dealing with Mr. High Maintenance was a little bit less enjoyable than I anticipated."

"Oh. Is the honeymoon over?"

"Thankfully, we haven't been on a literal honeymoon, so I don't have to continue to put up with it."

Holly winced. "Did you two break up?"

"Let's just say I spent more time with my ski instructor than I spent with him. And yes, we did."

"I'm sorry," she said.

"I'm not. You know, it starts with a guy paying all kinds of attention to you, but then all of a sudden they would rather just look in the mirror at their own reflection. Or, if not that specifically, at anything else but you just because they're tired of you," Elizabeth said, a bitter tinge in her voice. "Although Levi didn't seem to be bored with me. But then again, I was new."

"So... You think men just get bored?"

"I mean, it isn't like I *wasn't* bored. In fairness to the douchebag."

Holly's stomach sank. It was a good thing she and Ryan were finishing up, she supposed. Because it wouldn't take long for him to get tired of her otherwise. That was how things worked for her. Her parents had imagined she might fix their marriage, and all she'd done was add to their problems. And so what had started as a blessing, a miracle, had turned into a burden.

She would be that for him, too. She knew she would.

She cleared her throat. "It sounds like you need booze."

"I just might."

She walked into the kitchen and got a bottle of wine, pouring a generous helping for her friend.

"God bless you," Elizabeth said, raising her glass and taking a large gulp.

There was a knock at the door again, and after that, it didn't stop. Guests began to pour in, but still no Ryan and Margie and Dan.

Holly was starting to worry, even though she knew it was ridiculous.

Finally, the door opened, and there they were. But more important, there *he* was, the porch light behind him illuminating his masculine silhouette, the mist hanging low in the trees only adding to the drama of the moment. She could only see him. She only wanted to see him.

She was in so much trouble. How had she ever thought she was going to protect herself from this?

"Elizabeth!" Dan stepped in and tugged his daughter into a hug. "Holly," he said, smiling and hugging her too. Margie was greeting Elizabeth, then moved on to Holly. Holly almost cried when the older woman pulled her into a soft, gentle hug, the familiar smell of her perfume easing some of the ache in her chest. She'd last seen Margie a couple of months ago, compared to the days it had been since she'd seen her mother. And Margie didn't stare at her blankly.

"It's good to see you," Holly said, her throat too tight for many more words to escape.

"You too, honey," Margie said.

Holly stepped away, her eyes clashing with Ryan's. She tried to force a smile, one that he didn't return. A strange look was in his eyes, something thoughtful and deep, and it scared her.

She didn't want him to look at her that way. Because it would only fade. That was the one thing she wouldn't be able to stand. Not if he kept his word and ended things. But if she believed that it could be something more, if she allowed herself to love him—and not only that, but expect him to love her in return—she would be irrevocably broken.

Fortunately, the party kept her busy, and she wandered around the room making small talk with as many guests as she could. She made small talk with Sheriff Eli Garrett and his wife Sadie, who were expecting their first child in the spring, and with the sheriff's older brother Connor, his wife Liss, and their adorable baby. Along with Jake and Cassie, and Lydia Carpenter, the president of the Chamber of Commerce and frequent user of Holly's services. Half the town seemed to cycle in and out over the course of the evening, but as distracting as it was, as fun as it was, Holly's focus remained on Ryan and the sinking feeling in her stomach.

As the evening wound down, Ryan met her eyes across the room, moving toward her with intent. It was then that she realized she'd been avoiding him. It hadn't been conscious, but she'd definitely been doing it. He closed the distance between them, and was clearly about to say something when Dan and Margie unintentionally interrupted.

"Thank you so much for this party," Dan said. "It was so thoughtful of you, Holly. There are definitely some things we miss about Copper Ridge, and this is one of them."

"Yes," Margie said. "It's been so nice to see everyone tonight. It really is the best Christmas present we could've gotten."

"Holly worked very hard on this," Ryan said, his eyes intent on her.

"I can see that," Dan said, assessing Ryan. Holly felt like Dan saw a little bit too much.

Holly cleared her throat, tapping her glass with the side of her fork. It was tempting to get distracted, to let all the stuff she was feeling for Ryan eclipse the purpose of the party. But she wasn't going to let it.

"I just wanted to say a few words," she said when

everyone quieted down. "Dan, Margie, I wanted to do this for you because…well, it's for everything you've ever done for me. I don't know if a Christmas party is a big enough thank-you—no, I know it isn't—but it's a start. You gave me more happiness than I ever had before. You continue to give me support and love." Her words made her eyes feel scratchy as she realized how true they were. Dan and Margie loved her. They'd never betrayed her.

Because they were exceptional, not because she was. Those thoughts hammered against her temples, made her head ache.

She swallowed hard, pressing on. "And I love you, too. And thank you." She finished up as quickly as possible, before her emotions could get the best of her.

Dan and Margie pulled her in for hugs, and Holly extricated herself before she dissolved completely.

It wasn't long before they were co-opted by Elizabeth and a couple of other guests, leaving Holly with Ryan.

"Are you happy with how everything turned out?" Ryan asked.

"Yes," she said, surveying the room and the smiling faces of all her friends. Of Margie and Dan.

"You should be. It's great."

She lifted her shoulder. "It is kind of what I do."

"I know. But I think you outdid yourself."

She tried to force a smile, tried to suppress the giddy warmth that was doing its best to spread through her and turn her into a quivering mass of longing. "Well, it isn't a combination Christmas-birthday-Hanukkah-Valentine's party, but it's pretty cool."

"It's more than that. Margie said something interesting to me at the airport. She said that she's helped a lot of kids, but it doesn't go only one way. A person has to accept help. A lot of people can't, or don't."

"I'm not sure that a drowning person deserves credit for accepting a hand up," she said.

"You do. *We* do."

"You're being awfully introspective."

He leveled his gaze with hers, his dark eyes serious. "I am. In fact, I kind of want to talk to you."

Her stomach sank. This was it. He'd come to the same conclusion she had. Regardless of their original agreement, she knew it was over after tonight. It had to be, for her sanity if for no other reason. This was going to be goodbye. Whether it was marked by one last time together or a clean break, it was still goodbye. *It's better that it's now. You know it is.*

She took a deep breath and nodded.

She could tell him to wait until the party was over. But it didn't matter. It wouldn't make a difference. In fact, tearing the Band-Aid off might be for the best. Since they would have to act normally around each other and everyone else, they might as well start now.

"Will you come outside with me?" he asked.

"We can't talk in here?"

"No." He shook his head. "We can't."

She was afraid of that. "Okay." She moved through the living area, going to the back door, pausing to get her knitted hat and mittens and putting them on slowly, in no hurry to be alone with him. Stupid. She was being stupid.

Holly swallowed hard, her tongue sticking to the roof of her mouth. She was parched suddenly, nerves stealing all of the moisture from her body. She opened the door, and he followed her outside. She wrapped her arms around herself, walking to the middle of the yard, turning and looking back at her house, lit with white lights, looking every inch a holiday fantasy. And there was Ryan, in front of it all. Looking like he belonged. Which was unfair in such a major way.

"What did you want to talk about?"

"Let's go over here," he said, gesturing toward the small gazebo wreathed in lights at the back of the yard.

Tears stung the backs of her eyes and her heart pounded as she followed him across the grass, the frozen blades crunching beneath their feet.

He stepped into the gazebo, extending his hand. She accepted it, allowing him to help her up the steps and beneath the covered structure. It was so beautiful. Like a fantasy of some kind. They should dance next, or something. It should end with a kiss.

It wasn't going to end that way. She knew it.

Rejection was the only end. The only end for someone like her.

"Holly, I've been thinking."

"Don't," she said, holding up her hand. "You don't have to justify any of this. We set out the parameters of everything from the beginning. No apologies necessary. No need to look regretful."

He raised his dark eyebrows. "Do I look regretful? Because I guarantee you I don't feel it."

"Oh," she said, her stomach sinking.

"I also think you don't know what I'm about to say."

"Of course I do."

"No. Holly, when I picked up Dan and Margie at the airport today I realized something. There's a lot of life that I'm not living. A lot of things I've cut myself off from. Because of my dad. Because I never wanted to depend on anyone. I never wanted anyone depending on me. Not considering where I'd come from. I figured, I would work hard, redeem myself by building a life with some intangible."

He took a deep breath, then continued. "My dad was nothing more than a worthless bully. He didn't ever hold down a job, he never built anything. All he ever did was tear things down. I was so focused on being different than that, on finding my own way, and doing something. Anything. I missed a lot of things. I saw Dan and Margie standing there, looking as in love as they ever have, and I realized that in thirty years I don't want to just be fishing. I don't want to be alone. I want to build something bigger. Something that lasts."

He moved closer to her, his expression hidden from her in the dim light. But she could sense the intensity in his eyes, even if she couldn't see it. "I don't love Margie and Dan because they own the Farm and Garden. I love them because of who they are. Because they love each other. Because they loved us. There's only so much you can get out there and build with your hands, Holly. The rest I think you have to open yourself up to. You have to build it with your heart, and that's the hard part."

Holly felt lightheaded, breathless. "Did you... Did you spike the cider? Because it sounds an awful lot like you're talking about feelings."

"I am. And I'm sober. I guess it's a Christmas miracle."

"What exactly are you saying?"

"I want more. I want more, with you. I don't want us to be over. I don't want this to be over."

The twisting, intense mass of pressure in her chest burst, shattering into anxiety that burrowed beneath her skin, curled itself around her veins. "What? You're saying you want... You want some kind of copycat version of what Margie and Dan have?"

"Not exactly. But I think they prove it's possible."

"For them. But I'm not... I'm just me. When you get tired of it? When you realize that I can't just fix your issues, or the hole inside of you. Will you just get rid of me?"

"I'll never get tired of you. Of us. And I don't expect you to fix anything. I love you, Holly."

She felt like the ground had dropped out from underneath her feet. Like she was hanging from a ledge, with Ryan standing there holding out his hand. Except nothing inside of her could bring herself to take it. Because as wonderful as it looked, as much as it appeared like it could be salvation, there was a part of her that was afraid if she reached for him, he would only drop her.

It's Ryan. He won't drop you.

But she couldn't believe it. She couldn't. If her own mother had dropped her, why wouldn't he?

Yes, she was dangling from a metaphorical ledge, but she knew she wouldn't let herself go. That was the only thing she could trust. Survival. It wasn't comfortable, but it was sure.

"You can't," she said.

"What do you mean I *can't*? I do. I've lived my entire life knowing exactly what love *wasn't*. I went to Dan and Margie's, and I saw it for the first time. It's not something you can mistake. Don't tell me I can't. Don't tell me I don't know," he said.

"How can you? You're just as broken as I am." The words came fast, sharp. He drew back as though she'd attacked him physically. She might as well have. It probably would have hurt less. It probably would have hurt them both less. But she couldn't stop, not now. "Ryan, we could never make it work. Not you and me. If you were ever going to… And I know that *you* can… Then it would be with someone who isn't so damaged inside."

"You're not damaged. Your mom is. Your dad is. You aren't. They made you feel that way, because when you're surrounded by messed up people, you must look strange by comparison. I know what that's like. I didn't understand that not all fathers use their fists on their children. But that didn't make my dad normal. It just meant I didn't know better."

"Now it's your turn to tell me that I don't know better?" she asked.

"You don't," he said. "You must not. Not if you don't

know that you're lovable. Not if you don't know that you're worth something."

"I know that I am. Stop making it sound like I'm some emo teenager crying about imagined problems. My mother abandoned me. That's how I see this ending for me. And if I was ever going to believe it could be different, if I was ever going to believe someone might love me forever, I wouldn't believe it could come from someone who grew up the way that you did."

She wanted to cut her own tongue out as the words left her mouth. Hated herself for them, a thousand times over. But she wouldn't take them back. Not now. Not when she needed them to protect her.

"I know what it feels like to be a punching bag for somebody who isn't happy with themselves," he said, his tone harsh. "That's all this is. It's not about me, Holly. It's about you. I've experienced this too many times to doubt that."

She took a deep breath. "Maybe you should worry about your ego instead of mine," she said. "I don't love you. I told you what this was."

"You don't love me, Holly? I think you do. I think you have for a long time. I think I've loved you almost as long. What I also think is that we spent a lot of years being afraid. Because we knew if we ever touched each other, we would be lost. It would be all in. And it is. It is for me. I almost kissed you when you were eighteen, and I told myself I shouldn't because you were too young. Because I was no good. But that wasn't the reason. That was never the reason. It's because I knew that if I kissed you, I would love you. Forever. I would want to marry you, and stay with you all my days. I would want you to have my babies. Live with me. Be my wife. And I do. It's what I want. You want it too."

"No. I don't. Don't say it again. You keep telling me I'm worth so much, Ryan. You keep telling me I can have normal. So let me go find that then. I won't find it with you." *Stop taunting me with what I can't have.* She swallowed hard, moving away from him, pressing her back against one of the brightly lit pillars in the gazebo. She closed her eyes, turning her face away, willing him to leave.

She heard footsteps, first on the wooden steps, then on the grass. When she looked up, Ryan was walking into the house, closing the door slowly behind him.

She crumpled to the ground then, the cold from the wood seeping through her jeans, making her shiver. She closed her eyes, a sob wrenching through her, threatening to tear her apart. She'd thought that ending it herself would hurt less, but right now she couldn't imagine anything hurting more.

But she knew it was either now or later. Now or in a decade. It wouldn't last. Because it couldn't. Not with her. He wanted something to fix the emptiness inside him. She couldn't be that. She couldn't have that kind of pressure put on her. Couldn't fail at it again.

More than anything, she simply couldn't bear to love someone with all of herself only to be rejected again. Better to do it now. Better to stay in control.

It might break her now. But it would have killed her later.

She shifted her position, rocked back so that her butt

was on the ground, her back pressed up against the support for the gazebo. She tried to catch her breath, and couldn't. She watched it escape on a cloud in the cold air, a shiver working its way through her.

She looked at the people inside, could see them through the window, talking and laughing.

She had always felt like Dan and Margie had given her Christmas. Tonight, Ryan had taken it away.

That isn't fair. You took it from yourself.

"God rest ye merry gentlemen let nothing you dismay…" Her voice cracked and she sucked in a gasping breath as a tear rolled down her cheek.

She had always known it would end in heartbreak. She just hadn't thought she would be responsible for it.

CHAPTER ELEVEN

AFTER MOVING IN with Margie and Dan, Christmas Eve had become the longest night of the year for Ryan. They got Christmas presents for all the kids, no matter how long they'd been in the home, no matter whether or not they were staying for good. There was always Christmas dinner to look forward to, the tree, music. And all of it built anticipation for the main event that was Christmas Day, made waiting to open presents feel that much closer and that much further away.

Tonight, Christmas Eve was the longest night for an entirely different reason.

He looked across the room, at his entire living space. He was lying on his bed, the pitch and roll of the ocean just making him sick, where normally he found it soothing. But then, everything made him feel sick at the moment.

He had never told a woman he loved her before. Had never loved a woman before.

But he loved Holly. He knew he did. What he'd said to her in the gazebo was true. He had probably always loved her. He'd just been too afraid to admit it. Not only to her, but to himself.

She didn't trust him. He didn't believe she didn't

love him, but he knew she didn't trust him. He didn't deserve her trust, that was the bottom line. It was the truth. He wasn't sure he deserved anyone's trust. Had never done anything to earn it. He was untested when it came to relationships. He had a boat.

He didn't deserve her trust, no. He wasn't the perfect man. But he wanted to fight for it. Life, his boat, everything, seemed pointless without her. It didn't seem right that she was still holding herself back, still lost in the pain of her past.

He wanted to fix it. Wanted to fix her.

Wanted to fix himself so that he could be magically worthy of everything she was.

She had told him he wasn't good enough. Had confirmed everything he'd ever feared. He should be grateful. That she'd demanded what she deserved. That she'd let him off the hook. So he could slink back to his boat and his damaged life without having to worry about another person.

But he wasn't relieved. He was angry. He was…he was brokenhearted. And he would have thought that was impossible.

He'd offered love like it was a magic cure. She'd turned him down.

Maybe that was the problem. There was no magic. There was no fix. She was right. They were pretty broken. How could you come through everything they had and not be?

But they'd had help along the way. They had people to show them how it could be. They had each other. And they were damn sure capable of love. So, maybe he could never be the perfect man for her. Maybe they could never be unbroken. But maybe it didn't matter.

He wanted her broken or fixed. He wanted her even with every piece of himself smashed.

He didn't need magic. He just needed Holly. It wasn't about being worthy, or good enough. God knew he never would be. It was just about ending this vicious cycle they'd lived in for too long.

Being alone. Being bogged down in the past.

It was about making sure their parents—parents who had never loved them like parents should—didn't get a bigger say in who they were now than Dan and Margie did. Than the people who'd told them they were enough.

He stood up, the top of his head brushing the ceiling of the boat. He wasn't going to get any sleep tonight. But tomorrow morning, hopefully things would be different. Hopefully, he could get her to see things the way that he did.

Margie and Dan's house had always been a place of new beginnings. And tomorrow, he hoped the first day of the rest of his life would start there.

He would just have to convince Holly.

He went over to the kitchen cabinets, and got out a jar of peanut butter. It was a place to start.

HOLLY HAD ALMOST opted out of coming to the Christmas get-together today. But then Margie would worry about her, and she really didn't want to make Margie worry. Ryan had left the party without saying goodbye and Holly had spent the rest of the party with a smile pasted on her face that she knew looked as fake as the acrylic evergreen garlands hanging over her mantel.

At least Ryan would skip the party. He hated Christmas anyway. But apparently he loved her.

She ignored the stab of pain in her chest that accompanied that thought.

When someone loved you, was it supposed to hurt so very much? This was what it should feel like when someone rejected you, turned you down. This was what Ryan should feel like right now, not her.

But you love him, and you don't have him.

She gritted her teeth, shifting her hold on the stack of presents in her hand so she could press the doorbell.

The door jerked open, and her mouth fell open in surprise when she saw Ryan on the other side of it. "Oh. You're here," she said.

He crossed his arms over his broad chest. "Yes, I am."

"I thought you would skip, all things considered."

"I thought I would come, all things considered. Because I knew you would be here. And we need to talk."

"It's Christmas."

"Yeah, all the more reason for us to talk. Because I don't intend to spend Christmas with a broken heart."

"Did I break your heart?"

"Into about a thousand pieces, Hollyberry. You're the only one that can fix it, so don't look at me with those regretful eyes."

She tried to breathe around the pain, but she found it impossible. "Would you take these presents, please?" She shoved the stack of them into his arms without waiting for him to agree and pushed past him into the house.

"Margie isn't going to rescue you," he said, effectively stalling the progress she was making into the kitchen. "No one is. I told everyone what was happening."

"That is emotional blackmail, you bastard."

"Is it? If you don't love me nobody's going to pressure you to be with me. But if you're just continually punishing yourself for something you feel like you did wrong when you were a teenager, then yeah, people will pressure you to make a different decision."

"Ryan, I told you…"

He set the stack of presents down on the floor in the entryway. "I know you did. Now, I want to tell you. Let's go outside."

The living room was suspiciously vacant, and she imagined that the entire family had shuffled themselves to another side of the house to give Ryan privacy.

They were conspiring against her. And Ryan had a key and she didn't. She was tempted to determine, based on all that evidence, that they loved him best.

He led her through the room, out the double doors, to the back deck that looked over the tops of the evergreen trees, sloping down toward the ocean.

She walked toward the edge of the porch to lean against the railing.

"Okay," she said, her eyes resolutely fixed on the horizon line where the sea met the sky. "Talk. Make it fast, because I want my turkey and ham and pie. I don't want drama."

"How about a sandwich?"

She turned sharply to the side and saw that he was extending a plastic baggie with a sandwich inside of it toward her. "What is this?"

"It's a peanut butter sandwich."

Her stomach lurched, her heart twisting. "Why? Because you wanted to remind me of the worst day of my life? That accepting a little bit of peanut butter got me thrown out of my house?"

"No. I want to take care of you," he said, his eyes filled with such sincere emotion she had to look away again. She didn't deserve it. She wasn't worthy of it. "Take it. Take all the peanut butter I have, or ever will have, or can ever buy. Take whatever you want. I want to give you everything. All of me."

"Ryan…"

"Stop punishing yourself."

His words hit her with the force of a brick. Because she realized that he was right. It was exactly what she was doing. She was punishing herself. She wasn't afraid of losing his love so much as she didn't think she deserved it in the first place. "What kind of daughter sits in her mother's kitchen and talks with her father's mistress?" she asked, her throat tight.

"One who's hungry. Not just for food, but for affection. One who got dragged into games she didn't know the rules to. It wasn't fair. It wasn't your fault."

"You should have seen her face."

"I saw her face out on the street just last week. She's sad. She doesn't have any color. The life is completely drained from her. And that's all on her. She was wrong to send you away. She blamed the wrong person. She clung to the wrong person and let go of the one she should've held on to."

He leaned in, his expression growing more intense as he continued. "I'm not going to do that, Holly. Don't you make the same mistake. Don't you hold on to them, to that pain, and let go of me. Don't sell us short."

He swallowed, closing his eyes for a moment. "You're right, we're broken. We're never going to be perfect. You can't take away the fact that I spent the first few years of my life getting the crap beaten out of me for looking at my father wrong. That can't be erased. The neglect, the pain that your parents put you through, no one can wash it away like it was never there. But we can overcome it. Why do they get to decide what we are? Why are we giving them that much power? I'm begging you." He reached out to her, his hand held there, a lifeline she was scared to grab hold of. "Let go of them. Take my hand. Take my sandwich. Please."

"I'm afraid," she said, the words coming out a whisper.

"I know. I know, because I am, too. I want to be perfect for you, and I know that I'm not. I want to be able to promise you that I'll never let you down, because you've been let down enough. I want to promise you that I will be the perfect boyfriend, the perfect husband. I can't promise those things. I can promise you, though, that I will love you. I can promise you that I will never leave you."

She closed her eyes, a wave of longing washing over

her, tears streaming down her cheeks. "Will you stay with me? Will you really?"

"If there's one thing I know how to be it's loyal. If there's one thing I know how to do it's stay. I know you don't like my boat, but it's something I've been committed to for the past fifteen years. Even though it's hard, I keep at it. I do the work, even though it's tough on the body and the soul sometimes. Because I know in the end it's worth it. We'll be like that."

"Did you just compare me to your boat?"

"I do love that boat."

She laughed, a shaky, watery sound. "I… I want to believe you. I want to say yes."

"Then say yes. I might not be perfect, but I do think I'm the man for you. Because no one will ever love you as much as I do. I know you. I've known you for years. I've seen you at high points and low points. I watched you experience your first happy Christmases, saw your face when your parents didn't show up for your birthday. I know you almost better than I know myself. And I know that I want to spend my life feeding you, and giving you parties, and just loving you. Not because they didn't, but because I feel so much for you I can't do anything but show you. All the time. From now until forever. But I can't do it if you won't let me."

Joy and terror filled her in equal measure, her heart pounding so hard she could barely hear herself think over the sound of it. She stood and looked at him, at the grumpiest, strongest, most prideful man she knew, holding out a peanut butter sandwich and laying his heart in front of her feet. She knew in that moment if she couldn't match that offer, she didn't deserve him. He was being brave. He was risking everything. He was a boy who'd received more punches in the face than hugs all through his growing up years. Yesterday, he had offered love, and she'd given him nothing but pain.

"I'm so sorry," she said.

He closed his eyes, taking a deep breath, nodding slowly.

"No," she said, "I don't mean that. Just... For yesterday. I'm so sorry that I hurt you. I was so afraid, I didn't know what else to do. I thought if I hurt you, you would go away. You would stop asking me for things. My parents sent me away for a lot less. It should have been easy to get rid of you. But you're right, it isn't about being afraid you'll leave. I trust you. You've been here all these years, why would you leave now? That isn't it. I have been punishing myself. I felt unworthy."

"You aren't."

"Thank you. But...even if I am...I'm going to take it. Think of everything we've been given. All that Dan and Margie gave to us. Every Christmas present...we didn't have to earn those. Maybe we don't have to earn this either."

"Holly..."

"I love you, Ryan. I do. You're right, I have loved you forever. Whenever I thought of a life spent with someone it was always you. And I told myself that I didn't want to make a move on you because I didn't want to risk what I had with the Traverses. And if something were to ever go wrong between us it would ruin that. But I was just protecting myself. And I'm tired of that. A safe existence is nothing more than an existence. And I want to live. I want to live with you."

He pulled her into his arms, his hands—and the sandwich—pressed against her back as he leaned in to kiss her, hard and deep. When they parted, they were both breathing hard. "I think you destroyed the sandwich," she said, her tone slightly dazed.

He loosened his hold on her, holding the bag up, examining the squished bread inside. "So I did. But there's more where that came from."

"We really aren't normal," she said. "You know that, right?"

"Peanut butter sandwiches, purple condoms, and a Christmas-birthday-Hanukkah-Valentine's Day party aren't typical aspects of human courtship?"

"Who cares? They're part of ours."

He tossed the sandwich onto the deck, taking her back into his arms and pulling her in close. "You're damn right they are. And that's all that matters. I don't want normal. I just want you."

There were a few things Holly Fulton knew for certain. The first was that this was the best Christmas she'd ever had. The second was that she'd never been so happy in her entire life. But the most important thing of all was that she loved Ryan Masters with everything she had in her. And he loved her right back.

* * * * *

#1 *New York Times* bestselling author

LINDA LAEL MILLER

introduces you to the *Carsons of Mustang Creek*, three men who embody the West and define what it means to be a rancher, a cowboy and a hero in this enthralling series from the queen of Western romance.

Available March 28!

Complete your collection!

"Linda Lael Miller creates vibrant characters and stories I defy you to forget."
— #1 *New York Times* bestselling author Debbie Macomber

www.LindaLaelMiller.com

www.HQNBooks.com

PHLLMCMC

Celebrate the magic of the season with
New York Times bestselling author

RaeAnne Thayne

There's no place like Haven Point for the holidays, where the snow conspires to bring two wary hearts together for a Christmas to remember!

It's been two rough years since Andrea Montgomery lost her husband, and all she wants is for her children to enjoy their first Christmas in Haven Point. But then Andie's friend asks a favor—to keep an eye on her brother, Sheriff Marshall Bailey, who's recovering from a hit-and-run. Andie will do anything for Wyn, even park her own misgivings to check on Wyn's grouchy, wounded bear of a brother.

Marshall hates feeling defenseless and resents the protective impulses that Andie brings out in him. But when a blizzard forces them together for the holidays, something in Marshall begins to thaw. Andie's gentle nature is a salve, and her kids' excitement for the holidays makes him forget why he never wanted a family. If only he and Andie can admit what they really want—each other—their Christmas wishes might come true after all.

Pick up your copy today!

www.RaeAnneThayne.com

www.HQNBooks.com

PHRAT989

**Wish upon a Christmas star with
#1 *New York Times* bestselling author**

SUSAN MALLERY

in this sparkling Fool's Gold romance!

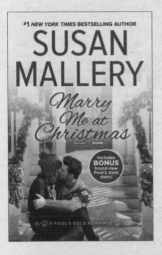

To bridal boutique owner Madeline Krug, organizing a Christmas wedding sounds like a joy—until she finds out she'll be working closely with the gorgeous brother of the bride, movie star Jonny Blaze. How will a small-town girl like her keep from falling for the world's sexiest guy? Especially with mistletoe lurking around every corner!

Available October 25!

www.SusanMallery.com

www.HQNBooks.com

PHSM935

REQUEST YOUR FREE BOOKS!

2 FREE NOVELS
FROM THE ROMANCE COLLECTION,
PLUS 2 FREE GIFTS!

YES! Please send me 2 FREE novels from the Romance Collection and my 2 FREE gifts (gifts are worth about $10). After receiving them, if I don't wish to receive any more books, I can return the shipping statement marked "cancel." If I don't cancel, I will receive 4 brand-new novels every month and be billed just $6.49 per book in the U.S. or $6.99 per book in Canada. That's a savings of at least 18% off the cover price. It's quite a bargain! Shipping and handling is just 50¢ per book in the U.S. and 75¢ per book in Canada.* I understand that accepting the 2 free books and gifts places me under no obligation to buy anything. I can always return a shipment and cancel at any time. Even if I never buy another book, the two free books and gifts are mine to keep forever.

194/394 MDN GH4D

Name   (PLEASE PRINT)

Address   Apt. #

City   State/Prov.   Zip/Postal Code

Signature (if under 18, a parent or guardian must sign)

Mail to the **Reader Service:**
IN U.S.A.: P.O. Box 1867, Buffalo, NY 14240-1867
IN CANADA: P.O. Box 609, Fort Erie, Ontario L2A 5X3

Want to try 2 free books from another line?
Call 1-800-873-8635 or visit www.ReaderService.com.

*Terms and prices subject to change without notice. Prices do not include applicable taxes. Sales tax applicable in N.Y. Canadian residents will be charged applicable taxes. Offer not valid in Quebec. This offer is limited to one order per household. Not valid for current subscribers to the Romance Collection or the Romance/Suspense Collection. All orders subject to credit approval. Credit or debit balances in a customer's account(s) may be offset by any other outstanding balance owed by or to the customer. Please allow 4 to 6 weeks for delivery. Offer available while quantities last.

Your Privacy—The Reader Service is committed to protecting your privacy. Our Privacy Policy is available online at www.ReaderService.com or upon request from the Reader Service.

We make a portion of our mailing list available to reputable third parties that offer products we believe may interest you. If you prefer that we not exchange your name with third parties, or if you wish to clarify or modify your communication preferences, please visit us at www.ReaderService.com/consumerschoice or write to us at Reader Service Preference Service, P.O. Box 9062, Buffalo, NY 14240-9062. Include your complete name and address.

Turn your love of reading into rewards you'll love with

Harlequin My Rewards

Join for FREE today at www.HarlequinMyRewards.com

Earn **FREE BOOKS** of your choice.

Experience **EXCLUSIVE OFFERS** and contests.

Enjoy **BOOK RECOMMENDATIONS** selected just for you.

PLUS! Sign up now and get **500** points right away!

MYR16R

LINDA LAEL MILLER

79999	ARIZONA WILD	___$7.99 U.S.	___$9.99 CAN.
78988	THE COWBOY WAY	___$7.99 U.S.	___$9.99 CAN.
78969	ALWAYS A COWBOY	___$7.99 U.S.	___$9.99 CAN.
78906	BIG SKY COUNTRY	___$7.99 U.S.	___$8.99 CAN.
78895	MONTANA CREEDS: DYLAN	___$7.99 U.S.	___$9.99 CAN.
78845	MONTANA CREEDS: LOGAN	___$7.99 U.S.	___$8.99 CAN.
77996	McKETTRICKS OF TEXAS: AUSTIN	___$7.99 U.S.	___$8.99 CAN.
77968	ONCE A RANCHER	___$7.99 U.S.	___$9.99 CAN.
77953	McKETTRICKS OF TEXAS: GARRETT	___$7.99 U.S.	___$8.99 CAN.
77870	THE MARRIAGE PACT	___$7.99 U.S.	___$8.99 CAN.
77866	THE BRIDEGROOM	___$7.99 U.S.	___$8.99 CAN.
77681	McKETTRICK'S HEART	___$7.99 U.S.	___$9.99 CAN.
77677	McKETTRICK'S PRIDE	___$7.99 U.S.	___$9.99 CAN.

(limited quantities available)

TOTAL AMOUNT	$_____
POSTAGE & HANDLING	$_____
($1.00 FOR 1 BOOK, 50¢ for each additional)	
APPLICABLE TAXES*	$_____
TOTAL PAYABLE	$_____

(check or money order—please do not send cash)

To order, complete this form and send it, along with a check or money order for the total above, payable to HQN Books, to: **In the U.S.:** 3010 Walden Avenue, P.O. Box 9077, Buffalo, NY 14269-9077; **In Canada:** P.O. Box 636, Fort Erie, Ontario, L2A 5X3.

Name: _____

Address: _____ City: _____

State/Prov.: _____ Zip/Postal Code: _____

Account Number (if applicable): _____

075 CSAS

*New York residents remit applicable sales taxes.
*Canadian residents remit applicable GST and provincial taxes.

HQN™

www.HQNBooks.com

PHLLM0916BL